ADVANCE PRAISE FOR *THE RESTORERS*

"Kick off from shore and enter the irresistible flow that takes us to the heart and soul of Pennsylvania, to the friendship of paddling pals, and to intrigue among the shady deals—all too real—that steal our precious inheritance of beauty. Best of all, at more levels than one, this is a story of love. Our great river now has a great story to fit our times."

—TIM PALMER, author of *America's Great River Journeys, Twilight of the Hemlocks and Beeches*, and other books

"Brook Lenker's *The Restorers* is a lot like the Susquehanna River on which it takes place: surprising twists, rapid turns, and more than meets the eye. We need more heroes like the sexy and green Reily Watters, both in fiction and in real life."

—TIM O'MARA, author of the Raymond Donne series and editor of *Down to the River*

"A tale held in one's hand, urging each of us to action rather than paddling on."

—R. JOHN DAWES, Executive Director Foundation for Pennsylvania Watersheds

THE RESTORERS

A Reily Watters Expedition

BROOK LENKER

Year of the Book
135 Glen Avenue
Glen Rock, PA 17327

Print ISBN: 978-1-949150-67-4
Ebook ISBN: 978-1-949150-68-1

Cover Image: "Moon Mist, Susquehanna"
Oil on linen 42" x 46" by Brian Keeler http://www.briankeeler.com and http://www.northstarartgallery.com

Frontispiece: "Island 109" by Margot Golba

DEDICATION

In memory of Pat, the river rat, and Bill, the West Virginia warrior –
saints of conservation – and my parents, David and Nancy, who
relished the beauty of the world... and a good story.

CHAPTER 1

Reily Watters paddled like his life depended on it. A large rapid – the biggest yet – loomed ahead. The bow of his canoe plunged into the trough, slamming forward, blessing him with a refreshing spray. Rivers enchanted like women but could tease and rip your breath away, yet the Susquehanna was a princess compared to his ex-wife.

Surviving the tumult, he ceased paddling, reached over the side, and splashed water onto his face. Droplets journeyed over the tight, horizontal creases of weathered cheeks and dribbled from the end of his beard. For the first time in years, he felt wholly alive... lost, now found.

A giant eddy tugged Reily toward the bank. He and fifty other paddlers were part of one big hippie family traveling in a temporary aquatic commune, a kaleidoscope of canoes and kayaks called the Odyssey. Over the previous two weeks, the river had been balm, healing him day by day. Farms and forests touched every meandering mile since Cooperstown. The towns were the way towns were supposed to be – friendly and walkable with an organic Yankee flavor. Little gifts filled every hour: a cow drinking along the shore, a beaver gnawing on a willow, a coyote crossing a side channel. That animal had fixed on him as if sharing a secret; it had found a way to persevere.

But today, clouds of dust obscured the mountain ahead while dump trucks carried it away piece by piece. A landform millions of years wise was being sacrificed for road fill. It was a sick world.

His days in landscape architecture contributed to such genocide. The majority of projects involved new construction and the eradication of nature. He'd overused the same introduced species with minimum benefit to wildlife. Burning bush and common barberry not only encroached on the native flora but were flat-out boring.

Lunch was served in a crowded community fire hall. Inside the sterile building, velvet paintings of deer and forest scenes dressed the walls, while faint odors of deep-fried poultry filled the air. Beefy men with names like Earl and Butch slopped coleslaw and macaroni onto flimsy paper plates. He felt queasy and claustrophobic. On the way out, he grabbed a peanut butter cookie the size of a saucer.

Behind the building, he found a waist-high wall and sat on top of it. Wil Wisnoski joined him.

"Gabriele is unbelievable. I can't believe we only met on the river two days ago, but I think I'm in love... and you know I don't get those feelings too often."

Reily gnawed the cookie. "Yeah, I know."

"You better slow down. You're chowing like a sugar-deprived diabetic."

He ignored the politically-incorrect insult. "You don't change, do you?"

"Thanks for inviting me on this thing." Wil's appearance fit the laid-back ambiance: Corona tank top, frayed khaki shorts, dollar store flip-flops on tanned, callous feet.

"You're welcome."

"Seriously, this is awesome. Much better than I expected. You don't know how bad I needed this. We've lost two writers at the paper. They've been working me to the bone for the last year. I have plenty of vacation days but no time to use them." Wil tasted his macaroni and shoveled another bite into his mouth. "Thanks for arranging the women, too. That was a stroke of genius."

"Glad to be of service." Reily noticed Gabriele and her friend Sol picnicking in the grass. Sol's dark-features were captivating in a natural, no nonsense way. Radiant eyes exuded intelligence and sincerity. He was moved by her presence. "Now, how do I peel that beautiful woman away from java stud?"

Wil swigged from a self-supplied twenty-ounce bottle of iced tea and spotted Reily's subject. "You mean her kayak buddy?"

"He might be more than that. He's been making her coffee in his stupid French press."

"I think she digs you."

"You've been puffing away too much with guitar-man." Reily had looked out for Roy Wilhelm Wisnoski, aka Wil, ever since they met at vacation bible school at the First Presbyterian Church. Raised Roman Catholic, Wil happened to be there because of a girl. It was a sign of things to come. Later they became better friends on the YMCA and high school swim teams. A year younger, Wil was the kid brother Reily never had, quick and cocky compared to his own deliberate, more reserved manner.

"A little smoking now and then with Alex won't hurt anyone. You should try it, but I guess that would impede your miracles. Remember my temporary blindness from the basketball pole collision? That scared the shit out of me." Reily almost overlooked the weird visor on Wil's head. On anyone else it would be ridiculous, but on Wil it was a stylish appendage.

"I'm not sure what I did that time, but I rescued your ass on many occasions."

"Not always. You can't take the one incident with a certain girl and make it sound like a regular occurrence."

Reily pictured the angry boyfriend, the fullback for their high school football team. "Her man was ready to kick your butt. I convinced him to control his angst. You couldn't help yourself. You were a natural-born weasel."

Wil grinned. "After that she disappeared from my life – or at least the dugout, but you're no saint, Watters. Don't give me that benign look."

"Saintliness is relative." Reily was always loyal to his friend but wouldn't hesitate to tell him that he had gone too far. He would follow up with suggestions for a better way to handle the situation and when things had settled down, Wil would usually say, "Thanks for the kind advice." Sometimes he felt like a probation officer counseling a client.

Wil reaffixed the cap on his bottle of iced tea. "When was the last time we did this?"

"Sat on a wall and talked?"

"No, when was our last expedition?"

"The Appalachian Trail Hike in '96?"

"You forgot the C&O trip."

Reily stood and stretched. "Sorry, that was a rough time." The trip had been cursed: two flat tires, a broken derailleur, and temps in the 90s every day. Those were minor challenges compared to the anguish of the divorce and being torn from his daughter. Beyond the sobering thoughts of that summer, Reily loved his adventures with Wil. The outdoors bound them together, especially in their youth. Whether it was hiking in a patch of woods or fishing in a farm pond, they spent much of their childhood experiencing what the countryside served. When college came, they parted ways but remained close and every Thanksgiving weekend would meet at steely bars in Bethlehem to recall their exploits in beer-enhanced color. There had been wives, a kid, careers, and other life distractions but a guys' trip every few years was mandatory. They were devout in their attendance.

The torpid day continued. Paddling solo in the back of the pack, Reily had a wide angle view of everything and everyone in front of him including java Rick and the luminous Sol Messina. Somehow Wil had already managed to lure Gabriele to share a kayak, too.

The whirling of double-bladed paddles made a dizzying perpetual motion machine. A congregation formed on the right bank and from the dispersion of bodies along the treeline, it could only be an impromptu bathroom break. A dozen or more ladies and men entered and exited rangy thickets of knotweed to relieve themselves.

As he nosed in to shore, the vegetation parted and there, like an erotic dream, was Sol clad in a solid black two-piece swimsuit. She nodded his way and trudged back to Rick's kayak. Her exposed back and legs could have been sculpted by Donatello. She paused to adjust her sandal and he noticed a tattoo on her lower left ankle. He strained his nearsighted eyes to discern the image. It was a sun – with goddess eyes and a grin.

CHAPTER 2

Hap Clay let off the gas and coasted past a parked Crown Victoria tucked behind a billboard. He craned to see who was inside. The last time he was stopped, a surly Negro trooper handed him a $150 ticket. With a democrat for a Governor and black cops, Pennsylvania had gone down a bad road.

Three days a week he zigzagged across the northern counties like a motorized bumblebee on uppers, racking up the miles between Sayre and Scranton. Infectious medical waste collection required determination and dependability; as a Korean War veteran, he had mastered both.

At 7:00 A.M., the lot was almost full at the Dushore Diner. He nosed into a space between a towering 4X4 and a familiar taupe sedan. Inside, the diner wreaked of greasy cooking, pheromones to the portly rear ends occupying the counter stools. The booths were full, too. Then he saw a chubby arm waving at him from the back. It was Lowell Orwell. His fellow township supervisor resembled George "The Animal" Steele.

"I drove by your place after supper last night and saw you leaf blowing your driveway. Didn't they teach you to use a broom in the military?"

Hap tried to imagine Lowell Orwell's hulk sweeping seventy feet of macadam but didn't rise to the bait. "What's the latest with Gert Bunting?"

"Nothing yet, but I don't think it will be long. That arthritis has her thinking about Phoenix. Her granddaughter lives there."

A slender, gum-chewing waitress walked up and hovered by the booth. "You know what you'll be having, boys?"

Lowell puffed his chest. "Sweetie, give me the number two, over easy, and can you warm up this coffee when you have a chance?"

The waitress scribbled the order with a pre-menstrual scowl. "Now, what can I get you, Mr. Clay?"

"How about two flapjacks and some orange juice?"

"You got it. Be right up."

5

As she moved away, Lowell's eyes followed. "What a little hotcake. She can lick my syrup any day."

Hap tried to empty his brain of the nauseating image. "When do we vote on the Bunting tract?"

"Next meeting."

"Why so soon? If this fellow needs Gert's land to make it a go, why don't we wait until he gets it?"

Lowell leaned toward him. "The longer we wait, the more time those subversive types have to raise a stink. Better to do it now."

Hap rubbed his forehead.

"What's wrong? Don't get weird on me. You know it's the right thing for everybody."

He met Lowell's sallow gaze. "It just seems like I've been hearing too much about it lately. I'm sick of it. A couple of people asked me about it last week."

"When it's all said and done and anyone asks, tell them you voted your conscience. Who can object to that?"

"Fine, but why did you want to meet me here? I know it wasn't to give me a pep talk."

"You're pretty perceptive in your old age." Lowell paused to finish his coffee. "Do you remember what we talked about after the last meeting?"

"Yep."

"Well, it's all wrapped up." Lowell began rooting through a worn leather briefcase at his side.

"Woodring gave it to you?"

"Shhh, gave it to us." Lowell laid a letter-sized envelope on the table and pushed it toward him. "Here's your piece of the shoo-fly pie." Hap snatched the envelope and folded it in half before stuffing it into his pocket with a pang of guilt.

"Why are we doing this here?"

"We rendezvous on some back road and odds are someone we know will drive right up. Then we'd have lots of explaining to do. Rumors would start flying that two of Conroy Township's finest are cupcakes. You want that?"

Hap chewed on his lower lip. Garth Brooks sang a patriotic tune on the jukebox. The waitress came with the flapjacks but made Lowell wait for his eggs. The food seemed fine but had no flavor.

Hap paid for breakfast at the register by the front door and fumbled for exact change. The envelope dropped to the floor. Before he could stoop, the waitress picked it up and handed it to him.

"Are you feeling okay?" she said.

6

"Why do you ask?"
"Because you look like you saw a ghost."

CHAPTER 3

The afternoon wore on. Reily didn't think about his motions, just did them without complaint mile after mile. While he sweated with each surging stroke, the river rested, oil smooth and silent.

At four o'clock the heavens collided, forcing him to seek refuge in a grove of saplings. Torrents of rain rinsed salt and grit from a bandana wrapped around his head. He shivered in futility to stay warm. The tree in front of him exfoliated bark – creamy on one side, russet on the other – seeking a better finish.

"Don't you love natural pyrotechnics?" The husky voice came from just a few feet away.

"You scared the shit out of me, Alex." Reily resumed breathing. "I didn't see you."

Alex Mueller laughed. Reily loved his constant happiness. Alex always looked lost but with direction and purpose.

"Deadly experiences can renew, make you feel like you're getting a second chance at things."

Reily weighed the comment. Soon the rain and canons retreated. He slogged through shoe-sucking mud back to his canoe and set his lanky frame on the cane center seat.

Alex inserted himself into his kayak. "You know what they say?"

"No, please share." Reily wrung the water from his shirt.

"A bad day on a river beats a good day at the office."

"You got that right." Reily had wasted twenty-two years, most of it confined indoors, with an unappreciative firm and the only upside besides his severance was the brevity of the termination. He may as well have been the day's paper taken to the shredder.

They navigated another mile until he lifted his paddle from the water and drifted, thinking about the rest of the day. A peppery cloud retrieved his consciousness.

"Hey, Reily," a sultry, scratchy voice greeted him from behind.

He turned to see Kim, a short, sexy, but married redhead from New York. A Newport dangled from raspberry lips. Wil had secretly labeled her "Adirondack Kim," more for her anatomy than her geography.

She paddled toward him. "That's a beautiful boat. Who makes it?"

"Watters Incorporated."

"Oh. Seriously, did you really build it?"

Reily straightened. "I did."

She slipped her pink kayak parallel to his canoe. "I love it. How long did it take you?"

"About six months. I saw an ad for a 'make your own canoe kit' and thought why not."

"You're quite the woodworker."

"Thanks, I've had a bit of free time." Kim was hot for someone her age and it was more than her looks; she had charisma. It was only the third time Reily had talked to her but he liked the kind words she spoke so freely. He never remembered his ex-wife saying anything complimentary or confidence-building... just verbal artillery – constant, loud, and painful.

Kim ran her lustrous nails along the hull. "What kind of wood did you use?"

"Maple and ash. They're a shade off one another, but they complement." He showed her the different strips. "The maple is lighter in color but heavy, stiff, and strong. The ash is slightly darker but has excellent bending qualities."

"I see. Did you ever canoe the Adirondacks?"

"About fourteen years ago, I went to Tupper Lake with my wife." He began to stroke his beard.

"The two of you should come back. Our inn is right on Blue Mountain Lake and we have a little log cabin for two with a big fireplace and an oversized Jacuzzi."

"I would love to check it out, but... we divorced."

"I'm sorry to hear that."

Reily wondered if that were precisely true as he watched her float away.

Back on the water, dehydrated and dead-tired, Reily approached the outskirts of Wyalusing, one of the many small, struggling Susquehanna towns with poetic Native American names. For once, he was near the front of the pack. A psychedelic string of trip mates stretched upriver behind him and out of sight. Somewhere in the mix were Wil and Gabriele... and the elusive Sol.

It was an easy walk to the high school, the night's campsite at a ball field carved into the floodplain. Reily pitched his tent on the infield between third base and home and crawled inside. From across the road, a John Deere puttered like a voice from the past. He closed his eyes and rewound the day.

"Reily, you better get your ass up." It was a familiar, booming voice. "You must have been having a hell of a dream. You were twitching all over."

He forced his eyes open to a face with cropped hair and lines etched on an oversized forehead. Alex kneeled in the vestibule.

"Dinner is over, but you can probably get some if you hurry."

Reily threw on a short-sleeved polypro shirt and rip-stop shorts and marched up the hill to a brick warehouse posing as a school. Architects had lost their imagination.

In the parking lot, a catering truck was backing up. He banged on its side. The truck halted, the driver's door slid open, and an obese woman with flabby arms stepped out. The vehicle creaked with relief. She was one of the ugliest ladies he had ever seen – with a net matted over curly hair and a chin hung low like the beard of a tom turkey.

He mustered the courage to speak. "You wouldn't happen to have a little food left? I overslept."

The woman said nothing, just scowled with hippopotamus eyes.

"Please, ma'am. I'm very hungry."

"There isn't much left. You people sure eat a lot." She pushed past him to the rear doors and gave them a tug. A greasy, appetizing odor hit him. "There are still a couple of legs." She assembled a paper plate with two chicken drumsticks and a side of applesauce.

He thanked her but she paid no attention.

While the sun cooled toward the northwestern horizon, Reily carried his dinner into the cavernous gymnasium where dozens of participants and a handful of locals had assembled for the evening program. He took a seat in front of Adirondack Kim and positioned the food on his lap. Along the front wall, a trim man with a tight beard fussed with the tripod legs of a movie screen, gazing through gold-rimmed glasses. Dr. Rob Murray was the Executive Director of Susquehanna River Conservation Society, or SURCOS for short. He hopped in and out of the Odyssey, yet he was its creator. Reily had thanked him with a beer two nights earlier.

The Doc began the night's presentation, "River of Possibilities." Reily tucked the grubby plate and a crumpled napkin under his chair, thinking that Murray seemed young to be a doctor. He leaned back and felt Kim's warm hands ticklingly massage his shoulders. Her perfume enveloped. It had been a long time since a woman had touched him there... or anywhere.

Content, he refocused on images chronicling decades of abuse of the Susquehanna – cleared forests, raw sewage, acid mine drainage. Some of the wounds were healed or under treatment but new ailments had emerged. From farms, lawns, roads, and rooftops flowed runoff laden with toxins, sediment, and an excess of nitrogen and phosphorus. The river suffered; the Chesapeake Bay reeled.

Reily recalled the times his Uncle Gus had taken him crabbing in the Bay. They'd spent most of the days lazing around in his runabout, anchored in shallow flats thick with seagrass. On lines baited with chicken necks, they pulled in more than a bushel of jumbo jimmies – hearty male Atlantic blue crabs. In the evenings, they picnicked under the big oaks outside his uncle's trailer. The steamed crabs were spicy and succulent, corn glistened with melted butter. Oysters were presented by the dozens, slimy sweet and salty. Since those days, crab harvests had fallen like a lead weight and the oysters were all but gone. It was an American tragedy.

Murray's lamentations continued. "We're paving over the watershed and as a result degrading our streams, destroying habitat, and displacing wildlife. We may be able to slow this trend but it's going to take action, major action, on many fronts and an expanded ecological consciousness."

The good doctor's eulogy spawned a headache. Reily guessed it was a combination of the magnitude of the bad news and a long day's physical punishment. Even though he was a card-carrying Sierra Club member and felt most comfortable in the outdoors, his own role in planetary stewardship was lagging. He could do better.

Murray described a place known as Whispering Heights, what he called "900 acres of greed" sitting atop a 500-foot escarpment along the Susquehanna River near the Vossburg Bend. Thick forest would be laid to waste to construct over 200 "sky chalets" overlooking a mile of river. More than 600 townhomes would cover the rest of the site, shoehorned into six artificial villages crisscrossing vernal wetlands where a dozen species of amphibians bred.

"All of these habitats support a cornucopia of wildlife – deer, bear, bobcat, turkey, coyote, fox – an A to Z of Pennsylvania critters," Murray droned on. "There are even rumors about a mountain lion although the eastern cougar is believed to have been exterminated a century ago. But the bottom line with Whispering Heights is this – it is a proposal for way too much development in much too sensitive a place. It needs to be stopped."

Reily felt like he'd been punched in the gut. He was driving a god-awful, gas-gulping Ford Explorer and still spreading poisons on his yard every spring. But the idea of a mountain lion thriving in Pennsylvania was somehow inspiring, and intriguing, all at once.

Doc Murray answered questions and invited the audience to sign a petition opposing the development. Reily waited his turn.

Murray handed him a pen. "Thanks for signing. We need all the help we can get."

Reily stood, towering over the man. "My pleasure, it's the least I can do and thanks for the excellent presentation. I spent a few summers in the Upper Bay and it breaks my heart to think about how badly we've screwed things up."

"I know what you mean. I live and breathe this stuff, usually through a scientific lens, but it still gets to me." Dr. Murray removed his glasses and cleaned them with a handkerchief. "Where did you go on the Bay?"

"My uncle's place was on the Bohemia River. Occasionally we'd do a full day trip down to the Sassafras, but most of the time we would fish the Bohemia."

Murray smiled. "I grew up in Elkton."

"I would ride with my uncle to Elkton to get Schaefer Beer."

"Schaefer, now you are dating yourself."

There was something affable about the doctor. "Speaking of beer, I could really go for one. Care to join me?"

"Sure, I'll just need to pack up first. It's been a long day. I had a marathon meeting with a foundation this morning then had to prep for tonight's talk. A beer would be great."

Reily laughed to himself. Every night was beer night on the Odyssey.

After Dr. Murray loaded his things into a small pickup, Reily led him into the sprawling encampment. They found guitar-man Alex and java Rick – with his sleek ponytail and diamond-studded ear – lounging in portable chairs engrossed by a flickering candle.

"You two look like you belong on the cover of an LL Bean catalog." Reily gestured toward his guest. "You all know, Dr. Murray."

Alex stood up and gave a friendly nod. "Super talk. I caught about twenty minutes of it but I had to leave to get *provisions*." He tipped his head toward a cooler. "There are two six packs in there, iced and ready to consume."

Rick rose and extended a flaccid hand toward Murray. "Good to see you again, Dr. Murray. You impress us."

"Please, call me Rob. No formality required."

Alex found a fleece blanket in his tent and laid it on the turf. Reily and Rob sat down. Rick handed them cold beers.

Reily held up his bottle. "Alex is a fine musician and photographer. Maybe he'll give us a concert?"

"Perhaps," Alex said before launching into a famous tune by the Allman Brothers.

Between songs and brews, they talked for nearly an hour about the Susquehanna, other notable rivers, and their own water-borne adventures. Reily was tiring. Rick rummaged for more beverages.

Alex looked around at the darkening tents. "Would anyone like to get high?"

Reily about choked for fear of offending the doctor, the person who had the ultimate say on acceptable Odyssey behavior.

"It's been a while, but sure," Murray said.

Apparently there was no need for Reily to intervene. "I'll come along but stick to my beer." In college, many of his friends employed pot and other mystical substances for entertainment but he exercised avoidance, more concerned about diminishment of his memory than any moral opposition.

They followed the trail to the boats. Riverside, Alex unzipped his hip pack and removed what appeared to be an enormous cigarette as elongated and chunky as a first-grader's pencil.

Reily gasped. "That's the biggest joint I've ever seen."

Alex beamed. "I call this the Ziggy – as in Ziggy Marley. Papa Marley's good name has been overexploited. I felt it was time to honor his son." He lit Ziggy, inhaled, and passed it on.

The smoking circle enriched the weirdness of the trip and it was tempting to capitulate. There was no fiendish spouse around to berate such behavior. A thick, cannabis haze, an intoxicating incense of burned juniper, hugged the ground. He sensed he might be suffering from indirect inhalation. He gazed over the water and upon the heavens.

"Looks like a planetarium," Rick said, almost reading Reily's mind.

"It's beautiful." Reily couldn't remember when he had last seen so many stars. The sky was a Christmas tree decorated with lights.

Alex attempted to sit on the cobbles but slipped. His backside hit the ground with a thud. They laughed in uncontrollable spasms.

"What are you men doing?"

Words stabbed from behind. The accent was proper British with a feminine spunk.

Reily spun around. "Holy crap, you almost gave me a heart attack." Even in the dimness, he could see the voice belonged to a slightly stooped senior.

"I'm sorry, but I needed to look for my water bottles. I believe I left them in my kayak."

Rick came forward with his hands in his pockets. "Do you need some help?"

"I don't think so and I don't believe you would be of much assistance right now. You've obviously been smoking a bit of marijuana."

"I'm Reily Watters." He decided to be spokesman since the others were too stoned. "Clove cigarettes. That's what you smell."

"Codswallop," retorted the British woman. "I know the difference between cloves and grass. People are so uptight these days. I'm glad you found a way to properly relax."

The tension drifted away with the vestiges of the smoke and the others came forward to meet the hip and witty old lady. Her name was Frances Collington. It was her first day on the passage.

Frances found her water bottles and went on her way, escorted by Rob Murray who was planning to spend the night in his pickup. Rick had a 'date' with his top of the line two-man tent. Alex and Reily remained, immersed in shadows and stillness.

Reily reclined and propped his head against a lifejacket. "How did you meet Gabriele and Sol?"

"At an Onondaga peace ceremony near the Finger Lakes. I knew you'd like them."

"Wil sure likes Gabriele. I've hardly seen him since they entwined. And Sol... she seems extraordinary but I have yet to have a substantive conversation with her. She probably doesn't want to spend much time with an old fart like me."

"Don't be so sure. That long hair makes you look young and you can party with the best of us." Alex hummed while assuming a prone position. "Just be like the river."

"What does that mean?"

"Follow the flow. You don't know what awaits you."

"Rejection, most likely." Yet Reily's optimism sparked. Blowing fifteen hundred dollars to paddle the entire Susquehanna in forty days might have been excessive... but it should be interesting. "Where are we headed tomorrow?"

"Meshoppen, I think, or... as the squaw said to her husband, Me-Shoppin."

"You're whacked, Alex Mueller, definitely whacked."

15

Reily listened to the soothing rush of the river then Alex's deep, slumbered breaths. Tranquility took hold and he closed his eyes in expanding appreciation of this wild, wonderful experience.

CHAPTER 4

A t 5:30 A.M., Sol Messina awoke to chatter. Crows were far more jarring than NPR. Last night's campfire Pinot Noir had left her parched. She unscrewed the lid and drank from her water bottle. At her Baltimore loft apartment, the city would be beginning to stir, the cobblestone streets of Fell's Point bathed in feeble daylight. There, tankers rested in the outer harbor; here, kayaks chilled in the grass. She was glad to be away.

"*Guten Morgen*," a groggy voice escaped the sleeping bag beside her.

"Good morning, Gabriele, and how are you feeling today?"

"My head hurts from too much wine. I told you we should only drink beer, yes?"

"Wine's better for you. When did you come to bed?"

"Much too late." Gabriele sat up and rubbed her eyes, smearing mascara.

"You need sleep. Wil needs sleep." Sol admired her friend, noting how she exuded sensuality even first thing in the morning. Gabriele wore a satin night shirt with the pattern of a zebra. Her golden hair was swept into a quirky pile high on her head. Even when they were in the hills of Zimbabwe and hadn't bathed for a week, she could turn the heads of male villagers, but sometimes Gabriele's accent drove her crazy, especially when American guys latched onto it, immobilized with lust. More than one drunken fool, thinking they were paying her a compliment, asked if she was a Swedish porn star.

Gabriele emitted an achy groan. "I need coffee."

Sol brightened. "Rick will have some."

They found Rick outside his tent. His French press released a soft sucking sound and, when opened, a puff of baked chocolate aroma. Backcountry breakfast brew was hot and ready.

"This is my favorite press. I have two of them – one for home and one for the road." He filled Sol's mug then Gabriele's with the caliginous liquid.

Sol savored the first steamy sip. "This is the best coffee I've ever had on a camping trip." She viewed the other trippers dismantling their temporary homes, packing their cars or lugging hefty loads to the Ryder gear truck for shuttling to the next campsite. A whistle reverberated across the outfield. It was the official outfitter, guide, and safety guru summoning them to the daily briefing. She and Gabriele were behind schedule.

Ten minutes later, they scurried to the circle of humans where the stubby, bulldoggish safety officer complained about lost and found items. In one hand he held a bent-shaft, carbon fiber paddle and in the other, a grill lighter discovered near some canoes. Alex stepped forward to claim the lighter.

The queasy litany continued with a description of the route to Meshoppen and hazards that might be encountered. Downed trees on bends in the river could act like spider webs entrapping unsuspecting paddlers. Sol pictured a worst-case scenario with overturned boats and submerged occupants.

At the river's edge, Sol prepared for another day on the water with Rick in his tandem kayak. She zipped her life jacket and watched Gabriele captivate Wil and his friend, Reily. Gabriele had a lithe left foot on Wil's kayak and rubbed generous gobs of creamy, white sunscreen down her illegally long legs. The ritual was heightened by the evocative scent of coconut and the metal stud that sparkled at her navel. Wil fumbled with his seat straps, his face flushed, but Reily moved his gregarious eyes away from Gabriele and slyly her way. She acknowledged him with a brief, polite smile.

Rick stretched headfirst into the cockpit to adjust the position of the foot pegs. Sol admired her young, free-spirited kayaking partner. She felt lucky to be paired with him. He was much better looking than the loser she left in Baltimore. This guy had a good vibe.

With gentle hands he helped her into the boat and gave her a double-bladed paddle. She breathed his musky cologne. He had his own custom carpentry business. Maybe he could build her a house?

They moved into the current. Tiny, lustrous clams bejeweled the bottom and fish of assorted size darted in surprise. Sol was amazed at the clarity of the water. The brown Inner Harbor was vile in comparison.

On the shore, she saw Reily stepping into his wooden canoe, too perfect for a rocky river. He was fit and handsome for an older man; the long hair, beard and beguiling gaze was a portrait of Hemingway in his prime. Until six months ago, she was living halfway around the world and had missed contact with men with whom she shared a native language and common experience.

Rick's soothing voice and instructive touch brought her back from the revelry and induced a pleasant, involuntary shiver.

Reily drifted like plankton on an inland sea. He reclined with his arms over the gunwales, his fingers dipping into the tepid water. The reflection of a bald eagle stole his attention. It glided from a low cliff on flattened wings as if powered by the gods. In this day of reckless disregard for the planet, it was refreshing to see a symbol of wildness alive and at ease. Eagles were returning to the river in numbers not seen for decades, finding refuge on verdant islands and craggy overlooks. Their rebound was one of the few environmental success stories – a glimmer of hope from a broken mirror.

Wil caught up to him and stoked the day's temperature with a well-oiled, buxom bow mate. Gabriele wore a ball cap, her ponytail poking out the hole above the adjustable strap. She looked fantastic but paddled pathetically.

She took a break. "Hi, Reily. Wil has been telling me stories about you."

"That can't be good."

"He said that people thought you were related because you looked alike and he told me how much you know about nature... how you describe the things you see with beautiful words."

"He's making stuff up."

Wil leaned forward. "He's a poet and doesn't even know it. He sees and understands things you and I don't. The man is astute beyond his years."

Reily dismissed the praise and replied to Gabriele, "I hope my friend is treating you well."

"Yes, very much so." Wil inched forward, rocking the kayak. "What are you doing, Wil?" she gasped.

"I think you need a little help with your technique."

"You will help me?" she laughed.

"Certainly." Wil placed his hands next to hers on the metal shaft and synchronously dipped the paddle from side to side, shedding silver droplets.

"I think I am getting it now, yes."

"You're doing great, Gabriele." Wil gestured to Reily with a tip of his head before stealing an over the shoulder view of her cleavage.

Reily shook his head at the crude gesture. "How old is she?" he mouthed the words to Wil.

Wil shrugged. "Gabriele, how old are you?" The question seemed too nonchalant.

"Why do you want to know?"

"Because Reily wants to know."

Gabriele turned so she could see both of them. "I am thirty-four." Wil's jaw dropped. "How old did you think I am?"

Wil hesitated. "I would have guessed twenty-eight."

Before she could ask their ages, Reily spotted bold letters on Gabriele's cap. "Do you work for US AID?" He pointed to her head.

"No, but Sol does. I work for the Lutheran Church."

Reily found it hard to believe Gabriele was a church girl but what did he know these days about churches and moral dictums? He was a faith-based soloist. The sliver of information about Sol was more interesting. "What does US AID do?"

"They are the US Agency for International Development. They do projects in other countries to help improve the economy, environmental conditions, and the quality of life."

"What country was Sol working in?"

"In the Republic of Zimbabwe, outside Mutare. That is where we both worked."

Reily envisioned a puzzle of the African continent. Where did Zimbabwe fit?

"We coordinated a coffee cooperative. Coffee is grown in the eastern mountains. The people are very poor, yes. There is seventy percent unemployment. We had good success with our program until Mugabe's crooked, evil government made our work impossible. Do you know of Mugabe?" She looked at him then to Wil, her pale blue eyes packed with conviction.

Reily shook his head, embarrassed but honest about the limits of his geopolitical awareness. "So you left the country?"

"Sol went back to Maryland and I returned to Germany but now I have a job in Baltimore on a visa." Gabriele seemed excited about her life trajectory.

He remembered the feeling.

Wil hijacked the mention of Baltimore to begin a new conversation with Gabriele. Reily floated away listening to flirtatious banter about a bar near the Inner Harbor and strip clubs along the infamous "block."

High above the water, Reily saw cars on Route 6 and minute people, distant and indifferent, spying from a roadside rest. His paddling comrades were dispersed a mile up and down the river.

"Are you enjoying yourself?" Frances Collington appeared from nowhere, her royal voice unmistakable.

"I am. Thanks for asking."

Frances was a sight – skin dark leather, hair polished silver. She raised a wrinkled hand toward Wil and Gabriele. "Those two seem to be having fun."

He discerned a teasing twinkle in her eye. "I'd say so. May I ask where you are from? I noticed your fine accent."

"Where would you guess?"

"Somewhere in the U.K., maybe England?"

"Heavens no, it's too dreary in the winter. I live on the lovely island of Eleuthera in the Bahamas. I've been there for the past twelve years but prior to that I lived in England."

"How did you end up on the Susquehanna River?"

'The sister of my late husband lives in Pittsburgh. I was planning a holiday to visit her and a few days later I found out about the Odyssey through my kayaking organization. I kayak twice a week at home. It keeps me fit and it's a nice way to meet men."

He failed to contain a laugh. Frances certainly was candid.

"Reily, you have a wonderful personality. Why isn't there a young woman with you?"

He shrugged his shoulders. "Probably because I'm old."

"You're much too dashing and charming to be going it alone. We just need to – how do they say it – hook you up."

Did Frances want to get him laid? "That's flattering but I'm closing in on half a century. I'm fine with that. I don't expect any miraculous affairs, but thanks for thinking of me."

"Look at them." She gestured downstream to two distant kayaks side by side. He made out Adirondack Kim's radiant hair and Alex's clean-cut, Boy Scout appearance. "They have been like that all day."

"They must have a lot to talk about."

"I believe they both have romantic intentions. I watched their body language, their nuances. I know love when I see it."

"She's married... plus she's probably ten years older than Alex. Kim is very amorous but I doubt she plans on sleeping with him."

"Dear, nobody plans these things. They just happen."

"You're a funny lady."

"If I'm not mistaken, you have your sights on a gal."

Reily coughed from embarrassment. "What are you talking about?"

"The blonde's friend, very attractive. I saw you assessing her this morning when we were all together."

"I was not assessing her." This old broad was bold. "I admit she's cute – but I don't know about assessing. That sounds serious."

"That's what men do, they assess women. They analyze our appearances, our bodies, our attitudes. They ascertain if they stand any chance of, well, getting lucky."

Reily threw back his head and sighed. "I think your assumptions are a little overboard."

Two damselflies, clasped in iridescent flight, flittered between them, and landed on the bow thwart of his canoe.

"That's a good sign," Frances said, "a very good sign."

CHAPTER 5

H ap wheeled into his driveway and noticed the mess. A wadded-up McDonald's paper bag and ketchup packet sullied his weed-free lawn. He parked and, after sanitizing the grounds, decided the asphalt needed another cleaning. Rains had delivered unwanted twigs and pebbles to his coveted parking surface.

In the back of the garage, he lifted the leaf blower off a shelf and filled it with two-stroke mix. Blowing was a fine way to unwind. His eyes caught the plans folded in the corner and his mood soured. *The envelope, how could I forget the envelope?*

With the concentration of a doctor performing a prostate exam, he probed under the car seat before scooting back to the privacy of the garage with his package tight in hand. A tug on a frayed string illuminated a single overhead incandescent bulb. He laid the envelope on his work bench and extracted ten exquisite $100 bills. They could have been printed that morning. NASCAR races in Charlotte had been on the wish list but they had lost their luster. He pushed the money back into the envelope and hid it under a dusty stack of Playboys from the 1970s. The Whispering Heights plans were to blame. He tugged them from the same pile and unfolded them. The sound echoed off empty walls.

Blue-line drawings showed two large parcels. One said "property of Donald and Gertrude Bunting" and the other "property of Woodring Holdings, LLC (formerly owned by William R. Corson)." The Woodring property was larger but had minimal road frontage. The Bunting parcel was under a tentative sales agreement. It provided better access plus space for a third of the housing units. If the parcel wasn't acquired, longer access roads would be needed and that would drive up costs.

The forest on the back side of the Bunting land was full of evergreens thicker than two people could wrap their arms around. Don Bunting had let Hap hunt there years ago. The deer were sparse but the trees would make fine timber if they were cleared. The open part of the land hadn't been farmed for a couple of years; it was scraggier than a bum's head of hair.

"Hap, get in here. I have supper ready." The voice came from inside the house.

"Be right there, Mim." He stowed the drawings.

Hap's wife adjusted a TV tray in front of his plaid recliner. She seemed thinner than he remembered but it had only been a nine-hour separation. He collapsed into the chair and fumbled with the television remote. Ever since they installed a satellite dish, he shuffled channel to channel to catch nuggets of hundreds of programs. It was mindless and relaxing after a long day of hauling.

She dropped a small stack of mail on his lap. "What in the world is that one?" She read the return label through horn-rimmed glasses. It bore the seal of a District Magistrate.

"Don't know." Hap winced at the thought of what might be inside. Did someone know about the township nonsense? His heart beat faster. Mim would be crushed if he got in trouble.

He opened the letter to find a summons for unpaid tickets in Pittston. Sometimes he had to wait centuries for the bags of syringes and bloody crap. He hated tickets more than liberals but at least it wasn't something worse.

He re-fondled the remote and found a commercial for hair replacement. The bald actor made him think of Lowell Orwell. A few clicks later, a pastor pranced and sermoned about temptation and weak flesh. Hap didn't wait for other ominous warnings. A movie looked familiar. Federal agents charged stockbroker Charlie Sheen with insider trading and led him away in handcuffs.

Mim placed a steaming plate on his tray. "The ham is from Engle's butcher shop."

Hap eyeballed the food wearily. He had lost his appetite.

CHAPTER 6

Reily dragged his boat up an icy stream that drained the mountain behind the disregarded town of Meshoppen. If the town was dying, the stream wanted nothing to do with it. The water was lively and refreshing – a tonic for the senses after the sapping rigors of a long day of canoeing. He repositioned the lightweight craft over his head and marched past fellow paddlers cursing and struggling with heavier loads. He caught up to Wil and Gabriele fifty yards further ahead.

Wil climbed a short bank carrying the front of his boat. Gabriele cradled the back. "This must be our campsite," Wil said between labored breaths.

It was another ballfield and, according to a hand-lettered sign, named after a local Bill who died prematurely in Vietnam in 1968. While it wasn't on par with taking a fatal bullet, Reily thought of the last few years as his own war. The past days were rehabilitation long overdue.

He dropped his minimal gear and plucked his car keys from a vinyl dry bag. Two vans courtesy of the Gifford County Conservation District idled in a gravel parking lot ready to return to Wyalusing where Odyssey participants could pick up their vehicles.

The striking westerly vista demanded eloquence and Reily internally scripted what his eyes confided: *a golden ribbon, mellow as fine bourbon, lively as champagne.* It was entertainment as the van negotiated Route 6 high above the river.

Kip, an employee of the conservation district, steered the overloaded Dodge. He looked like Gilligan from the old TV series. "How long are you on the river?" he asked through snuff tucked behind his lower lip.

"About three more weeks," Reily answered. "Folks come and go, some are only here a few days."

Reily glanced behind at the other occupants. Sol was tight beside Rick who was mushed against a driver's side window. She was whispering something in his ear.

"So Kip, what kinds of things do you do for the district?" He hoped small talk would erase Sol from his mind.

"We give advice and assistance to farmers." Kip paused to spit in a soda can. "Things like proper planting techniques, barnyard management, manure storage, stuff like that. I also help enforce erosion and sedimentation regulations at construction sites."

"Do you know about that proposed development near the Mossburg Bend?"

Kip chuckled and caramel drool dribbled down his chin. "You mean Vossburg. Sure I know all about that plan. It ought to keep us real busy."

Reily was surprised at the indifference in Kip's voice, like it was no big deal to bust up acres of wildlands. "You think they'll get the approvals they need?"

"This is Pennsylvania. Everything gets approved. It's all about tax revenue and jobs in Conroy Township and every rural township. Can't say I disagree about the jobs. Most people around here have to commute a long way to work... if they have work."

Reily gazed out his open window and felt the breeze against his face. A loud pickup passed on the right sporting a gun rack and a bumper sticker reading, "My kid beat up your honor student." He frowned. Even with all he had been through, he wouldn't channel his disenchantment toward the academically successful children of others. He loved kids, especially his own daughter, Casey. She was becoming quite the independent woman.

Reily turned back to Kip. "So where do things stand?"

"Excuse me?"

"With the development. What happens next?"

"Well, I think they have to get it rezoned, at least part of it, but that isn't a big hurdle. Most places around here don't even have zoning. There's also a property dispute. The developer is wheeling and dealing with an old lady about her farm. He wants it for more access and houses. Claims they had a verbal agreement, but she hasn't made up her mind."

"Who's the developer, this *he*?"

"Carl Woodring. He has a company called Woodring Holdings. I think they're based in Wilkes-Barre, but they have properties all over. They sell real estate. They develop, too."

Reily scratched at his beard. Was murdering the land a learned behavior or a genetic defect?

Lost in thought, Reily drove his own car back to Meshoppen and parked adjacent to the ballfield. He proceeded to erect his tent next to Wil's along the home run fence within earshot of the cascading stream. He stomached another poultry dinner and was tempted to skip the evening program until he saw the speaker hunched over with a gleaming bald head and youthful exuberance. Morris was the man's name and he shared his lifelong collection of Indian artifacts and an encyclopedia's worth of knowledge about the people who once used them.

Reily watched from a park bench. Wil passed him a beer. The cold, amber liquid refreshed while poor Morris's lips became sticky with drying spit as he held up arrow points, pipes, bowls, and implements. The old man took short breaks to catch his breath and sip from a cup of water while his wife, of like size and stature, sat on a folding chair beside him in proud adoration. The two were soul mates. Morris had passion, too. Reily remembered the similar rush he received from ogling clients enthralled with his meticulous plans. That was a long time ago.

After Morris's departure, devilish noise drifted from the Wild Waters Inn, the only bar in town and a dangerous temptation to civilization-starved river runners. It called to Wil and Reily.

Reily grabbed his wallet from under the driver's seat of his car. "Where are the ladies?"

Wil motioned with his head toward the river. "Last I knew they were planning to bathe outdoors."

"And why aren't we with them? I could stand a good washing."

"We weren't asked... plus you couldn't get it up for both of them."

They started walking to the bar. "It has nothing to do with that. I don't even know if the machinery functions anymore. All I know is that it would be a truly cleansing ritual – much better than a pricey spa – to immerse with Sol."

Wil stopped. "You're doing it again."

"What?"

"You're playing with your damn beard like you're trying to find something."

"Whatever. I didn't know it was a problem."

"No big deal. I just don't remember you doing that in the old days."

The inn was hard to miss. Paint peeled in slivers off wood siding. Beams of light escaped around a sagging main door.

Wil pointed to a grimy sign above the entrance. "Wild Waters and Reily Watters – a perfect match."

"You're mistaken. Wild and Wil are synonymous the world 'round."

Wil tugged on the handle and they were enveloped in a caustic cloud of tobacco smoke and loud music. Reily surveyed the barscape. A warped pine floor struggled to support a half dozen tables, mismatched chairs, and a pool table stained ugly by years measured in spills. A frizzy-haired barmaid emptied the ashtray in front of two people at the bar. Along the wall, an oversize couple in leather kissed and grinded. It would have made him sick if it weren't for the pleasing décor in another corner of the room: a freshened Sol and Gabriele waving at them. Rick was waving, too.

Reily stood beside Wil at the bar.

The barmaid approached. "What will you two have?"

Wil spoke over the heavy metal, "Five liquid valium shots."

"What the hell is that?" The barmaid flashed teeth as yellow as the floor.

"Throw together some vodka, Crown Royal, and cranberry juice. That's it." Wil sounded like a mixology teacher.

Reily shuttled the drinks to a lopsided table where his friends sat. Wil robbed two chairs from an empty table and brought them over. The ladies were drinking gin and tonic, Rick a cosmopolitan. No one protested the shots.

Wil tipped his glass at Gabriele. "To new friends and cheap drinks."

Reily closed his eyes and swallowed the concoction. When he opened them, Sol was staring at him, her shot glass still full.

"How bad was it?" she said. "You looked like you were in pain."

"Not bad at all," Reily answered.

Sol wore no makeup but her eyelashes were thick and opulent. Freckles spotted burnished shoulders. A scar – overwhelmed by the woman's abundant breathtaking features – slanted across her right cheek. "Alright, I'm going to trust you." She threw her head back and slurped with eyes tight shut.

"What do you think?"

She drew a deep breath. "Excellent. Let's have another one."

"Really?"

She bought the next round.

Drunkenness arrived unannounced. Sol moved closer to Rick who had switched seats with Gabriele so she could be near Wil. Fortified with alcohol, Rick became more social, telling Sol details about himself – his two-bedroom row house, his herb garden, his favorite cafes in New Hope, a pet cat named Harvey.

Wil grasped Gabriele's hands to read her palms or do something less innocuous. Then they stood and stumbled toward the pool table without issuing an invitation to join them. Gabriele sat on the edge of the playing surface and hooked her legs around Wil as he explored her mouth with his tongue. The leather couple, still conscious, cheered them on.

Reily couldn't take much more. He went to the bar and asked for a single-malt scotch. They didn't have it. The barmaid didn't even know what it was. He settled for a glass of Johnnie Walker straight up.

A small, bony man swiveled on his stool and surveyed him. Reily felt like a giant.

"I ain't ever seen you in here, has I?"

"No, you hasn't." The guy was oblivious to his teasing.

"My name is Hap Clay. Nice to meet you."

"I'm Reily."

"Now, I don't think I ever heard that name before."

"Me neither." Reily didn't want to get trapped in conversation with a chatty drunk. "Are you a township supervisor?"

"Hell yes, I've been one for twenty... wait a minute, how did you know?"

"It's on your shirt."

The lines loosened on Hap's face. "Oh yeah, I forgot."

Reily sipped his drink. "Where's Conroy Township?"

"Gifford County, where the river makes a sharp bend – about eight miles from here."

"Is that where the big development is proposed?"

Hap's friendly, alcohol-softened demeanor vanished. "It isn't that big. Projects like that are a dime a dozen in the Poconos. We aren't that far from the Poconos, you know."

"Yeah, I know."

"The locals, including myself, we want this thing. It'll be good for the area."

"That's not what I heard. Sounds like it will screw things up first class."

"Bullshit, wacko bullshit. Who's telling you that? A few houses aren't going to hurt anything."

"Hundreds of new houses is a different matter." Reily felt himself getting primed from the booze.

"Where did you hear all this? Look, damn it..." Hap jumped to his feet and teetered. He grabbed the bar for support.

"I didn't mean to make you mad."

"I don't need this." Hap dropped a ten on the counter. "See you later, Glenda."

Reily finished his scotch at the jukebox. What made the old guy snap? He scanned the selections and for a dollar picked a trilogy of Neil Young songs.

Sol and Rick prepared to leave. Reily held up his empty glass and saluted them, sad to see her go. The bar was empty now except for Wil and Gabriele who continued to share saliva and a sixteen-ounce Budweiser. The leather couple was gone, and the barmaid counted money.

His watch read 11:40 but it seemed much later. It was time to go. Neil Young hadn't even finished playing.

Chapter 7

Sol knew the drinks were distorting reason but she couldn't help her mild attraction to Rick despite his negligible response. He was lean, strong, and sentimental... and for some reason, always made her laugh.

"Cool spot, huh?" From the rock, all she could hear was the burbling water in Meshoppen Creek. She'd had to plead to get him to stay up with her.

"Yeah." Rick didn't budge. He rolled a bottle cap between his fingers.

The air was fragrant, the stars radiant; it was a good night for romance. Sol pulled his shoulder toward her but he subtly resisted. She was mystified. They'd had an excellent day together and she was hoarse from the endless conversation. "Are you okay?"

"Sure," he replied.

She moved closer and without pause, slid her left arm to the back of his neck. It was moist with perspiration. Three weeks earlier, the day before her birthday, her egotistical ex-boyfriend had acted similarly but more bluntly, terminating their brief but fervid courtship without notice.

There was one more thing to try with Rick. She twisted her body upwards and pushed her lips against his, horrified to find them taut and unwelcoming. "What's wrong?"

"I'm sorry." His voice was barely audible.

"I'm usually pretty good about deciphering emotions. I guess not this time."

"I don't know how to say this. I'm not very good at it."

She prepared for the 'girlfriend' confession.

"I like your company. I know they don't make women any nicer. Unfortunately, I am not attracted to women. I can't help it."

She couldn't find words. Her stomach was in a knot. Rick caressed her back with his right hand.

"I had a partner, guess I still do, but we decided to give one another more breathing room. He moved out. We'll see what happens. I didn't mean to mislead you. I hope you'll still be my kayaking partner. I had fun today."

Sol wiped tears with the backside of her hand. "No problem, I'd be glad to remain in your kayak."

"Good. Well, I better go. See you tomorrow." He kissed her on the cheek before lowering himself from the rock and disappearing streamside.

She sat and stewed about her miserable luck with men. The water offered little consolation but she welcomed the counsel of nature. Maybe it could bestow the gift of discernment.

CHAPTER 8

R eily awoke to abbreviated laughter and unmistakable voices. "We have to be quieter," Wil said. "Our sex is too loud, yes?" Gabriele confirmed they were doing the forbidden deed, yet again. Only Wil could meet a centerfold foreigner years younger and bed her regularly.

Reily considered the possibility that the whole thing was a dream but there were more sounds from the tent next door – unmistakable vocalizations of lovemaking, feverish squeals of coital momentum. He couldn't sleep through this. He put on a shirt and left the tent barefooted.

He heard strumming as he approached the port-a-johns. Two silhouettes were sitting under the pavilion. One held a guitar.

"Is that Reily?" The seductive voice was a giveaway.

"Kim? Who's that with you?"

"Hello, Reily." Alex sounded mellower than normal.

"Was that some Grateful Dead I heard?"

"Indeed."

"Mind if I listen for a while?"

Alex turned a tuning peg and tested a string. "Only if you pretend you're Jerry Garcia."

Kim supplied Reily with a beer from a cooler while Alex laid into another Dead tune.

Reily was curious. Were they working on romance? Alex mentioned a girlfriend more than once. Kim was older than Alex, probably in her early forties. Why wasn't her husband on this grand adventure? Alex was a good guy. He deserved to get laid, or better yet, fall in love.

What about his own situation? Such a fair summer's eve was primed for passion but sleep was a more critical pursuit. After another song, Reily drained the last drops of beer into his mouth, thanked Kim, and slipped away from the pavilion. Alex kept on playing.

Stars drenched the sky and the ground radiated a belated chill. Away from the music, he heard the stream's invitation.

On damp sand, below an infant waterfall, he was native among ferns and stones and surrounded by the alien trill of American toads hoping to beckon a prospective mate. His toes wiggled in the fine grains, mitigating his companionless funk. The water urged him to urinate and so he did, turning away from the current and showering the vegetation. A feeling of being watched crept over him. He pulled up the front of his shorts and glanced around. At first he saw nothing then caught a shape upstream, slipping away. It appeared to be a woman. He wanted to say something but refrained out of shame. The water remanded him to his tent; he obeyed.

Reily stirred from a bad dream, more frightening than normal. Abby rode a tidal wave on a personal watercraft trying her best to drown him. But it had also included a strange, enchanting female who seemed familiar, a gardener wearing a sleeveless sundress and a wide-brimmed hat.

The sun was beginning its daily climb as he emerged from his tent, the sky dusted a watermelon hue. His watch said a quarter 'til six. Others stirred: a child whimpered to his parents; a sneeze was followed by flatulence; whispers came from the tent next door – the one with boxer shorts lying in front of the entrance flap.

At the pavilion he found Alex sitting on a picnic table. His upper torso attended to a small camp stove, his legs remained in a sleeping bag.

"Good morning, Alex."

Alex twitched. "Yo Reily, you gave me a startle."

"Serves you right."

"You up for a little green tea? It'll warm your bones."

"No thanks, I'll find coffee."

"Did you know that green tea was the preferred beverage of Mahatma Gandhi?"

"No, I didn't know that." Alex had random access insights. "But it makes sense since tea is a common thing in India."

Alex nodded. "They say green tea makes you wise."

"It must. Look at Gandhi. He was prophetically wise and an overall great man."

"I wonder if Jesus drank green tea." Alex poured a steaming cup.

"Mostly wine, I imagine."

"Did anyone ever tell you that you resemble the manger man?"

Reily laughed at loud. "Once, many moons ago, a drunken girl at a party told me I looked like George Harrison. She even made me talk to her with a fake British accent."

"I'm serious, you do look like the Messiah."
"Those are big sandals to fill."
Alex held up his cup, "To our new Messiah."
Reily shook his head. "That stuff is skewing your reality."

Reily returned to his tent and noticed how the dew drops clung to it like a thousand transparent beetles sleeping on its surface. Short blades of mowed grass stuck to his bare feet. He put on socks for the first time in days, then wind pants, hiking shoes, and a long-sleeved shirt bearing the logo for the Key West Sailing Center.

Breakfast and coffee wouldn't be served for another hour, so he took the book he'd started a week ago and walked to the shores of the creek. He found a sitting rock and turned to page forty-six of Thor Heyerdahl's autobiography. It wasn't on the recommended pre-Odyssey reading list distributed by SURCOS but he had relished *Kon Tiki* years earlier, an account of the famous voyage across the Pacific on a balsa raft. A river trip would be a fine time to gain a deeper understanding of his favorite explorer, even if the clerk at the bookstore hadn't a clue about him.

A rippling of the water pulled him from a page. The glistening back of a fish perhaps eight inches long darted up a riffle. Thanks to years of coaching from Wil, he knew it was a brook trout – shy residents of unassuming mountain streams. It had signature orange and white on the pectoral fins and a calico body. Brook trout needed cold, clear water to live happy lives. They preferred simplicity, familiar surroundings and favorite holes of ample depth – underwater islands in an otherwise shallow world. The handsome fish traveled solo. Maybe he had a lady trout friend waiting for him in an upstream pool?

A vitriolic song caught his ear. High in an ash tree he spied a flash of Halloween color and the troubadour. It was an oriole, one of the most beautiful songbirds ever made. The last time he'd seen one was on an Audubon walk led by an octogenarian who could have been sixteen. There was something about nature that fostered longevity. Little marvels kept life interesting and numbed the irritations experienced along the way. For being pickled and sleep deprived, his brain was in overdrive. He stood up, stretched, and walked to breakfast with Heyerdahl in his head and hand.

Church Street was lined with century-old oaks and plain, two-story wood-sided homes. Porches dressed with gliders, flags, and flower pots touted community pride. The Methodist Church blended with the rest of the buildings; he nearly strolled past.

Inside, rows of folding tables were surrounded by empty folding chairs. Kindly parishioners prepared him a plate with scrambled eggs, two perfect strips of bacon, and a mild cup of coffee in a Styrofoam cup. It tasted wonderful.

Others began to arrive. The Watson family from Johnstown accompanied their delightful daughter, Carly, who was always querying him with overly complex questions for a seven year old. Today she wore a yellow hat and matching rain slicker as if she had disembarked a fishing boat from the Grand Banks. Then Wil snaked in.

"Sit down, my friend. You look like you need a seat."

"You're a perceptive one, Watters." Wil dropped into the chair next to him. He wore sunglasses, disheveled hair, and his crusty visor.

"I'm surprised you can walk."

"I didn't drink that much."

"I'm not talking about the alcohol." Reily lowered his voice. "You two were screwing like newlyweds."

"Have I mentioned that she's unbelievable? She's off the pages of the swimsuit edition of *Sports Illustrated*, but it's not just her body or her looks." Wil grabbed his arm. "This woman rocks. She's my intellectual equal. I'm feeling young again."

Wil swooned but Reily had seen him in this same state of mind before. "Good for you but be careful. Maybe she's just curious about what it's like to seduce a vulnerable old guy." Reily didn't want to see his friend get burned. The pain lasted too long.

"No way, I have her captivated. She's head over heels." He jabbed Reily in the ribs. "And I had her heels over her head, too."

Modesty was not one of Wil's defining traits and he was pretty sure the cocksure attitude had contributed to the demise of his marriages. "So where is your wonder woman?"

"I don't know. I told her I was going to breakfast and she said she'd come, too, after she found Sol."

Reily raked at his eggs. "Do you think Sol hooked up with Rick last night?"

"Maybe, but don't be so down."

"I'm not down."

"Yes, you are. You look like a scolded puppy. Even if she bounced on Rick's broomstick, there's no need to fret. Maybe tonight or tomorrow night it will be your turn."

Reily wielded his last strip of bacon like a sword. "Don't you ever shut up? First of all, I'm not looking for anything, especially not a one-night stand. Secondly, even under the remote possibility I was given the chance, I wouldn't want to bat cleanup to Rick."

"Suit yourself, but I think she digs you."

Reily cast a doubtful frown. "You better get your food before the hordes arrive."

Wil stood. "Good advice. By the way, I'm not paddling today."

"What?" Wil always had a detour.

"It's going to rain but mainly I want to write. Gabriele has inspired me."

More likely Wil wanted to plunk Gabriele in the back of his car. "Let me guess. She's staying ashore with you."

Wil suppressed a most devious smile.

CHAPTER 9

Gertrude Bunting fed her tabby morsels of leftover bacon and finished hand-washing the breakfast dishes. From the window above the sink, she could see the corner of the barn with white, weathered boards and a faded declaration of John 3:16. Just beyond was the pond where her boys and kids from nearby farms would swim on dripping hot days. The new field, as her late-husband had called it, rippled golden and holy in a fresh, gusty breeze. Her dresses and underthings flapped on the clothesline tight to the house. A Jesus sun catcher projected prisms on her arm. This was her place, every broken down square inch of it, but it still gave her comfort.

A knock from the main hallway was predictably followed by loud barking thanks to Schnitzel, her plastic guard dog. The battery-powered Rottweiler replica was activated by sound. His thirteen inches broadcasted a short series of guttural woofs to repel would-be intruders.

Puffing from exertion, she opened the seldom-used front door. Glaring back at her was a slim man wearing sunglasses and dressed in a button-down denim shirt. His mustache seemed mismatched against pallid skin. His hair was slicked-back and rusty as a hinge.

"What can I do for you?" she asked through a cracked storm door.

"Are you Mrs. Bunting?"

"Who wants to know?" She didn't want a salesman harassing her at 8:30 in the morning.

"I'm Carl Woodring. You met my attorney months ago." He paused as if expecting an acknowledgment. "This is regarding your farm. We're anxious to settle so that you can reap the rewards of this special property. I was hoping we could talk in more detail about my proposal." He dropped his sunglasses onto the bridge of his nose and stared beseechingly.

She opened the storm door and moved into the sunshine, her face scrunched in a scowl. "I don't think we have much to talk about. I'm not ready to sell yet. I've been on this farm a long time and I might want to stay for a while longer."

"I can appreciate that, Gertrude. Is it alright if I call you that?" She heard a little southern drawl in his words.

"The folks that know me call me Gert." She turned to pluck weeds from the window box. "You can call me Mrs. Bunting."

Woodring laughed with irritation. "Fine. You should know that the supervisors are voting later this week on the zoning change for your corner of the township. Then shady people, not decent businessmen like me, will be hounding you and you could end up losing out. Do you want that to happen?"

"I'm not so worried. A spray of hot lead shot will take care of the pesky ones." She chuckled at her own audacity.

"My offer gives you financial security and the plan for my development maintains the things you like about Gifford County."

"I only listen to one man and that's the Lord Almighty. He's given me many good years and pretty soon it'll be time to wrap it up. Then I'll call you – if you don't bother me too much in the meantime." She made eye contact with him for the first time and didn't blink.

Woodring folded his arms and sucked a breath through flared nostrils. "Mrs. Bunting, the offer is only good for 180 days and we're up to 150 and counting. If you don't sign and we don't settle, I don't know if my investors will endorse submitting a new offer. They may lose interest and that would be unfortunate for both of us."

Gert felt an inkling of remorse for the man's predicament but she knew he had used the plural 'investors' for pity and leverage. It was his rear-end on the line – restitution for sodomizing God's creation. "Well, I don't know what I'm going to decide but I'll tell you what I will do, I'll pray about it. Maybe ridding me of all this worry makes sense but I just don't know yet. You and the township can do what you must. So will I."

Woodring walked to his big car, deflated as a flat tire, and opened the door. She thought he might have a crying fit, but he drove away without a tantrum, his tires moping through the gravel.

CHAPTER 10

Precipitation arrived late morning, starting as scattered light taps, growing into the deafening beat of a billion raindrops on an aqueous drum. Cold rivulets seeped down Reily's spine. He shivered in futility.

Conditions were miserable by most measures, yet stimulating. Without occasional hardship an expedition lost its value, its significance; the joy was cheap and meaningless. Life required suffering to foster appreciation for the serenity of the routine. He paddled on.

The river swept left in a gradual but detectable arc: the Vossburg Bend. The right bank reached upward – a towering rock wall shrouded by sheets of rain. The paddlers below appeared miniature. Sol and Rick were absent from view. He had trailed behind them all morning and from his distant surveillance, they weren't talking to one another very much. Perhaps it was a symptom of the somber weather more than a deviation in their relationship.

Boats were ashore, tucked at odd angles against the left bank. He landed and flipped his canoe upside down to keep out the dripping sky before regarding the steep, stone face. The development would be an abomination. He imagined garish homes lining the upper rim. Hunger displaced incredulity and he set off to find lunch at the camp hidden away on the peninsula.

A spongy path twisted through waist-high ferns and scattered pines out of *Grimms' Fairy Tales*. The rain lulled. He saw a long cabin ahead with sixty of his group mulling, eating, and talking on a timber-railed porch with a green shingled roof. A wood-burned sign decreed the structure Mehoopany Lodge of YWCA Camp Sullivan. It was a life-size Lincoln Log creation. He remembered the set he had given Casey fifteen years prior.

Inside the cabin, warming pans bubbled. One was mounded with spaghetti, another purveyed oily meatballs and sauce. He filled his plate. His Italian food addiction could be blamed on his mother's one-quarter Umbrian ancestry.

From the far corner of the porch, he ate and watched others courier apple pie and chocolate cake to loved ones. The lurid sights and smells summoned. On his way inside, he held the screen door for Sol and saw that she was carrying a small plate with a square of cake centered upon it. The skin on her hands was barely a shade lighter. "That looks pretty good."

"I know. I love chocolate," she said with a flex of her brows before walking away. *Poof.* Gone.

He retrieved the last piece of cake, shuttled it back to his porch seat and devoured it in three bites. Somehow it tasted better knowing that Sol liked it, too. She enthralled without pretention. He hadn't thought endearingly about another woman for months and now he was becoming irrational about one much too young and unattainable.

As he arose to return his plate, Alex approached with Sol at his side. Reily's fork slipped and clattered on the decking.

"Great Messiah, we wondered if you wanted to join us for the tour."

"What tour?"

"The non-violent pilgrimage to Whispering Heights to pay homage to the absolute and omnipotent power of the American dollar."

"I see." He looked at Sol who shrugged her shoulders. "How could I have forgotten the Whispering Heights field trip?"

"Are you in?" Alex said.

"I wouldn't miss it for all the green tea in India."

His heart vaulted as he zipped his rain gear. Sol may have lobbied for his inclusion or at least supported it. The afternoon offered promise.

Rob Murray and his pickup were parked in front of the lodge. The camp had been named for a general who sanitized the region of its indigenous inhabitants but a peaceful mist and sunburst kayak poking out the back of Murray's truck tempered – for a moment – injustices of centuries past.

Reily, Sol, Alex, and eleven others gathered round to get the lowdown on the tour. The brutal hike would provide a unique chance to see the threatened land firsthand but they would be trespassing on private property. The volunteers were undeterred.

Murray surveyed the lot of them with a gleam of appreciation. "To the boats, folks. We'll paddle across and tie off."

"If I'm prone to a heart attack, I'll find out today."

"Come on, tall man, it's not that bad," Alex said.

Reily caught his breath. "I didn't say it was bad, it's actually quite good. I'm just out of shape."

"A few more weeks of this and you'll be ready to climb Everest."

"If I don't flatline first."

Sol was ahead of him and turned around. "Check it out." She pointed to the view behind them. A thin blanket of fog shielded Camp Sullivan hundreds of feet below but the sun was winning the battle. The bending river sparkled in applause. A warm breeze luffed her hair.

The ascent grew precarious. Thorny greenbrier covered sections of the scant trail. Loose rock succumbed to gravity. In a world of overzealous lawyers, Reily was surprised Doc Murray would let them do this hike. SURCOS must have decided that exposing candidate activists to an atrocious development scheme was worth the risk. Good priorities. They earned his donation.

Reily had Sol directly before him and could now, as Frances had surmised, assess her physically and intellectually. He noted the perfection of her buttocks through the thin, tan fabric of her hiking pants. They appeared firm and divinely proportioned to the rest of her. Fearing the consequences, he refrained from touching them but it was their conversation that impressed him most. There wasn't any shallow, time wasting talk. She engaged him like a long lost friend, speaking over her shoulder and asking him about the places he had trekked or traveled. Her tone was one of genuine interest. He was spellbound. Alex mused far behind them, shuffling like a snail. Perhaps it was on purpose to leave the two of them alone together. Clever.

Sol paused to pluck berries from a shrub. "Are these blueberries?"

"Yes, the lowbush kind. They're my favorite fruit. Are you going to eat them?"

"I should but I'm superstitious. I'm feeling far from blue today. Being out here in the fresh air makes me feel good. Something red would better fit my mood. Think we'll find any of those?" There was mischief in her eyes.

He laughed. "I'll keep looking."

Sol resumed hiking. Out of the thick heath, a black snake raced across her foot. She jumped backwards; her left foot skied off the edge. Reily lunged forward and scooped her across the back with his arm. She fell onto the trail, and he tumbled on top.

For eternal seconds they laid there. He felt his heart hammering... or maybe it was hers. He rose to a kneeling position. Sol's lower lip was smudged with blood, her hair tousled.

She rolled onto her elbows and lifted her head. "Wow, that was scary."

"I'll say." He reached into his pocket for a bandana. "Here, you might need this for your lip."

"Thanks. And thanks for saving me."

"Anytime."

She offered her right arm and he pulled her to her feet. They resumed hiking. He recounted the moment of peril and his response. Had it been demure or awkward? They squeezed past a sofa-sized rock and the land went horizontal. The others were there gathered in a clearing.

Rob Murray spotted them. "Is anyone else with you?"

Reily stumbled up to the group, Sol beside him. "Alex is back there somewhere but I wouldn't wait on him."

Rob regarded his followers. "Alright then, let's take about a half hour to explore. You've already heard a bit about the site. Now you're on it. There aren't any trails except for the poorly maintained one coming up and it continues behind me for over half a mile to the road. I suggest splitting into small groups and carefully poking around. Please don't step on nor pick any wildflowers and do keep an eye out for rattlesnakes. There's a neat rock garden that begins roughly 150 yards that way or if you follow the trail for about 100 yards and turn left you'll find some exceptional wetlands. Soon they'll be dry for the rest of the summer. That's where I'm heading. Plan to meet here at 2:30. If you run into anyone that doesn't look familiar, try to get back to this spot. I'll do the explaining. Any questions?"

"I can already tell that this site has a lot to offer." An older man had spoken. Reily knew him as Cal from Ohio. "But why throw all your potatoes into this kettle? What makes it more important than the next parcel down the road?"

Rob dropped his head to compose a response. "There are many reasons why this place is worthy of protection – size, biodiversity, proximity to the river, the view it affords. I could go on but the gentleman raises a good point. There are hundreds of Whispering Heights... places that stoke our souls, burgeoning with wildlife and resplendent with beauty... but there's a limit to how long we can look the other way. For me, it isn't just about this property *per se*, it's about the future. Wallace Stegner called it the geography of hope. I believe we need to be couriers of hope and bring some solace to the land. The preservation and restoration of our collective home is our cross to bear."

Rob's eyes were moist. It was good to see a scientist inflamed with passion. They were trained to be cold and objective but this guy was different. Reily appreciated the disgust about desecration of the environment. He'd experienced it almost daily during his career. There was still no sign of Alex but it was time to roll. He turned to Sol. "Shall we explore?"

They set off in the direction of the reported rocks. He spotted a colony of teaberries clinging to the ground and picked three, sharing them with Sol. "I believe these would be the red fruits you requested?"

"You're very resourceful."

"The forest spirits present them as a gift – for the close call on the way up."

She sighed with false exasperation. "I accept." He watched her nibble on one of the berries. "I haven't had a teaberry in years. I forgot how good they are."

He put one in his mouth and tasted wintergreen. "Very good. I think Native Americans used them as a breath freshener."

"Interesting." They continued onward, Sol following him. "So where did you learn about plants?"

"It's part of being a landscape architect. You have to know them. I was always partial to the local species. They understand the soil and the climate and get along well with the other living things in the area."

"So you're a landscape architect?"

He stumbled on a Beech root. "I consider myself in remission. I'm a recovering LA."

"I see."

It was time to learn her dossier. "I understand you work for a foreign aid organization?"

"Yes, I worked with Gabriele in Zimbabwe. Now I'm in Baltimore. Complete culture shock. I coordinate international fair trade coffee programs. From time to time I get to travel but I'm easing into the traditional office thing. It's a little sad knowing some of my greatest adventures are behind me, but I'm ready for stability. At least, I think I am."

"So you're becoming a conformist?"

"I didn't say that."

He stopped. "Is that what I think it is?"

Sol looked where he pointed. "Yep, poop and a lot of it." The oblong pile was partially covered with pine needles and humus. It had an oily glaze. "Do you think it's from a bear?"

"That would be my guess but what do I know?"

"You mean you're not an expert on feces, Mr. Watters?"

"I've been told I'm full of shit but that hardly qualifies me as an expert."

They approached the outcropping promised by Doc Murray. Fractured passages bled moss and lichen, winding between house-sized slabs of bedrock erupting from the ground. Garden of the Gods had been transplanted to Pennsylvania. He felt like a kid in a maze. Sol scampered out of sight.

Minutes passed. "Okay adventure girl, just because you know African jungle tactics doesn't mean you can stalk me like prey." A shadowy crevice between stacked boulders made a probable hideout. He gripped the coarse sandstone with his fingertips and climbed. "I know you're in there." There was no response. He caught a rancid scent from something nearby, dead and ripe.

A figure pounced from the void. "Gotcha!" Sol landed inches from his hands.

He made a lighthearted scowl. "I just aged ten years."

She sat down and dangled her legs from the ledge. "I'm sorry but it was the perfect setup. I was on the rock and realized you were right below me. Please forgive me." Her eyes begged with canine sincerity.

He pulled himself up and rested beside her. "You're forgiven – this time." A geologic freak show surrounded them. The place was unworldly.

Sol whistled like a child then paused. "I hate to interrupt our outing, but I think it's time to go back. We might not be able to find our way out of here."

"No worries." Reily led the way, bushwhacking through rhododendron. Branches scratched his face and arms but he couldn't have cared less. This was the most fun he'd had for eons.

"Reily, look." Sol crouched to the ground. A tawny, speckled songbird lay dying, it's plumage unscathed. "I wonder what happened. There aren't any windows to crash into."

He stooped to examine the bird, a wood thrush. "Maybe it hit a tree? I can't see any blood." He lifted it in cupped hands and stood to show it to Sol. It flew out of his palms, skimming past her face in hasty departure.

She shook her head in disbelief. "What did you say to it?"

"Nothing, honest. Maybe it was late for a bird seed sale or a hot date."

She studied him playfully. "No doubt, but that was borderline miraculous. Do you have special powers?"

"If I do, they're yet to be discovered."

CHAPTER 11

"In Ezekiel 34, we read '...Is it not enough for you to feed on good pasture? Must you also trample the rest of the pasture with your feet? Is it not enough for you to drink clear water? Must you also muddy the rest with your feet?'"

Hap tuned out the radio preacher, the religious rabble and brainwashing of WGOD of Waverly, New York. In ten minutes, a new country station would come into range but his mind focused on the upcoming Conroy Township meeting. Woodring, the red-headed rat, would be dressed like he came off a dude ranch and argue like he was before the Supreme Court. He'd beg the supervisors to approve a zoning variance for the Bunting place. Fat Lowell would insist that development is necessary and that they must honor this reasonable request. All he had to do was second Lowell's motion. Wilson would stammer in opposition but two yes votes would push it through.

Ahead, on the right berm of the road, a young lady in blue jeans stood by a Chevy Blazer. She looked upset and waved a reluctant hand. He felt obliged to stop but feared the repercussions to his schedule. Either the gal had a beer gut or one in the oven; the bulge in her blouse was hard to miss. He eased to the side and turned off the car. A "Save Farmland" sticker squawked from her bumper. He hoped she wasn't a greenie.

"What's the trouble?"

She smiled as he approached. "I'm not sure. All of a sudden there was a big boom from underneath and then it just shut down." A crucifix shimmered on her bosom.

He squatted behind the vehicle and peered underneath. Black liquid dripped from the middle of the rear axle. "I think you blew out the differential. She's losing oil."

"Is that bad?"

"Yep, I'm afraid so. I know we're surrounded by state forest but your truck won't go anywhere until that's fixed. It needs towed."

"My husband's going to cry. He loves this old truck." The cute lady chewed her lower lip. "Where's the closest garage?"

47

"I have to think about that one. There's a place in New Albany called Creeson's on the right side of the main road. Look for all the junked cars."

There was panic in her gentle, blue eyes. "I hate to bother you but do you think you could take me there? I don't have one of those cell phones to call anyone."

He had two more stops to finish the day's route but duty elsewhere sometimes called. "I'm in a hurry, but we can run up there."

"I really appreciate it. I'm glad there are nice people like you around. I'm Mary Kambic, by the way."

He extended his hand. "I'm Hap, Hap Clay." The situation was setting up to be a fine story for his buddies at the Wild Waters Inn.

CHAPTER 12

The campground was a sliver of green stretched along the river and backed by the Route 6 bypass. Cars streamed across the bridge into Tunkhannock. It was a Monday and people were returning home from their day jobs in the Wyoming Valley oblivious to the occupation of their community by a band of itinerants.

Reily positioned his canoe alongside the other boats, guessing the night's rest would be fitful. Walking along the narrow park road, he found a few of his comrades setting up tents. Then he sighted Wil's SUV and Wil getting out the driver's side.

"Hey, can you give an old man a lift?"

Wil strolled up to him barefooted. "What old man?"

"Actually, I'm feeling spry right now. I probably had the best day I've had in years."

"Outstanding. What happened?"

"We connected."

Wil's eyes brightened. "I told you."

"You did?"

"Yes, I did this morning, but you were adrift in a sea of self-doubt."

"Your motivational speech was about sex. I'm just pleased the woman liked hiking with me. I'm telling you, Wil, it was really nice."

"For what it's worth, I think you're going to have big sex on this trip. When, I can't predict, but it will happen. Just watch those emotions, brother."

Reily absently pulled at his beard. "I have no expectations so I'll be fine."

"I had a pretty outstanding day myself."

"Oh no, what deviant act did you commit on Ms. Gabriele?"

"Nothing, I was as pure as Reily Watters. I went to this cozy coffee house in town, had a fine lunch, and ended up spending three hours writing. This whole deal has me primed."

"What did you do with your woman? Your visor's pretty filthy, by the way."

Wil shrugged. "She was way tired, almost narcoleptic. She spent the afternoon snoozing in my Trooper."

"And what are you writing these days?" Reily looked past Wil hoping for a glimpse of Sol.

"Just you wait and see. My Machiavellian mind has surreptitiously contaminated another manuscript."

"Oh no."

"Oh yes. Something tells me I'm on to something good."

"Speaking of something good, have you seen Sol?"

"They left."

Reily's heart dropped. "Who left?"

"The people who have cars to move. The vans left about five minutes ago with your sweetie aboard, along with Rick, Alex, and other hooligans."

"What about everyone else?"

"There's another talk. This one's at the courthouse a few blocks thataway." Wil motioned with his chin. "The rebound of this little Mayberry is the topic *du jour*."

"So how am I going to get upriver?"

"Fear not, I'll take your slowpoke ass to Meshoppen."

"Thanks, but I'm contemplative, not slow."

"Like molasses with a brain."

Reily attempted to place Wil in a headlock. Wil shook free and went to the back of his vehicle, popping the tailgate to reveal Gabriele curled in the back. She twitched and unfolded from a fetal position, her skin flushed. The car was as stifling as the Everglades and reeked of wet shoes. Reily was amused by her willingness to nap under such conditions. She must be in love.

Gabriele squinted. "What time is it?"

"Almost five," Wil said.

"I was so tired." Strands of hair remained pasted to her cheek.

"Hey, I'm going to run Reily back to his car. It might take a while, so would you mind setting up the tent? When we get back, we can all go into town for dinner."

"Okay, but you trust me with your tent?"

Wil pecked her on the forehead. "Absolutely."

Reily watched the affection in disbelief. "Is there anything happening tonight that we need to know about?"

"Nothing." Wil reached in his pocket for keys. "It's a night on our own. I checked the schedule."

"Great." Reily appealed to Gabriele, "Could you see if Sol wants to go with us to dinner?"

She unloaded a supermodel smile. "Certainly, yes, just hurry back. I'm getting hungry."

With the windows down, the radio cranked, and Wil at the controls, Reily felt eighteen again. He closed his eyes and enjoyed the breeze.

"You're not obsessing, I hope."

"Nope, more like dreaming."

When he opened his eyes, they were approaching the crossroads of Russell Hill. On the right was a multi-acre spread with a ranch house, detached garage, and a for-sale sign at the end of the driveway. The sign said Golden Ring Realty. There was an agent's name below it. "God, please no."

Wil shot him a confused glance. "What?"

"The real estate sign said Abigail Gordon."

"I'm sure it's a coincidence. The name's not that unique."

"I have a sick feeling."

"What was the latest on her?"

"She's back with her mom, left Jim for good and took up real estate." Reily sank lower in the seat. "I get sparse details from Casey, even fewer from Abby."

"Where's Abby's mother these days?"

"Scranton. That's not that far, is it?"

"No. Not really."

Reily sorted bad memories the rest of the way to Meshoppen.

Wil dropped Reily next to his Explorer. "Are you stopping for a shower?"

Reily reanimated. "Now that's an original idea." It had been three days since his last cleansing. "Where do we do that?"

"They opened the middle school for us but doors close in half an hour."

"I'll follow you."

In Formula One style, Wil led the way back to Tunkhannock and a school with coveted plumbing. The locker room was empty but antiseptic smells filled Reily's head with teenage flashbacks, quelling a portion of his name-spotting discontent. An endless torrent of nuclear hot water did the rest. He was determined not to let Abby bring him down but resistance was never easy. He brushed his hair, trimmed his beard, polished his teeth, and dashed himself with an archaic aftershave. Wil, preening at an adjacent mirror, told Reily he looked refurbished.

"Thanks. What time is it? You told Gabriele we'd hurry back."

"We did. You could hardly keep up."

"But this was an extra stop."

"Relax." Wil zipped his toiletries kit. "They'll be waiting for us."

Reily learned long ago that urgency was an emotion foreign to Wil but the calm assertions of the ice man were often well founded – like now. From the park road, certain bodies occupied a playground and they didn't appear hostile. Sol and Gabriele lounged on a pair of swings. Kim and Alex balanced on opposite ends of a teeter-totter. Rick slumped at the bottom of a sliding board, a beer in hand.

Reily rolled down his window. "Good to see you delinquents."

Sol pouted. "We're hungry."

Gabriele kicked at the dirt. "We had no choice, yes, but to eat all of Wil's potato chips."

"We were about to barbecue Rick," Alex said. Rick ignored the comment.

The posse walked into town where they found an enticing Italian restaurant. Stools and tall round tables were painted Mediterranean colors, speakers delivered Luciano Pavarotti. They gorged on crusty, complimentary bread. House Merlot flowed by the carafe.

Reily noticed a smear of olive oil on Alex's chin and eyes blazed with illicit, scarlet trails. Mr. Mueller was indubitably gone. "Alex, were you smoking?"

Alex smiled froggily. "A delightful blend of two varieties but my friends wouldn't join me."

"We already had the munchies," Kim said.

Sol turned to Reily. "The berries didn't tide me over."

He sighed. "I should have given you more. Adrenaline speeds up metabolism."

Wil leaned closer. "What are you two talking about? I think I missed something."

"I nearly fell to my death but Reily saved me," Sol elaborated.

Rick left the table, posture sullen. Reily saw him standing outside talking on a cell phone.

Wil was oblivious to the sudden absence. "I was working on my book today with unbridled energy thanks to all of you characters." He paused and lifted his wine glass. "You're excellent fuel for the creative process. I'll even confess that my protagonist elicits some of the quirks of my old friend." He tipped his glass at Reily.

"I can relate to your gleanings of Reily," Alex said. "The man touches us all."

Reily shook his head and laughed. "Don't say that so loud."

"Alex is right," Sol said. "You have a nice way with people. You're very personable and genuine."

He reddened. "Thanks, everyone. You flatter me, but my ex-wife would be pounding her gavel in objection if she heard your statements." He wanted to kick himself for referencing dark days past. Thoughts of his former spouse clung like soggy cotton and he didn't need Sol to hear about the implosion of his marriage.

Gabriele began to inquire about the *verboten* subject but Kim interrupted. "We all know why Reily is a character in his own right but, Wil, I'm curious, how the rest of us might be seeping into your book?" She rubbed the rim of her wine glass with her thumbs.

Wil folded his arms in slow motion, evaluating how much to say. "In the wife of the protagonist, I can envision your forthrightness, Kim. No nonsense. Polite but bold. Obviously, she had such qualities before I met you, but now it's been refined."

Kim cackled disproportionately. "You're good, tell us more."

"Alright, the same character – her name is Sara – presents an outer mesmerizing grace. She reminds me of Sol." Wil acknowledged Sol with a wink.

Reily was surprised by Wil's candor. He usually kept his writing to himself.

Rick returned to the table and stared at his plate as if examining it for cracks. Kim patted him on the back. The chemistry titrating between Rick and Sol the night before was long gone. She was now watching him with sisterly pity, not drippy concern. Maybe they had slept together, maybe not, but any residual bond was weak. Who had Rick talked to on the phone? Then it struck Reily like a paddle in the face: Rick must have a girlfriend at home and he'd confessed to Sol. The girlfriend must have sensed that her boy was exploring new territory and issued a not so subtle notice to cease and desist. Reily remained worried – if Rick had been intimate with Sol, how could he ever match the abilities of the young buck? They probably did it for an hour.

Satiated on wine and pasta puttanesca, Reily waited inside the front door of the restaurant while the others settled their checks. He spied a rack of real estate guides and picked one up, curious to compare local prices to those in southeastern Pennsylvania. The top of one page read "Golden Ring Realty: Engaging You with the Property of Your Dreams." Such sappy, pathetic marketing. He scanned down and stopped. There were six agents pictured on the page and the fifth one – second row, middle photo – was Abigail Gordon. He knew that shrewd, made-up face anywhere and the listing of her name confirmed it. Her hair was longer than he remembered and she had bulked up, but those soul-slicing, coal pellet eyes never changed.

Wil approached and Reily handed him the publication without comment. Wil glanced at it for a moment, nodded with a frown, and laid it on the counter. Reily's stomach knotted.

Outside the restaurant, mayflies swarmed a street light. Wil took him into the shadows and grabbed him by the shoulders. "Look at me. Tonight's your night. Don't schiz-out because that sophisticate, skanky ex of yours staked a claim somewhere in this piece of Pennsylvania. Who cares?"

"Relax. I won't schiz out." Wil had a point but he didn't need to be so hyper-incredulous.

"Purge her from your thoughts and fill them up with nothing but that ravishing, little river goddess. She's waiting for you." Wil let go and turned away.

Reily adjusted his shirt and saw Sol watching from the corner. She must have viewed the entire exchange.

He walked in discomfited silence back to the waterfront, trailing behind the others. He needed to prepare his tent, but all he wanted to do was escape inside its hexagonal walls. As he unloaded the Explorer, Sol appeared wearing an Arizona State sweat jacket over her sun dress. Her hair cascaded over the hood like taffy.

"So how are you?" Her voice was warm and diffident.

"I'm fine." He wanted to say more.

"That was a good dinner but I didn't know we were infiltrating Wil's story."

Reily managed a slight smile. "He's such a bullshitter." He realized he hadn't seen her tent. "Did you put up one of these?"

"Nope, I'm going tent-less; just me, my sleeping bag, the stars, and the river."

"Sounds like fun."

"Then join me. You can help me interpret the sky."

"I may require my Therm-a-Rest." It was all he could think to say.

"It's permitted, actually required. Do you think I'm planning to sleep on top of rocks without one?" She began to back away. "See you down there."

"Give me five minutes."

Reily exalted. Cosmic forces were in his corner. He was about to bed down next to the river goddess and Wil wasn't there for vindication. Reily could elaborate on every magnificent chunk of the deal later. He brushed his teeth with fury and put on deodorant. With a long arm wrapped around a sleeping bag and air mattress and his pillow in the other hand, he alighted to the river, feeling high and mighty on the Sol train.

CHAPTER 13

Hap blasphemed the $1.90 per gallon displayed on the pump. Having a Republican President hadn't done a damn bit of good; the Arabs were still calling the shots in 2004. He jammed the nozzle into the Ford and through clip-on shades spied a skinny, sour face with a ball cap coming his way.

"Hap, I want a word with you."

It was Roger, one of the township leeches who slimed their way to every meeting and fed on each decision. The codger was a real pain in the ass. "What can I do for you, Rog?"

"That would be us, not me." Roger pushed his face too close. The overhead lighting at the Citgo cast a greenish tinge on his complexion. "We citizens of Conroy Township don't want you or Lowell Orwell selling off our homes to speculators and profiteers. We like things just as they are."

"I'm not selling off anything. You're not making any sense."

"Both of you are planning to vote for that zoning change to the Bunting place." Roger stepped back, his eyes misty. "That would be a darn shame."

"My mind's not made up. I know you don't agree but there might be a good side to more growth up here. I live here, too, and I like the same things you do."

"You're so full of manure you might explode at any moment. Orwell's told half the county about his screwed-up intentions and you always follow that idiot's lead."

Hap didn't know what to say. Rog had a point about his habitual deference to Lowell's judgment. He needed to be more questioning and independent. The episode – another in the intermittent but constant pissing from constituents – was aggravating his ulcer. He decided to say nothing.

Roger retreated. "Hap, do the right thing. You know what that is."

Hap tried to top off his tank as Roger drove away. The gasoline erupted, spilling on the concrete and splashing his trousers. It appeared as if he had urinated in his drawers. He stood listless, smelling of petroleum, wondering what rumors Roger and other folks were catching or throwing. It didn't matter. He just wanted it to go away.

CHAPTER 14

R eily nearly missed her on the shoreline. Sol nested beside a chunk of driftwood, hidden from the world. A stump doubled as a nightstand. He began to unroll his air mattress on the opposite side.

Sol cleared her throat. "You don't need to go over there. I'll feel like I'm talking to the tree."

"It could serve as a sound wall. I have an affinity for snoring."

"I'll take the chance. It can't be worse than the trucks braking on the highway."

He dragged the gear to her side and prepped his bedding. She laid there quiet as a stone, riveting his nerves. Two minutes later, he reclined with his hands under his head and took in the infinite sky. A mosquito whined by his ear. A firefly ignited inches overhead. It made him laugh.

"You know why they do that, don't you?" Sol said.

"It's a mating thing, right?"

"Yeah, but every species has its own pattern."

"That's creative."

Sol propped herself up on her elbow and turned to face him. "But you know what's even cooler?"

"What?" Even in the dimness her eyes were brilliant, collecting the scattered light.

"There's a species that mimics the female response patterns to the males of other species and when they make their move, it eats them. They call it *femme fatale*."

Reily positioned himself toward her. "Scary. So how did you become the firefly authority?"

"From my dad. He's a scientist, actually an astrophysicist. He knows a lot about everything, insects included, but he really knows what's out there." Sol tipped her head to the sky but kept her eyes locked on his.

"A star man."

"Yes, but mostly the dynamics of the solar system and the sun's influence on the earth. I can tell lots of stories about Dad. He's my Superman. But first I want to know what was up after dinner? You looked distressed." She sounded like his mother.

"Well..." he paused, hating to share his biographical horror story.

"We do have all night. You're going to have to enlighten me sooner or later."

She's persistent. He sat up on his sleeping bag. "Let me caution, it's not a cheery tale – quite bleak, actually. You see, I was married for nearly eighteen years. Our years together, especially the latter ones, were a matrimonial treadmill. I'm astounded I survived the workout."

"How long ago did you divorce?"

"Two years ago next month."

He waited for her to say something profound. Every word that floated from her lips had purpose and poignancy. Then she sat up, too, and worked her legs into a matching Indian position. Her stare penetrated as if she were a therapist. It was good to be her patient.

"So what was the argument with Wil about?"

"Ah, that. Well, I guess my ex still haunts me at times..." He filled her in on the details. "Evidently, Abby's peddling houses in these parts. Wil was telling me to buck up and ignore her recurrence."

"That's her name, Abby? Tell me more about her – and you. What happened?"

"You sure you want to hear all that?"

"Yes." Sol maintained a serious but gentle gaze.

He leaned back. "But what about your relationship history?"

"There's not too much to tell. My latest ordeal was with a single-minded guy who worked in the development office at the National Aquarium. I can take rejection but he was cold and calculating. He found out that my father was co-author of a landmark study about astronomical influences on coral reproduction and asked if I could convince Dad to join the aquarium's prestigious Chesapeake Council and make a $25,000 contribution. I resisted – I know my dad too well – and suddenly this guy had an aversion to spending time with me. What a coincidence." Sol stuck out her tongue in disgust. "Now it's your turn."

"I met Abby my junior year at the University of Pennsylvania. She would constantly ask the professor questions, annoying all the students, but I guess I found it amusing. One day we were paired on a project and she interrogated me. The conversation ended with us declaring we should go out sometime. By my senior year, we were living together, two years later, married. I thought her black and white ways balanced my mild-mannered, open-endedness... at first."

"Did I hear that you have children?"

"Just one – a girl. It was a whirlwind. I landed my first job with a firm called Alan Sutton and we bought a row home in Manayunk just a few blocks from the Schuylkill River. Abby's parents bought us a canoe, a Grumman, as a housewarming gift, then we had Casey.

"That's a nice name."

"I picked it." He liked Sol's compliments. "So city life was good to us, but after nine years, I was transferred to be the lead associate at a satellite office in Allentown. Abby was irate. Said there was no way she was moving to Hicksville, PA."

"Then what happened?" Sol seemed intrigued.

"We settled in Nazareth, northeast of Allentown. For me, it was a homecoming, close to my birthplace and roots in Bethlehem. For Abby, it was hell. Our place was small but it had charm and mature woods right behind it. Occasionally, I'd escape solo or with Casey for a hike on Blue Mountain or a paddle on the Lehigh – anything to get away from you know who."

"Let me guess, she left and went back to Philadelphia?"

"Nope, she found solace in the Assembly of God Church and its pastor, a fire-breather named Jim Gordon." Reily pictured the hypocrite at the pulpit, tongue-lashing the political left while ogling his wife. "Seven years later, she divorced me and married the blasphemer. The canoe went with her, bound for a still and dusty life in the garage of his McMansion. Worst of all, she got primary custody of Casey. Our daughter was sixteen at the time." He took a deep, cleansing breath. "That's the crux of my woeful biography."

Sol reached out and patted his arm. "That stinks. You seem too good a soul to have deserved that. If you don't mind me asking, where's your daughter now?"

"Liberty University. She just finished her freshman year, even made the dean's list." His voice trailed off.

"Is there tension in her relationship with you?"

"For some reason she targets her resentment at me like a firing range. Most of the time, she prefers to ignore me."

"Eventually she'll soften and realize what a fine man her father is." Sol unzipped her sleeping bag and burrowed inside.

"I don't know." He got into his bag, too. They both looked skyward as if on cue.

"I liked our time on the mountain today," Sol said.

"Me, too. I want more mountain time."

CHAPTER 15

Hap stood before the mirror in regretful self-reflection and flossed stringy flecks of chicken from the gaps between his discolored teeth. A few landed on the glass and stuck like bad publicity – the kind that might erupt from this week's vote. He could deal with the county weekly but the big papers from Williamsport, Scranton and Wilkes-Barre made his intestines curl. They thrived on controversy. One story would lead to another and that was seldom good.

His cheeks had wasted, hair thinned, skin tags multiplied. Dishonesty was taking its toll.

He centered himself atop the cool, crescent seat. To his left hung Mim's mint-green curtains embroidered with umpteen identical log cabins. They framed a window begging to be washed and a spacious backyard where he once grew a garden. Anymore, the only planting he did meant sitting his butt on a barstool. Hap remembered his beagle and groundhog chases and scattered neighbors offering a hand. This place had been good to him. Now he was going to betray it. Central Indiana had nurtured his early days and how grossly it had changed. The whole place had been swallowed by Indianapolis – an ugly, land-eating melanoma. Maybe he'd be encouraging the same sort of cancer here? He wiped himself and wiped again. It seemed harder than ever to wipe clean.

CHAPTER 16

W il worked his double-bladed paddle in overdrive and strained to keep pace with Reily. "This headwind sucks, but look at that sky. I swear we never have skies that indelibly blue in Jersey."
Reily wasn't listening.

The trees along the shore expressed greater animation. Wil knew how to get his attention. "Summer solstice, my ass. It's chillier than Abby."

"Thanks for bringing her up, but good comparison." Reily showed a smile. "She can't touch me today."

"You must be healing."

"Sol therapy could cure any man."

"I already miss the ladies." Wil visualized glistening Gabriele catching rays without him. He couldn't wait for more time with her and more time to write. The situations the past week were delicious page fodder. This novel would be a winner. Getting it published a cinch. His other novel, well received by critics but lagging in sales, had gained him marginal notoriety like his regular exposés in the *Ocean Press*.

"You gents ready for a fill-up?" Rick surged into peripheral view. "I know you love coffee. Let me see your cup." He drew his boat to Reily's and presented a stainless steel thermos. "Hold on to my seat and I'll fill you up."

"Okay." Reily foraged his mug from a dry bag. "Are you missing your paddling mate today?"

"Very much. Sol's a good kayaker – excellent stamina – and fun to talk to." Rick dispensed the coffee without spilling a drop.

Wil chuckled to himself. For describing someone who may have been the lay of his life, Rick was pretty casual. It reinforced his suspicions.

"Wil, would you care for some of this?" Rick gestured with his thermos. "It's a Costa Rican dark roast."

"No thanks, I have my tea. I'm set." Wil flashed a bottle.

"What are you fishing for?" Rick pointed to a fiberglass rod on the deck of Wil's kayak. "Trout, I presume?"

"Nope, it would be bass. The water's too warm for trout. I assume you don't fish?" Wil examined him smugly.

"Never tried it. I don't think I could get past the whole worm thing. Strikes me as cruel, messy, and unusual punishment."

"Use artificial lures," Wil suggested.

"I guess I'm not very interested."

A burst of wind raced upriver, pushing their congregation apart. Reily labored to a position parallel with Wil and caught his eye. "You're being harsh with the boy, aren't you?"

Reily was right. Always right. Wil shrugged. "I've been more of a prick with others."

"You've been way worse, but what's Rick's offense?"

"I don't know, I guess I shouldn't be such a dick but there's something about the youngster that has me wondering..."

"Wondering what?"

"I think he's a hip grabber."

"A what?"

"A rear paddler." Wil snickered at his own phraseology.

"You mean you think he's gay?"

"That's what my intuition tells me and that's based on more than his hyper-enthusiasm."

"He likes paddling with good looking women."

"That doesn't mean anything. I know several tippy-toe types and they relish women. It's who they yearn to be." Wil sensed his presumptions were a tad caustic. "But it's no big deal if he is homosexual."

"Bet you two shots of Wild Turkey he isn't."

"Mr. Watters, you're about to be ten bucks poorer."

CHAPTER 17

R eily lay with his head sticking out of the tent, the breeze tickling the trees. He was comfy as a panda at two o'clock on a summer afternoon while back at his former office the farm ants were carrying the weight of too many projects. This was a much more satisfying existence. Wil was fishing along the river, practicing his passion, and he was doing the same by reeling in a book. The last great work of Thor Heyerdahl was moving him, amplified by the mighty conveyor of people, places, and experiences on which he found himself.

"Yo Reily, what tis that manuscript before thee?" asked a pair of tanned and crusty feet.

Even in the glare of the sun, he knew that shadowed face. "The memoirs of Thor Heyerdahl. Alex, are ye familiar with him?"

"Of course, the leader of one of the greatest expeditions of the twentieth century."

"Wow, I'm humbled by your erudition."

Alex sat down and reclined in the grass beside him, laughing prodigiously.

"Are you high?" There was a ninety-nine percent chance Reily was correct. Alex smoked pot as routinely as kids chewed bubble gum.

"Not yet, but I just remembered what Kim said."

"Said about what?"

"About you, tall, quiet one. She said she wants some of that." Alex poked his finger into Reily's sternum.

Reily shook his head in disbelief. "Why do you mock me?"

"She told me about her yearnings as we were heading back to the campsite after dinner last night."

"I thought you were wooing her."

"She's had me sizzling, but I must forego her physical nourishment. My heart is occupied in State College. A tryst with an older, married woman could be counterproductive, but I must tell you what else she said about you."

"Oh no."

"'He's as smooth as soft ice cream'." Alex attempted to impersonate Kim's rasp.

"And as silky as a chocolate parfait," another voice chimed in. It was Frances Collington, the barracuda of gossip, sharking into view from the other side of her tent, her hair a whirling dervish, her voice wicked but jolly.

Reily got up. "You surprise yet again. You're a master of stealth."

"Have to keep men on their toes... or at least their best behavior."

"You don't have to worry about us," Alex said. "We're as pure and white as whipped cream."

"Well, my boy," Frances said. "I'm sure you know many of the decadent things one can do with whipped cream."

Frances was one degree north of surreal but Reily appreciated her style. Even a senior, albeit a spunky one, comparing him to dessert made him feel good, and sexy Kim, calling him smooth? Now that was titillating.

Based on the mouthwatering cut before Reily, the Loyal Order of Moose had mastered the art of roasting meat. The local lodge, adorned with a token moose head, dark paneling, and burgundy drapes, reminded him of a cheap horror film or a steel town sports hero movie. The dim surroundings were irrelevant; he was feeling brighter than a sunroom.

"Reily," Sol spoke in a whisper. "Do you really think this is roast beef?"

"I think so."

"What if it's moose?"

He sat across from her at the end of a long table populated by others in their group, but as far as he was concerned they were on another planet. His attention was funneled to the woman before him. "Just so it's not a Moose Lodge member." He leaned closer. "What if it's the outgoing Grand Bull?"

They both laughed. Sol rubbed her temples with her fingertips.

"What's wrong?"

She grimaced. "I'm getting a migraine, probably from sunbathing with Gabriele today. The glare gets to me. They start with little tremors and end as an earthquake in my skull. I can be knocked down for hours."

"Stargazing might cure you."

"I wish. I better go sleep this off. If I'm lucky, it will go away and I can revel under the stars with you later."

Reily didn't want the night to end. "That would be sublime."

"Thanks." She patted his hand and rose to leave.

He got up, too. "Let me walk you back."

"I'll be fine. Stay here with the others. It'll make me recuperate faster knowing one of us is having fun."

He was left lamenting by the table, rolling the end of his beard between thumb and forefinger. He noticed Kim watching him. She must have seen Sol's departure.

She called to him above the din, "Come sit by me," and waved him over.

Reily obliged as Sol would have wanted him to.

"I'll get you a drink – anything you want." Kim had gaping, clandestine eyes.

He occupied the chair beside her. "That's a very nice offer. What are you drinking?"

"Beer, but I'm ready for shots."

"Sounds like trouble."

"How about a pair of buttery nipples?"

"Excuse me?" Reily struggled to remain unstirred.

"Butterscotch Schnapps and Baileys." She summoned a waitress.

Kim talked about her day and leaned too close, displaying freckled breasts yearning for liberation beneath an underperforming top. She stretched out her legs and crossed them. They were lithe, smooth, and hazardous to men under the influence.

"Reily, did I tell you that your beard is quite handsome." She bit the tip of her finger in devious contemplation. The drinks were adding up. "Let me touch that beautiful face of yours." She reached out and he acquiesced, her warm fingers tracing his jawline. He avoided her eyes. Wil and Gabriele remained at the bar in alcohol-soaked conversation. He hoped they wouldn't see Kim's hands-on activities.

The face feel was interrupted by the arrival of two buttery nipples. Kim raised her shot and cajoled him to do the same. "Did you ever have these?"

"It's a first for me."

"You'll love it. Drink up." She slammed the shot like a veteran barfly.

He emulated her technique. The nipples were dangerously sweet and creamy.

"Want more?"

"One and that's it. I don't think I should have more than two in one evening."

"I bet you can handle a lot more than that." She tried to pinch his backside as she sighted the bar.

Reily considered a direct and unequivocal walk to his tent. Was her perfume fogging his thinking? The far wall was festooned with black and white photographs of Moose leaders past – all portly and cheerful. Was drinking away your evenings in shadowy, musty confines a ticket to happiness? Maybe they had streamlined aspirations and minimized distractions, lives free from an abundance of red-headed temptresses like the one handing a twenty to the bartender.

Reily corralled Kim at 10:00 P.M. They were the last patrons at the Moose Lodge.

Outside, she rested the weight of her head on his shoulder. "We must go to the beach."

He pictured a pink crescent of Bermuda sand but knew she meant the river. "There's not really a beach here."

"No really, Reily?" She cracked-up at the alliteration. "There's a beach with little rocks along the river."

They passed a string of cottages in the community known as Falls. Most were dark. They were props on a movie set, too tidy and quiet to be real, but it reminded him of the Chautauqua village where he'd spent many summer weeks as a child. The ice cream at the Hemlocks Inn was cold and sweet and the air smelled like an evergreen wreath; behind the counter, high school girls scooped with smiles and matching t-shirts. Years later, he'd taken Abby and Casey there. Casey asked if she could make ice cream cones when she was grown up. Abby said the mosquitos were driving her crazy. Maybe the truth was the other way around.

Silent throngs of tents filled a wide, grassy lot like cavalry assembled before a decisive battle. These environmental warriors traveled by boat and were too friendly to fight. Alex would pass his peace pipe and forge far-reaching alliances. Reily told Kim his spontaneous tale as they wobbled down the lane.

At the beach, he stopped to count the boats, an orgy of endless watercraft one against the other on their sides.

Kim pivoted and pressed her body to his. "Do you like the moon?"

He struggled to admire the waxing golden sliver. "Sure, I love a good—" A moist tongue flickered in his ear. "Whoa."

Kim pulled away and stared, her lower lip distended in a frustrated pout. "What's wrong? You're not attracted to me, are you?"

Reily's mind raced. He didn't have a firm grasp on his momentary desires. On a whim, he took her flushed face in his grasp. "You're a spectacular woman, Kim, but you're also married."

"And your point?"

"We shouldn't go any further. It's been a fun evening, but let's leave it at that."

"I may as well be single." She turned her eyes to the sky. "My husband's a two-timing jackass. I think he's currently in remission from philandering but it's just a matter of time until he has a relapse. This is my time to finally live a little. I deserve it." Tears trickled down her cheeks.

Reily delivered a kiss of compassion, maintaining contact for several seconds. Her sticky lips tasted like butterscotch. "That was to tell you how cool I think you are. I can't have an affair or even a one-nighter with you and I'm not sure why, but let's commit to making the most of the remaining weeks in other ways – whatever the hell that means."

Kim closed her eyes and, after a long hushed moment, agreed. She failed to veil her dejection. "I guess we better go get some sleep. I can already tell I'm going to have a hangover."

CHAPTER 18

Sol awakened from a vivid dream and studied the ceiling of her tent, her forehead damp with perspiration. She tried to recollect the details. The man in it had been Reily, no doubt, and she was amused by the realism of their kiss. There was something very nice about him. He was injured emotionally but very attractive. While older than any man she had considered dating, his attributes outscored others in an audit of former relationships. She sat up without pain and gulped from a water bottle. Her headache was vanquished. She put on sandals and went out to savor the evening.

The tents were an obstacle course. She picked her way over tie-downs to avoid becoming a human projectile bombing someone's slumber. Sneaking past Wil's tent she heard only dissonant breathing – the dull reverberations of a male plus Gabriele's muted, marmot whistle. The lovers were recharging.

In the last row, close to the road, she found Reily's tent.

"Reily, are you up?" A great horned owl replied with deep and lonely hoots from a nearby tree.

She called his name again with greater volume. No response. Like a CIA operative, she inched the front zipper along its track until she could fit her head inside. There was a sleeping bag – smooth, unrumpled, and unoccupied. Where would he be so late?

Absorbed in self-cogitation, she shuffled along the road. It had a lunar glow, luminous on her feet. The night stoked rambles of long ago: Michigan summer evenings when twilight lingered longer than the days, and teen years in the muggy Virginia tidewater when her dad was doing research at Wallops Island. She would sneak off in the earliest hours of the morning when everyone but her scheming friends were unconscious in their beds. Boat slips and backyards cried for investigation and the ploy of sleeping on the porch provided easy access. The behavior hadn't been motivated by a boy, but the adventure – because you could. Big Dipper swims, low-tide smells, even the splinters from Reigle's dock were innocent joys, the memory of which imparted no sadness, just profound appreciation. As if on cue, a bullfrog groaned near the river, a guttural, monotonic complaint. Bullfrogs preferred ponds but maybe this fellow was a wanderer like her, sipping and sampling life but never quite full.

She tiptoed down a set of metal stairs stepping onto a distended beach that elbowed to the right and disappeared. Her feet pushed gravel with an alternating swish. The boats were ahead, all pushed together and so were two figures, a shorter person leaning against a taller one. The silhouettes kissed.

Sol peered harder; her body went numb. It was Reily and Kim, the same Kim lurking down the table when she'd left the Moose place. Sol stood still as stone. The guilty parties left the beach, hiking up the bank, walking beside one another but not close together. They never saw her.

She sat down right where she stood, feeling as empty as a good bottle of wine.

CHAPTER 19

A bleak winter descended upon Reily's Odyssey. When he scooched into the breakfast line, Sol left for the port-a-potty and when she returned, she refused to look his direction. The avoidance couldn't have been more blatant.

He placed his tray next to Wil's on a folding table, one of ten arranged in rows across a vacant, groomed lot. "What did I do?"

"You tell me. I had another humdinger of a night."

Reily wrestled his chair forward in the turf. "Show a little sympathy, I may have obliterated something extraordinary."

"You must have upset her."

"We didn't talk this morning."

"What about last night?"

"Things were cooking at the Moose." He poked at the crumbly pancake on his plate. "Then she got a migraine."

"You did something, my bearded friend." Wil pointed at him with a plastic fork. "What might that be? No holding back."

"I'm not holding back." His elevated voice spawned a handful of stares from those nearby. He leaned closer to Wil. "Kim made a move on me. We were down by the boats. I told her thanks, but it wasn't a good idea."

Wil was amused. "Did she kiss you?"

"I gave her a quick smooch."

"Any tongue?"

"No, it was pure and innocuous."

"You kissed that sexy kayaking mama just to comfort her? How noble. Who are you, the Pope?" Wil liked to vitiate his Catholic childhood.

"It was absolutely in the clear. Harmless and munificent."

Wil raised his eyebrows. "Did Sol see?"

"It was late and dark. She had to have been asleep."

"We've got to get moving but things are undeniably awry. I'll get the juice from Gabriele. She'll know what's going down."

"I'll be further indebted."

Wil stood up. "Damn right, Watters."

The safety officer ranted, more nasally and grating than normal, at the morning briefing. Reily blamed his own encumbered state of mind. The diatribe continued.

"If you can't see the boat ahead of you then you better paddle harder. It isn't a race but it's not an inner tube float either. In other words, stay together and look out for one another."

Another person stepped into the circle. The figure wore pleated trousers and a mauve t-shirt touting rainforest protection. The glasses flagged him, but Reily did a double take to be sure. It was Rob Murray. He could have been a corporate plant. His hair was neat and side-parted, his beard closely trimmed. A leather briefcase hung on his shoulder. Amongst the scraggly gang, he looked lost.

"Is everyone enjoying themselves?" Murray asked loud enough for all to hear.

Members of the group answered with varying levels of enthusiasm. Some appeared burned out by the daily labors of paddling and camping. Like any good host, the doctor casually elaborated on a few of the comments.

"When will the fun begin?" asked a recent federal retiree suffering from self-importance.

"Isn't being with all these fantastic people fun enough?" Murray masterfully outstretched his hands. "Well, if journeying on the finest river in the Eastern U.S. doesn't have you pumped, there is a public meeting you're welcome to attend. Tonight, the leaders of Conroy Township, Gifford County, decide on the zoning for the proposed Whispering Heights development. Two vans will depart Wilkes-Barre at 6:30 tonight." Murray turned stoic. "We can sure use the support."

Sol was MIA. Adrenaline Rick had whisked her off, leading the group to who knows where on another stifling day. Wil was frisking upriver with his bombshell. Kim was back there, too, hiding behind sunglasses and a wall of embarrassment. Reily appreciated her late-night maneuvers; Sol was the only reason they hadn't done it like wild raccoons.

Riffles complained about trespassing boaters. Gawking gulls spoke nonsense. Nature always had an opinion. Out of nowhere, a fish flopped into his canoe with a startling thump. It was a smallmouth bass nearly two feet long and showing the scars of age. Reily applied a firm grasp and returned it to the currents. His pulse normalized while he brooded over the symbolism of the event. Was it a metaphorical suggestion that his soul starved for nourishment, or that he was in need of a kindred spirit?

Pittston appeared extemporaneously, a hilly mirage on the river plain. Traffic groaned, sirens wailed. Church spires – gothic and grim – frightened more than soothed. It would have to do; it was the biggest town he'd seen since Binghamton.

The group spilled into the streets in search of restaurants. He stayed behind. The only hunger he felt was for a certain suave, good-natured brunette. He crunched an apple from his dry bag, oblivious to its sweetness but not to the black BMW bouncing through the lot of the municipal boat ramp. Music shook the tinted windows while the driver braked to the beat. He watched as the car backed into a parking space expecting it to discharge one or more blimpy, gold-toothed gangster types. Never had he seen a bad-ass rapper cruising with a kayak strapped on top. His curiosity remained unquenched when a short man emerged from the car dressed in penny loafers, khakis, and fancy shades. The dude had crazy, curly hair like a Collie with a perm and was headed his way.

"Yo, my man," the dude said with a cocky drawl. "Are you part of this Odyssey gig?"

"Yes, indeed." Reily didn't bother to get up.

"Excellent, I just had to check this out. Sounded yowzy."

The guy was high on something, maybe himself. His name was Michael Blackman and he had "skidded into town" from New York City but that was only his east coast "party port." He was a movie producer, or so he said. Reily guessed his specialty was cheap skin flicks but Mr. Blackman rattled off legit titles, one of which Reily had seen.

"You made *Eb and Flo*?"

"Yesiree, my man." Blackman snapped his fingers. "One of my favorites."

It was a good one. A quirky couple busts up a mob-led industrial development scheme. The film received award nominations, but was only a modest success at the box office.

"What's your name, tall man?"

"Reily Watters."

"Well, aqua man, mind giving this cat a hand with his kayak?" They went to the car. "This is my lazy river boat. I have two others to match, one for the bays and a little sucker for whitewater... although that one's a super-doozy plastic."

Blackman's kayak was gorgeous and expensive – a custom Kevlar layup with a sleek hull. "Sweet boat." He dreaded the scratches the river might inscribe.

"Yesiree."

Paddling with this wily one would be a good diversion. Reily was still down but now a little up. Why had a rogue movie producer joined their humble voyage through Northeast Pennsylvania? The better question was probably "Why not?"

Reily almost tackled Wil when they finished the day at a park opposite Wilkes-Barre. He immediately asked about Sol.

"She's as angry as a quadriplegic."

Reily cringed. "Don't say stuff like that. Seriously, how pissed was she?"

"I thought she was a dragon. Flames could have squirted out her urethra at any moment."

"Stop messing with me, Wil. Your friend is infirm."

"She spoke to me through Gabriele."

"That working through a medium thing is always a bad sign." He felt nauseous. "How did you ask her?"

Wil cast a 'get-a-grip' expression. "I didn't. I was probing things with Gabriele when Sol and Ricky came along, only this time he's in the bow and she's paddling like she's on steroids. Then she said to Gabriele while I was standing there, 'Tell your friend that his friend seems to have created a new measure for shallowness'."

"That doesn't even sound like Sol."

"Exactly, it was her supernatural archetype. She drank in that scene last night like a bad potion. Gabriele told me that Sol saw everything – your temptation in the wilderness moment – and figures you had it plotted all along."

"God, this is awful." He had to sit down but Wil wouldn't let him.

"As you know, my friend, I'm a two-timing animist atheist but if there is a God and he works in mysterious ways, then this would be one of those moments. Yahweh has revealed Sol's true feelings."

"You're blabbering."

Wil removed his funky beach visor and held it upright at arm's length in front of him, peering through the opening and aligning it with a building on the far shore. "Look at something in a different way and sometimes you see something different. You now have the gift of knowing that Sol is enthralled with you. You may have sensed and hoped it before, but now you know. Sol never would have been so distressed, so *obsessed*, if you hadn't already moved her in a big Watters kind of way."

Wil's observation had merit. "If you're right, how do I get things back to where they were yesterday? Time machines are out of the question."

"Give her something good to drink, figuratively not literally, although a little alcohol might help. Tell her what happened, let the words flow, tell her how you feel... become Shakespeare incarnate. Throw out the kind of prose you did back in the day."

This time, Wil had *his* back.

CHAPTER 20

"**D**o you like bumps in the road?"

"They aren't as exciting as they used to be, but every once in a while one will make me feel like I'm floating and give me a good tickle inside."

The child grinned so wide her cheeks might crack. "Big bumps do that to me, too."

Reily liked Carly's simple-minded questions. She reminded him of Casey at that age. They even dressed alike: bright-colored tops, pint-sized jeans, and sneakers that could fit in the palm of his hand. Carly was squished safely beside him but he wasn't a hundred percent sure of his own daughter's whereabouts. She had mentioned a summer waitress position in Virginia Beach and reluctantly provided an address and phone number. He pictured hair the color of wheat and skinny legs standing on the sand. If only he could hit rewind.

The van lurched and refocused him on the meeting coming up. The fate of innumerable creatures and untrammeled forest would boil down to the inclinations of a council of three people whose only context for the word 'preserve' might involve a mason jar. He would say something. He just hoped he could contain his outrage.

In one of the backseats, Blackman bantered about the meeting. The guy had only been here for a few hours and barely knew the details about Whispering Heights yet he proselytized like a crusader. He spoke maniacally, citing REM lyrics laced with his own words. Soon the whole van knew how he'd met guitarist Peter Buck "when the 'boys' were recording Losing My Religion."

Conroy Township didn't waste money on capital improvements. The municipal building was a pre-cast aluminum structure poised upon a concrete pad. An oblong, simulated wood-grain table occupied one end of the meeting room and was lined with three metal chairs cushioned in black vinyl. The set faced a room full of molded plastic chairs in two retro color varieties: tangerine and lime green. A coffee percolator burped bitter steam from a table along the back wall welcoming attendees as they arrived.

They came alone or in small groups of two or three. Most were older, over sixty, and predominantly male. With hands in their pockets, they joked about weather and wives, or recapped plans for the weekend. Reily watched their moves from the back row, nibbling a ginger snap from a cookie tray. He felt like a social scientist, only he didn't intend to be a neutral observer. Salvation of the planet was everyone's business.

The crowd was a flock of multi-hued, variable-sized sheep waiting for dubious shepherds to decide their fate, but a wolf was lurking in the form of an American-made developer. No country bred them more cunning or ravenous.

Reily's eyes turned to the door where, to his surprise, Wil and Gabriele entered... and to his mortification, Sol. Wil typically avoided civic involvement as if it might cause impotence.

Sol was stunning, the embodiment of natural grace. She wore an airy sunflower-print skirt with a white blouse and seemed superbly over-coordinated for a river runner. Eye contact was brief but definitive, her expression mirthful. More Odyssey people turned out, including Doc Murray, who had his comments ready on a tablet, and Alex with a camera and long lens sure to make the board of supervisors ill at ease.

The chairman of the supervisors was ruddy, broad, and profoundly bald. His nameplate said Lowell Orwell. To his right was Lawrence Wilson. He looked like a Larry – in his fifties, buttoned-down in a short-sleeved plaid shirt and built like a pole. His gaze was forthright, albeit tranquilized. The number three supervisor, seated closest to the main door, was unforgettable. Hap Clay was the skinny, shrunken drunk from the Meshoppen bar, though his nameplate identified him as "Harold." Would he be as testy this evening?

After a droning, insipid recitation of the pledge of allegiance, the board approved a contract for salt and anti-skid material for winter. The gluttonous chairman cleared his throat for further pontification.

"The next item before the township is the request by Woodring Holdings, LLC, for the rezoning of the 410-acre tract in present ownership of Gertrude L. Bunting. Woodring Holdings is requesting a change from agricultural status to R-4 Planned Residential Status. Would Mr. Carl Woodring approach the microphone in front of the supervisors?"

A mustached guy with carrot hair, denim shirt, and western boots came forward exuding condescension with every step. The developer bellyached of painstaking delays, nervous loan officers, the agony of uncertainty, and building projects in hiatus before providing a sanitized description of his plans. As he spoke, he made contrived gestures with his sunglasses, striking them in the air with each point like a bad imitation of a Bill Clinton speech.

"The upzoning of the Bunting land to the special R-4 district will mean some new and very attractive housing opportunities for Gifford County. As has been so astutely recognized by many community and business leaders, growth will bring jobs and, like it or not, that is exactly what this county needs." Woodring paused to let the remark hyper-resonate. "I implore the board to approve my request for the betterment of all. I rest my case." He ceremoniously folded his designer frames and placed them in a shirt pocket.

Reily was unmoved. It had stage quality worthy of applause if only the stakes had not been so high. Between hearing such foul utterances and watching the chairman nod and gloat, he was disconsolate. To allow such garbage to flow unchecked was an environmental crime and a violation of someone's commandments. He had to say something.

The floor was opened for audience comment but Blackman was already at the microphone. The chairman was annoyed.

"Please give us your name, sir."

"The name is Blackman, Michael Blackman." The movie maker mopped his brow like a southern-fried lawyer. "Ladies and gentlemen, you certainly realize that I'm not from around here but I may as well be because if this stray cat—" Blackman diverted his eyes to Woodring, "morphs your paradise into Matchbox City, there will be a torrent of transients, New Yorkers, and other odd-speaking outsiders as crazy as me setting roots in Conroy Township. You'll see a wagon train of wilders, and I do mean wilders, wanting big houses on your prairie. Understand?" There were scattered nods in the room and all was hushed. The audience was enthralled with Blackman's speechmaking.

The chairman glared. "Mr. Blackman, I suggest you skip the disparaging references to Mr. Woodring." He mispronounced *disparaging*.

"Got it, boss."

Reily despised confrontation but wallowed in Blackman's assault. Stoking xenophobia was a brilliant move.

Blackman was just getting warmed up. "Stemming from New York as well as the left coast, I have seen land changed forever, overnight, and the cause is always the same. You know what makes these things happen?" The question was met with perplexed faces and a few more nods. "Well, I'll tell you: greed-infected politicians and developers. The developers call themselves *businessmen* to improve their stature, but they aren't the hard working shop owners that built this country. They are predators consuming everything we like about America."

"Mr. Blackman." The chairman detonated. His eyes bulged like a porcupine fish on the defensive. "Enough. You have thirty seconds to finish your statement."

"Here's the message to remember. If he builds it, it will cost you. Taxes will go up. Studies prove it. You seem to be good, smart people so please think about what I've said and consider, maybe even investigate, what motivates your elected officials to tolerate such a bad idea. You may not like what you discover."

The rabid chairman leapt from his seat, spit dripping from his jowls. "If you're suggesting something improper, you're off your rocker. Consider yourself censored. This forum will accept nothing further from you."

The crowd buzzed and bodies shifted. Neighbor whispered to neighbor. Hap Clay looked caulked, his skin milky, his expression sour as if he were being squeezed. Lawrence Wilson seemed startled by the exchange and fumbled with his pen. Adding to the mayhem, Alex began shooting pictures of the supervisors. Blackman saluted them, turned and bowed to the audience. Scattered applause was curtailed by the carnival gavel of Chairman Orwell.

A slender, senior gentleman ambled to the microphone, favoring his right leg. He, too, usurped an official invitation to speak. The man crooned for five minutes warning of a "scourge of flatlanders" and a "sowing of problems unforeseen." He closed with an impassioned reading from Leviticus 25. "...Because the land is mine and you are but aliens and tenants. Throughout the country that you hold as a possession, you must provide for the redemption of the land." There were a handful of *amens* and they emboldened the speaker. He approached the supervisors' table and implored each of them to do the right thing and "follow the wishes of the Lord."

Reily was touched by the man's earnestness and authenticity. Now, it was his turn.

CHAPTER 21

"That was some meeting."

Sol cracked a heart-melting smile. "You were impressive."

"Hardly."

"I mean it. What was that you said? Sometimes you get one chance to get things right? And then that whole story about the farm you grew up on. It was very profound. I almost cried when you talked about the pond they filled in."

"I went slightly overboard. The eyes were rolling in there." Reily tipped his head toward the township building, his hands stuffed nervously in his pockets. They were leaning against Wil's Isuzu, just the two of them, illuminated by a security light. Only a few cars remained in the gravel lot.

"You were a poet and all that matters is that we won... well, for the time being. But I disagree with one point you made. I think people and even the land at times get second chances. You have to be receptive to that prospect; the belief in possibility."

"I'll try." He was entranced by her metaphysical tidings. She deserved a thorough confession about last night's debacle but first he had to sort out the circus that had ended twenty minutes prior. "So why do you think the old supervisor motioned to table the rezoning request?"

"I'm not sure, but did you see how mad the chubby one became?" Her voice was happy, melodic.

"I thought we'd be calling a funeral director." Reily sifted for new words. "I want to apologize..."

Sol made a false frown. "No, I was a bit impetuous. Wil told me everything."

"He did?"

"Yep, but I can't be mad at Kim for having good taste." She exhaled for dramatic effect.

"I shouldn't have drank so much nor allowed myself to go wandering with a strange woman on a deserted, moonlit beach."

"Perhaps, but do you have something against moonlit beaches?"

85

She was an angel of forgiveness. "Not a thing. They deserve the best company – too beautiful to take in alone, you know."

She nodded. Her eyes were attempting to mine his emotions. "Where's that moon tonight?"

He broke away from her stare and considered the sky. "It has to rise soon. We must find a good place to enjoy it, don't you think?"

"I'm not sure." Her voice trailed and his hope listed. "I'm not sure I should be alone with Reily Watters. He has quite the reputation, you know?"

"Boy, do I know." She was even witty.

Wil and Gabriele spilled into the parking lot from the building, cookies in hand, offering to share the remnants. "We pilfered the last ones." Wil spoke with a mouthful. "So where should we go? I need outdoor time after listening to all those long-winded fools." He glanced at Reily. "I'm not impugning you, of course. You made me proud, Watters. Way to hit them."

Reily shrugged. His public remarks had been cathartic. If he believed in the cause, he could deliver a homily like an itinerant preacher. "What about a drive to Whispering Heights?" He looked to Gabriele, as sexy as usual but absent makeup. "You and Wil haven't been there yet, but you'll love it: big rocks, lots of ponds, wonderful old trees. You can't help but like it although it's probably not as impressive in the dark."

Gabriele tugged Wil's hand. "That will make nice fun. Wil, let's all go, yes?"

Wil smirked. "Yes, yes, we all go."

Reily stood close to Sol feeling strangely debonair. "Does that work for you?"

"With one condition."

"And what would that be?"

"No falling off the edge."

Hap chewed on what had just happened while at the urinal waiting for a trickle. It wasn't the fact-throwing so-called Doctor Murray that gave him doubts, or the wise-cracker from New York who pranced around; the humdinger was Mary. The look on her face was so kind and innocent. It was like he could read her mind. She was telegraphing him, probably thinking about her baby and wishing the area would remain as it was. Hap had no qualms about what he'd done, but Lowell Orwell had nearly ruptured like a frozen pipe. Woodring expected a guaranteed result and didn't get it. The developer was well connected and had a cutthroat reputation. A drink would scrub the worries.

Lowell almost tackled him when he left the men's room. "What the hell were you thinking, Hap?" He clenched his fist. "Carl is ornerier than a sow with cubs."

"He can go hibernate for all I care."

Lowell swallowed and steadied himself. "Look, I suppose your conscience snuck up on you tonight but Carl means business. He has a lot riding on this. He was a hell of a lot calmer than I would have guessed, but he wants to meet tonight at 11:00 at his property to sort things out."

"Out there? In the dark? We won't be able to see a damn thing... not to mention that we shouldn't be anywhere, especially on his land, at the same time. I think Woodring's spilled a few of his beans."

Lowell looked around fretfully. Everyone was gone from the innards of the municipal building. "That bastard knows all kinds of bad people from what I hear, and I don't want any part of me or you spilling." His voice dropped to a growl. "Take that dirt road in and bear right at the split. A little further, there's a turn around. Park there and be sure to keep your lights off."

Hap stared at the floor. "This is a bad idea."

"Maybe, but things will be worse if we don't show up."

He watched Lowell labor toward the door. "This all stinks." He probed his pocket for a Rolaids.

CHAPTER 22

Reily served as navigator, a state gazetteer splayed on his lap, but his experience in reading plans and blueprints was futile. Road signs were an endangered species and spotting them and the roads themselves in a land devoid of artificial light was akin to locating a toothpick in a stack of firewood.

Eventually there was a break in the trees and an intersection. Headlights revealed an uncultivated field, glowing eyes of a few ambient deer, and a distant barn and farmhouse looking lonesome and impoverished. A hundred yards up the road, weathered letters on a corrugated mailbox spelled Bunting.

"This is it," Reily said. Wil slowed the car.

"I think we need to go to the next property." Sol spoke from the back seat. "That's how I remember Doc Murray's explanation."

Reily nodded. "There's got to be a driveway up ahead somewhere."

Moments later, Wil made a hard right on a muddy, rutted road. When it forked, Reily told him to veer left based on nothing but intuition. They parked where the road terminated at a padlocked gate. Beyond the gate, the road narrowed to a path.

Sol insisted they take off their shoes. "Barefoot in the woods is the best."

"Until a rattler impales your big toe."

"No wimping out on us, Wisnoski." Reily didn't wholly disagree with Wil's point. "But we should stay hushed so the rattlers won't know we're here."

Moss tickled underfoot – a strange, spongy sensation – as they carried their shoes along with them for later. He felt as energetic and playful as a newborn kitten; a predator leading his pride. The forest was a black netherworld and since the batteries in Wil's glove compartment flashlight had long expired, their only illumination was from a penlight on Sol's keychain.

Unseen chirps and unknown clicks dosed the imagination. Sol held on to the back of his shirt and from the whispers, he gathered that

Gabriele had a hold on Sol in the same way. Wil evidently had latched on to Gabriele's bra strap. They probably looked ridiculous.

Abruptly the trail opened to a sky slathered with stars. They had reached the escarpment carved by the river.

Wil peered over the edge. "What do you say we scout these denizens? Up here, not down there."

Reily rested on a rock rising above a coarse thicket of blueberry. "And what are we looking for?"

"Whatever you seek."

"Should we not separate into two groups?" Gabriele's accent seemed out of place in the backcountry.

"Reily and I will investigate this direction." Sol pointed southeast, parallel to the flow of the river. "You and Wil can go the other way."

Without saying another word, they put on their shoes. There was a frivolous urgency to their motions and it wasn't motivated by prudence. Reily could taste the anticipation. It was overpowering. Only once before had he felt this emotion: the last night of a two-week adventure course in Maine. Shannon was an assistant leader who spent inordinate time at his side teaching him about coastal ecology and outdoor skills on the islands of Casco Bay. On the last night, they'd exposed their burgeoning feelings. With softness and purpose, she'd asked him to walk to the point where she kissed him and wouldn't stop. He could still smell the spruce needles and hear the applause of the ocean. Last he knew she was somewhere outside Manchester, New Hampshire, with three kids and a professor for a husband. The memories had crystallized but time cushioned the melancholy. The return of the 'love high' was worth the wait.

Wil already had a hiking stick in hand. "See you two back at the car in, say, half an hour?"

Reily took Sol's hand. "Good plan. If we get lost, I'll hoot like a barred owl."

"Whatever you say, Huckleberry Finn." Wil tugged his lady into the shadows and disappeared.

Reily led Sol along the rocky edge, always staying a few feet back from the precipice. Her hand was warm, smooth, and wonderful. They pushed through tangled thickets of pitch pine and mountain laurel; a branch thwacked him in the cheek but he was temporarily invulnerable to pain.

They came to a flat-topped chunk of sandstone, spacious and inviting. With near perfect contours for two people to recline upon, they positioned themselves side by side above the great chasm. The silence was implausible.

"Are these our box seats?" Sol said.

"Very expensive ones but as you can see they're well worth every dollar."

Without words, they regaled in their creative perspective of sky and nature – an elevated, dizzying awe – like a king and queen seated at the table of the universe. The big dipper was extra big, ready to ladle them up.

"Look at Ursa Major."

He was impressed with the constellation and Sol's astronomical repertoire. "Do you see Ursa Minor?"

"Wait, it's hard to pick out with all the other stars."

"Let me show you." He grasped her right hand in his and helped her trace the pattern. It was a high voltage touch.

"I see it. Thank you, Reily." Her voice was a whisper.

He loved the way she spoke his name. "The big dipper is me and you're the little dipper pouring out good karma which I gladly receive." The words streamed out of nowhere.

She pressed close. "That is the most eloquent thing any man has ever said to me." In one deft motion, she turned and loped her arm around his neck, leaned on her knees, and kissed him, deeply, lovingly. "There, see, I believe you are good karma, too."

"I guess so." He floated. Her lips were luxuriant, the nectar of a tropical orchid. They kissed again and again for minutes at a time, pausing when necessary to breathe. The euphoria continued until he heard consecutive whinnies from a gravely-ill horse or, he finally deduced, Wil Wisnoski trying to summon them.

CHAPTER 23

"That was the worst screech owl imitation I've ever heard."

"It got your attention, didn't it, Watters?" Wil was standing before him with Gabriele.

"I thought something was dying."

"We saw lights."

"Like a UFO?"

"As in car lights, close to where we parked."

"Probably teenagers parking." Sol was holding his hand. He hoped the grasp would fuse permanently.

"Likely, but we should head back. They might want to vandalize my Trooper."

"That might improve its appearance."

They started back on the same trail. This time Sol took the lead pulling him along. "More car lights," she said. They couldn't be missed – two beacons penetrating the woods like a scene from a Stephen King movie. Then they disappeared as if someone had flipped a switch.

Wil froze. "What do you think?"

"You're suggesting we sneak up on them?" Reily already knew the answer. An innocent mission couldn't hurt, but he wanted minimum distraction from his current state of ecstasy.

"I want to impress our lady friends with fearless, guerilla tactics."

"Gabriele and I already saw enough guerilla tactics in Africa," Sol said.

They tip-toed another few hundred feet; voices were close by. Wil motioned for Reily. He reluctantly released Sol's hand. "I'll be right back."

"Just don't make me have to rescue you."

"No worries." He smiled in the dark and followed Wil.

Wil scanned ahead. "Let's head toward my car. It should be in front of us. I think they're on the dirt road that veered to the right. We can backtrack and come in the way they did."

Rednecks were dangerous, especially when screwing or drinking, but this was classic Wil. Reily felt a jolt of nostalgia. They passed the

93

gate and Wil's car and merged left on to the other so-called road. He could feel the adrenaline. He felt badly about leaving the ladies behind but they were safer back there.

Suddenly the darkness lightened. The moon was up and the new illumination unveiled the faint silhouette of a car, then two more. He and Wil dropped to the ground slithering like GIs behind a large tree. The voices came back in range.

"It's very disappointing. I can't emphasize that enough." The person speaking seemed vaguely familiar. The man didn't have the tonal qualities of a teenager or the syntax of the rural disenfranchised.

"Well, I'm sorry, too," said a different voice. It sounded deeper and more indigenous.

"You can't push this thing down our throats. Give it some time and we'll probably see it your way. Just give it more danged time." This was a different person. Reily lifted his head and could discern three upright bodies in the clearing.

"More time?" the first voice said. "Why the hell did you think I paid you?"

"Do you have to talk so loud?" the indigenous voice said.

"Lowell, please shut up for once. Are you worried about a deer hearing us? All I care about is Mr. Clay here clearly getting my message. His lack of follow-through has me deeply distressed."

It was the supervisors and the developer. Reily pegged it. He twisted his neck to look at Wil who nodded back. A mosquito drilled his lip and he pinched it into mush. With his tongue, he traced the welt beginning to form.

"It goes against my better judgment," Woodring said, "but I sense that Mr. Clay needs more of an incentive to comprehend the virtues of my project. Am I right?"

"No, you're not right," Hap Clay said. "You're so damned used to throwing your weight around, but it just doesn't work that way all the time."

Lowell Orwell stepped toward his elder colleague. "We made a deal with this man."

"I mistakenly accepted some of his money and I think I ought to give it back."

"Hap, this has been a long road," Woodring said, seeming artificially calm. "I appreciate your propriety but you can feel alright knowing I'll do a good job on this land and help the township in the process. Hell, you've said as much yourself."

Orwell hoisted up his trousers. "He's right, Hap."

"Anyway," Woodring said. "I am asking a lot of you. A thousand bucks isn't much. You deserve a little more."

"What if I don't want more?"

"That's your decision." The developer reached in his back pocket. "Here's an additional $1500 to do something nice with." He waved the money in front of Hap Clay as if it were a dog treat.

Even at a poor angle in stunted light, Reily saw the anguish on Hap's face. Poor guy probably needed the money.

Hap tugged the thick wad from the developer's hand. "No promises."

"If you don't deliver, I'll want all of this back and more. You'll owe me for pain and suffering."

Orwell shuffled his heavy feet. "Carl, you didn't forget about me, did you?"

Woodring retrieved more cash from a shirt pocket. "Here's your extra prize, now take up a gym membership and work off that tonnage." Orwell ignored the insult and snatched the money.

This was real life, hillbilly-caliber John Grisham material. Woodring didn't instill fear but any person handing out bribes could only be bad news. Reily reached to nudge Wil, but there was something on his own face. Instinctively, he slapped at it.

"You hear that?" Orwell said.

Woodring frowned. "I think we're up past your bedtime. Give me a damn flashlight."

Reily grabbed Wil's arm. "Let's move." Escape was now the objective. They scrambled to their feet and down the old logging road. A beam of light bounced off them and the surrounding trees. "We should split up." He turned right into the woods. Wil stayed on the road.

Reily bounded and crashed like a deer eluding hunters until he deemed there was no one in pursuit. There was something alien and inanimate ahead. He crept closer. It was a drilling truck, incongruent in the forest, with vertical rigging fixed in place. He leaned against it to rest, listening to his own quick, wheezing breaths and sensing the sting of lacerations on his shins and arms. The wild world around him was dead still. Where were Sol and Gabriele? He restarted himself in the assumed direction of where he'd left them. Three minutes later he met Wil peeking around a tree.

"You alright?" Wil said. Somehow he'd managed to retain his visor.

"Fine except for a complimentary collection of leg wounds, but I'll survive. It's the ladies that I'm worried about."

"Me too, let's keep walking."

"So what the hell did we just witness?"

"That would be called a crime."

Woodring let the others drive out first. He had restrained Orwell from chasing the trespassers... although it would have been a sight to see. Who would be out here in the dark? The running nimrods didn't look like juvenile delinquents and if they did hear any of the conversation, they wouldn't say a peep; they were the ones breaking the law.

At the split, he performed a three-point turn and nosed up the other road. The headlights revealed grasshoppers and dual tracks ending at a parked Isuzu wearing a New Jersey plate. He removed a fountain pen and memo pad from the center console and scribbled the license number. The vanity tag was easy to remember: BCHBUM1.

CHAPTER 24

Except for the alt-country serenades of Jeff Tweedy from a home-burned Wilco CD, the Trooper's interior was mute on the drive back to Wilkes-Barre. Reily attributed it to exhaustion, but the state of sedation was fused with exhilaration. His girl was curled-up beside him in the backseat, her flushed cheek and delicious hair tucked snugly against his shoulder. The window was rolled halfway down feeding them a current of tangy air. Heaven was as simple as an endless summer drive.

A haze of lights indicated they were approaching the city. A sign pointed eight miles to the airport, and airports made him think of his father. Dad would have found his antics this evening much too careless. The regimen of a military career and years as a fighter pilot had made Keith Watters a steely man, but he would have courted the likes of Sol like Humphrey Bogart. He had radar for the ladies but was a devoted husband. Despite protracted days at Willow Grove and weeks at bases in Florida, his dad loved his mother with the same ferocity with which he'd served his country.

Reily missed his parents and the small farm where he grew up. It was eleven acres of gold: the vegetable garden with homemade tomato cages; the bank barn with the sagging roof; the raspberry patch murderous to shoeless feet. The thoughts glistened in brilliant color like his mother's oil paintings. After his dad died, his mother subdivided the property. Reily considered buying it, even moving the Lehigh Valley office of Alan Sutton, but Abby suppressed the proposition. Soon the farm vanished beneath bedrooms and blacktop. His slug of the proceeds felt like blood money.

"We're home, kiddos." Wil looked at Gabriele in the passenger seat and him and Sol in back. "You're all more contorted than a nursing home full of rheumatics."

Reily stretched. "He has a gift for words, doesn't he?"

Sol opened her eyes. "We're back?"

"Yep, and it's not even 1:00 A.M."

"Did you slip me a sleeping pill?" Her voice was coarse from slumber. "I dreamed I was running around a dim forest in the middle of the night with two fearless studs and a German secret agent."

"I assure you it wasn't a dream." He loved her sense of humor. His ex would have been as bristly as a porcupine.

Sol slid out of the car. "Where did you set up?"

"I'm at the edge of the clearing, last tent before the woods."

"I'm near the bathrooms, not exactly the quietest place."

"Then come stay with me, I'd be happy to share my home."

"You sure there's room? Gabriele told me I whistle like a pika when I sleep."

"I always wondered what one sounds like. Guess this is my chance."

"I'll meet you there." She scurried off with alpine enthusiasm.

Reily stewed inside the tent awaiting her arrival. The orange glow from town penetrated the nylon skin around him. A rooftop condenser buzzed industrial white noise. Someone squealed their tires to compensate for a secret inadequacy. There was a shadow and then a willowy face smiling through the unzipped door.

Sol crawled inside and without saying a single word, kissed him. He caressed the back of her head, neck, and shoulders. They parted and began to disrobe. He worked hurriedly, leaving on his boxers. She shed her outer garments with the same awkward zeal then assumed the position she had taken on the shores in Tunkhannock, laying on her side, propped on one elbow. Black panties and a sports bra were the only things covering her supple skin. Her stare was tender but fiery; she summoned him with a finger.

He wouldn't make her wait a second longer.

Hap Clay drove a back way home to afford more time to sort and settle his mind. Relief was elusive. He returned to the safety of his garage and the familiar smell of turf fertilizer. When the din of the automatic door abated, he approached the work bench and undid three buttons of his Sears dress shirt. Near his abdomen, brushing past the scars of hernia surgery, he removed a slim cassette tape recorder and pressed rewind. The recorder had been a gift from his late sister who thought it might be a handy device for listening to books on tape during all of his driving. A plop of sweat struck the vinyl case, punctuating his frazzled condition. He pressed play and adjusted the volume control.

The voices came out garbled but decipherable; Lowell's inane words were unmistakable.

CHAPTER 25

The lovemaking was impeccable. Reily could feel her galloping heart and deep exhalations transmitting fulfillment. For being deprived of meaningful female companionship for so long, he graded his endurance as commendable. Sol won the gold medal for how to delight, and not for audacity. It was the little things: the whisper in his ear, the voluminous sigh, a zinger of a kiss. She even said, "Thank you." No woman had *ever* thanked him for sex. He rolled off but lay close, putting his arm under his head so he could admire her.

He studied the perfection of her breasts and neckline and the speck three inches above her left nipple. "That is a lovely mole."

"Oh, that one. I have many."

"Are they all that exquisite?"

"Doubtful. Aren't you going to ask about my scar?"

"What scar?"

Sol tapped her cheek. "The one right here. You don't have to pretend you didn't notice."

"Let me see." Reily ran a finger along her face. "Oh that. I find it interesting... another thing that makes you, you."

She gave half a smile. "My dog bit me – it was pretty scary."

"I'm sorry." Reily pulled a part of his sleeping bag over their lower halves. "Sol?"

"Yes, Reily?"

"Did I, um... this... meet your expectations?" The question came out more serious than intended.

She looked straight up as if the tent weren't there, probing for the right words. "I don't think I had any expectations, except that you'd be a passionate, energetic, and sensitive lover."

"Can you check off those boxes?"

"Nope," she turned her head and peered wide-eyed at him, "because they would be inadequate. I'd do a write-in with phrases like 'immensely satisfying,' 'knows how to please,' etcetera."

"Really?"

"Really."

He had a spontaneous thought. "Sex is like hiking a good trail."

"Oh?" She scrunched her face with a 'what made you think of that' look.

"The anticipation builds as you approach the summit or an alluring destination. You're overwhelmed when you get there and then you hike back to the trailhead. The last leg, you're drained but completely recharged from the whole experience."

"And what trail did we just hike?"

"Let's see? That's hard. It was incomparable. I'll use a Pennsylvania trail... maybe the Golden Eagle by Pine Creek. It goes up and up, ever higher, adrenaline surging, full of rocks and wildlife surprises, and the Pine Creek below you looking so good you think it's a painting, something surreal. When you come down, your mind lingers up there on the rocks at the vista and you feel good for days."

"Wil's not the only one with a gift for words."

"I don't know about that."

"You do. Now, I'm trying to think of one of my hikes. How about this: Maryland Heights at Harpers Ferry?"

"I've been there."

"Good, then you'll be able to relate." She covered herself with a corner of his sleeping bag and inched closer. "First, there's the crossing of the Potomac. It's not dangerous but it has that feel to it. There are swift currents below and rocks make sneaky eddies. The moving waters are stimulating. As you walk along the C&O, there's a prolific sense of history that sweeps you up and lifts you. The hike, at that point, is routine but you know the best part is yet to come... and it doesn't disappoint," she said with a smirk.

Reily scratched his beard. *I just hope she's still talking about me, and not Rick.*

"The trail up the mountain is well worn and can't hide that it's been trampled on too many times. You learn more and more with every step and, just to please, wildflowers explode in color and the trees pose with chiseled expressions as you walk past. Finally, breathing hard and fast with sweat oozing from every pore, you reach the heights and the rivers, mountains, and town unfold below you like a giant welcome mat. And even there, the excitement doesn't cease because if you don't watch your step, you could get seriously hurt."

Yeah, Watters. Better watch your step.

"The view inspires and fills you with content and appreciation for all the good things in life."

"Wow. You just made Walt Whitman cry with joy, but 'prolific sense of history?' Are you suggesting I'm an artifact?" He poked her with a finger.

Sol laughed. "Certainly not. Are you anxious about your age?"

"Just when I'm with someone as extraordinary as you."

"That's very sweet. So come clean, how old are you?"

"And your guess is?"

"Forty-two."

"You're warm."

"Forty-four."

"You're a winner."

"You look very young for your already young age."

"Aren't you the diplomat?"

"You know who you remind me of?"

"Abraham Lincoln."

"Very funny," she poked him back. "George Clooney. You're not a clone, but give him longer hair and I bet you'd have the paparazzi confused."

"Great. I can look forward to being chased by leeches with cameras."

"In kayaks no doubt, but with the Clooney thing let the record state that you are much more handsome."

"If you say so, but now it's my turn. I'd have to say you resemble Liv Tyler."

"As in the Aerosmith Tyler?"

"Yes, as in Steven's daughter, the one with the gorgeous lips, eyes, and everything else. She's definitely a Sol wannabe."

"That's generous. Aren't you curious about my age?"

"You're a minor, aren't you? I was afraid that might be the case."

She grabbed his shirt from the floor of the tent and snapped it at him. "You're full of it."

"Alright, I know you're over eighteen. I'd say twenty-nine."

"Try thirty-three."

"I'm dumbfounded." He wasn't kidding. She didn't have a detectable wrinkle. "What's your secret to looking so radiant?"

"River mud. I slather it on daily, often unintentionally."

He laid back and closed his eyes, folding his arm beneath his head. "We should package it. We'll make millions." A blanket of contentment settled over him. "Tomorrow I want to take you to Ricketts Glen. The waterfalls will blow you away and a trail circles the entire gorge."

Sol stifled a yawn. "Another hike with Reily, how can a girl pass that up?"

"Many have, trust me, but you won't want to."

"You don't know this but I'm a great admirer of waterfalls, not the Niagara kind – they're much too garish – but the out of the way ones that you have to seek. Did you ever notice how a waterfall can make a million sounds?"

"I don't know but I promise to listen intently."

She reached over and ruffled his hair. "One of the best waterfalls I ever encountered was in Maui along a crazy road to a place called Hana. This plume of white, misty water was backed by the blackest rock and the greenest mountains I've ever seen. It was unreal."

"I've been to Maui but not to Hana. I hear it takes a whole day."

"It does. We'll talk more about Hawaii but it will have to be tomorrow. I'm afraid I'm fading out."

"I can't imagine why." He kissed her forehead. "Good night, Sol."

"Good night, Reily."

He laid there and listened. Her puffs of breath were more satisfying than the tumble of waves at Lahaina at sunset. The Pacific had been calm and clear on that June day two years earlier when he'd fled the disintegration of his marriage and placed his immediate future in the hands of United Airlines and the Pioneer Inn. At the edge of the sea, he'd slurped an oversized frozen daiquiri while a sea turtle breached not ten yards offshore. It waved a flipper at him, two distinct flaps. Friends later questioned the observation but the moment was overpowering, like he was being recruited by unseen Polynesian gods. As he breast-stroked towards Lanai, he'd been filled with a precipitate sense of conquest over his marital plight. There would be many more dark days ahead but at that sliver of time, he was a climber on Haleakala and the semi-tropical sun bathed him in abiding light.

Tonight, he was mentally back in Hawaii, on the big island, and Sol had guided him to Mauna Loa – the tallest mountain on earth. Nothing mattered in the world below. He traveled into an infantile slumber, happy and heavy, like someone who had treaded offshore currents or trekked the trail of a lifetime.

CHAPTER 26

H ap awoke to the hum of the window unit he'd purchased in July 1988 when the plastic thermometer melted and his well went dry. His head was anchored to the bed from an unsettling fog deeper than routine insomnia. The Emerson sputtered when it deemed necessary, pushing a cool, stale blanket of air. Army jeeps had a similar, pervasive drone. Fifty-three years later they visited uninvited, delivering cruel memories of the skirmish northeast of Pusan: the deafening blur of gunfire, molten pain in his shoulder, soil painted sticky red. Six men died – butchered like cattle. He was one of five who survived. It was a horror he never spoke about.

He threw off the clammy sheet and nursed his way to the kitchen, searching for coffee at the Formica counter patterned in swirls of yellow and green. It had aged better than he did. Where was the coffee? Where was Mim?

For the past four years, Mim slept in the guest room to escape his disturbing habit of yelling in his sleep, yet she could be counted on to have a pot of Maxwell House ready to go. Something was awry. Her bedroom door was shut tight. He twisted the loose knob and pushed inward, his mind conjuring possible explanations for her tardiness. She appeared to be sound asleep, her mouth gaping as if awaiting a feeding hand.

He nudged her arm. "Wake up, Mim, you overslept."

She didn't move.

"Come on. I have to work today." He noticed a pasty trail of dried saliva tracing from the right corner of her mouth.

"Mim." He gave her two good shakes. The next few moments compressed in his mind like the time-warping confusion of a Korean battle where every movement, every instant might be your last. He pressed his ear to her breast and his fingers to her neck and prayed for a heartbeat. Nothing. He pushed harder. Something was ticking inside and her chest was moving up and down, barely. "That's good, sweet pea. Keep that up."

He scrambled to the phone, dialed 911, and told the efficient young lady on the other end everything he knew about the situation. Then he waited by Mim's bedside, her mouth still open in an awkward way and blanket tight to her chin. It was a gloomy premonition of what she might look like in a coffin. He stood there panting, thinking, *I haven't called her 'sweet pea' in forty years.*

CHAPTER 27

Reily blinked his eyes with the clumsiness of a bruin emerging from hibernation. The brightening world was a rude reminder of a slim night's sleep. He inched his neck to the side to verify Sol's presence. His butterfly was asleep in her cocoon. Air drifted softly from her nose, her mouth drawn in a calm, complacent expression.

Sol stirred. "What time is it?"

"Wait a minute." Reily felt for his watch beneath his pillow. "Any guesses?"

"Eight o'clock?"

"Not even close. Try nine thirty."

"We must have been out of it. I never sleep this late."

He shook his head in agreement. "Me neither. I bet the group left us behind. Safety man probably ruptured when we weren't at the morning briefing." They heard the aeronautical whir of a weed whacker. "I better investigate."

Wearing only his boxers, Reily confronted the outside world, finding a deserted urban park and a gritty stare from a member of the lawn crew. There were no paddlers, only one other tent, and just two cars in the lot. They had been marooned.

The drive to the state park was docile compared to the precarious descent they were making into a most rapturous gorge. Ferns gilded rock walls. Crusty hemlocks, a century or more wise, weaved a spired fortress. First there was a murmur, then a roar. Water exalted, tumbling ninety feet, tossing spray that swirled into an electric mist and painted their bodies with tiny droplets.

Sol gazed at the top of the waterfall. "Incredible."

Reily shivered. "I'll second that." He wasn't sure if he was talking about the natural wonder or the female at his side.

"Cold?" Sol pointed at the goosebumps on his arms.

"No, I'm ecstatic."

"Good for you." She leaned up to his ear. "I am, too."

He felt light and gooey inside, Teflon and tempered steel outside. A boulder could have bounced down the mountain and smashed him flat. It wouldn't have mattered. Sol had morphed him into a lovesick super hero. He shared his feelings candidly, being careful not to use the word love.

"So what should we call you?"

"I was partial to Spiderman."

"How about... Captain Feelgood?"

He wrapped his arms around her. "I don't know, that's kind of weird."

"Then I'll stick to calling you Reily. It's a very nice name and has that aura of Irish luck."

"I think it's actually Welsh – something about woods or meadows."

"It fits you well."

"Yours does, too."

Sol flashed a surprised look. "You know what my name means?"

"Sun. It's Spanish."

"Very good. It's unique, but kind of odd, don't you think?"

"It fits your disposition."

She smiled. "You obviously don't know me very well."

Ricketts Glen was a natural cathedral, testimony to a creative and omnipresent force pulsing through everything, everyone. Reily was humbled. Neither he nor other landscape architects could replicate such spectacle in any grandiose plan they might contrive. Sol looked heavenly – veiled in a peculiar, enchanting light. He felt divine.

Their hike ended at the concession on Lake Jean and a rack of seventeen-foot Grummans, his canoe of years ago. Reily's fingers followed the tiny keel where rivets joined the aluminum hull. He handed a gangly male teenager working the stand two twenties to cover a half-day rental.

Sol stepped into the bow. "Think we'll get bored out there for so long?"

"No, you haven't been on this lake." He shoved off but noticed the teenager was fixated on Sol. "Dock boy is staring at you wantonly."

"Glad I can give him a thrill." She peered ahead and kept her stroke on rhythm. The boat surged forward.

"You actually have two admirers."

"Who would be the other?"

Reily couldn't hide a smile.

CHAPTER 28

If there was one thing Woodring detested, it was the way Purillo always trimmed his nails when they were meeting. The big clod would sit and nod, his belly spilling over his trousers while he worked his clippers surgically, finger by finger, in furrowed concentration. The crude habit smacked of disrespect but Woodring tolerated it because "Mikey P." had a talent that he revered and invested dearly in: building houses on the cheap. Purillo's company was the preferred contractor for ninety percent of his communities and knew bargain suppliers of siding, drywall, lumber and paint from Brooklyn to Bayonne. Some of the stuff was absurdly inexpensive and he didn't want to know why, assuming ignorance was a plausible future defense.

"Do you think you'll be ready in the fall?" Woodring studied his wall calendar.

"You mean with the big project looking down on the river?" Purillo spoke without eye contact, inspecting the cuticle on his left thumb.

"What did you think I was referring to?"

Purillo shrugged. "Maybe Mt. Pocono?"

"Mt. Pocono should be simple by comparison but plan on the spring for that one. As far as the river project, I want us framing phase one in September, October at the latest."

"You think everything will be approved by then?"

"It better be." Woodring glared.

"We'll be ready. Most of my crew will have finished other jobs. We'll roll."

Woodring remembered something else he wanted to ask Purillo. "How's your bother, Sid?"

"Fine, I guess. We don't talk that much."

"Think he'd mind doing me a favor?" Woodring pushed back from his king-sized, black cherry desk and dug through his attaché. "I'd like to know who owns this car. It was parked at Whispering Heights last night."

He handed Purillo a piece of paper with a license number scrawled on it.

"Sid's a state trooper, not a private investigator."

"C'mon, he's got those resourceful Purillo genes."

"Alright, I'll give him a call. You want to grab an early dinner?"

Woodring lit a cigarette. "Dinner? It's not even three o'clock." Purillo must live to eat.

CHAPTER 29

The ambulance whisked Mim to the Tunkhannock Clinic where an Indian doctor yawed in an accent about getting her to the hospital in Wilkes-Barre. Hap waited frantically and when a new ambulance finally arrived, the driver had slanted eyes. Considering the circumstances, he decided not to let the Asian's presence bother him too much.

Wilkes-Barre's emergency room was busier than the Dushore Diner on a Sunday afternoon. A specialist name Schindle asked a bazillion questions, blinking and frowning. Hap wondered if Schindle was short for Schindler, like the movie about the Jews.

Dr. Schindle eventually shared an opinion. "Mr. Clay, your wife must have had a stroke. We can't be certain if and when she'll emerge from this coma. We're going to do our best to keep her stable while we continue to run tests." The doctor said it matter of fact, like she was merely suffering from a sore throat.

Hap was bedside in the ICU. Mim's eyes were closed, mouth open, and both arms stabbed with IV tubes. Automated medicine machines blipped and beeped. Behind him, hidden by a curtain, lay a young man whose car had been compacted by a tractor trailer. The visiting priest left with tears in his eyes. The prognosis wasn't any rosier than Mim's.

For another hour Hap sat there, every minute sending him into a more acute sadness. Tears came to his own eyes and he couldn't remember the last time that had happened. In a world that was getting crazier by the day, Mim was the only constant of any value. Life would be grayer than February sleet without her around. His head throbbed and he craved coffee. Slowly he peeled himself from the chair and walked off in search of a cup of solace. The hall clock said it was 3:00. The horrid day lacked the decency to end.

CHAPTER 30

L ake Jean delivered on its shoreline promise. Like a tidal slough, a winding channel pushed far into the fringing marsh. Lilies floated on still water, asking to be touched. Teaberry grouped on hummocks. White pines buttressed by virile roots reached for the stratosphere and the air, tempered by shade, was redolent of sap.

Reily and Sol probed further until his paddle sank into soft bottom and the keel began to drag. The passage was narrowing, too – he could touch land on both sides.

"I'd turn around if I could, but I think we may need to back out."

Sol was preoccupied. "Are those more blueberries?" She coveted a sprawling bush ten yards away dripping with fruit.

"May I collect a handful for you?"

"That would be delightful."

Reily stepped onto spongy ground and headed for the motherlode. Sol shouted. A bear the size of a picnic table emerged behind the bush. Time froze. The brush exploded. Five hundred furry pounds never moved so fast.

Reily stood breathless and lightheaded as the black bear vanished in getaway mode.

Sol jumped out of the canoe and came to him, administering a comforting hug. "Please don't get eaten. I'm just getting to know you."

The berries remained, so they picked them together. Reily fed Sol a few, one at a time, dropping them onto her tongue. He was stirred by her delicate breath. The feelings blended with the warmth of the sun on his skin and the slow beat of water lapping the shore. He kissed her again.

She eased her lips from his. "Want to go for a swim? I know we're not allowed, but I'm a prisoner of unconventionality... being with an older man and all."

Reily took a deep breath. "Someday I will recollect the time a young mermaid asked me to swim. Others will think it's a fable, only I will know it was true."

Without another word, Sol peeled off her shirt, stepped out of her shorts, and entered the cool water. "Get your butt in here, you strange and handsome man." She swam away unhurried.

A descending trumpet, the call of a Veery, rode over their genteel arm of the lake announcing it was time for a lacustrine christening. Reily obeyed, disrobed to his boxers, and walked into the enfolding liquid. Sol waited, treading water, her face as bright as the sun. He approached under the surface, spotting her alabaster hue through the tannic broth. Like an octopus he enwrapped her, his hands landing on firm glutes. His head broke the surface inches from her face.

"Do you work out?" He squeezed his hands.

"Now you're asking for it." In the dancing light, her hair and eyes glistened like dark maple syrup. A fat, flattering drop of water clung to the tip of her nose.

Her sumptuous feel suddenly made him wonder if Rick had enjoyed the same pleasure. "May I ask you something?"

"Certainly."

"Did you and Rick spend the night together?" Reily dropped his head knowing he had crossed a precarious line.

"Nope." Sol stared over his shoulder. "Let's go back to shore."

He followed her with quiet motions, stewing over his blunder. They found solid footing by the canoe at thigh depth and she wheeled around wearing a puzzled, almost sad expression. He felt an uncomfortable wave of self-consciousness. Water dripped from his beard.

"You know, even though it would have been irrational and perhaps sleazy, I might have slept with Rick the other night," Sol said. "He's very good looking and I know I was charmed. I'm on the rebound from a loser with a capital L and may still have pent-up feelings to shed... but Rick didn't give me the chance."

"How could he resist you?"

"I don't think it was me. It was my gender."

Reily threw back his head. "Damn. Wil was right. I hate when he's right."

"Wil knew Rick was homosexual?"

Reily nodded. "Yeah, but he used less acceptable terminology."

She frowned. "I'll let this one slide, but next time he'll hear about it. Let's get in the canoe."

Reily complied and went to the stern seat. Sol maneuvered to the bow and sat facing him. She showed no interest in putting her clothes back on.

"I believe all things happen for a reason. Do you?" She locked eyes, excavating his thoughts.

"Yes, most of the time."

"So you are wondering why I didn't go for you initially. Well, I noticed you right away, and Rick, too, but he asked me to share his kayak. We had great days together. Everything was so new, I was enthralled yet I continued to watch you on the river. You have a unique presence, Reily: gentle but strong, seasoned but ageless, and a quiet confidence. And you already know I find you attractive. Next thing, I'm drinking with Rick and alcohol muddled my reasoning." She directed her left eye at him in squinty insinuation. "But I'll forget about your prying and paranoia if you kiss me. You have fifteen seconds. I'll close my eyes."

They made love in the canoe, his first time making it in a boat of any variety. Why he had waited so long was bewildering.

It was Sol's first boat sex, too. "The closest I came was at the aquarium with my short-term boyfriend. It was against the shark tank late at night. He got me drunk on tequila. You know, I can't believe I just told you that."

"Now I'll never look at a shark without thinking of you." Reily's back began to kink from the awkward position. Sol had her head on the bow seat with a life jacket as a pillow. He was wedged below the center thwart, his body against hers. A faint breeze brought clean mountain smells. Sol traced his chest hairs in a silent trance. He admired her. "How do you describe your eye color? You have intriguing, complex irises."

"Sometimes they're green, sometimes brown. There's even a little amber-yellow that appears from time to time."

"They're a kaleidoscope, the seasons of Sol." Reily rolled onto his back and squirmed into his wet boxers. His head was next to her waist, the field of vision limited by the sides of the Grumman. The rays of the sun were oblique, the sky cloudier. The feathered branches of a pine dressed the foreground.

"Sol, thanks for saving me."

"I didn't know you were in danger."

"Just my soul... you've given it a second chance." He waited for a response but there was none, only a hand stroking his cheek and hair.

"I hear something," she finally said.

"Sounds like an outboard."

Sol sat up. "There's a boat coming this way."

"Guess we better get dressed." Reily hopped out and grabbed the rest of the clothes, tossing Sol what she needed. They scurried about in a breathy tangle of limbs and garments. A john boat and its male occupant puttered by the cove, faking preoccupation with the motor.

Reily's watch was in the car, but his stomach told him it was getting late. They began the paddle down the lake and tossed around ideas for dinner, reciting cuisines they craved. Sol told tales of lousy Zimbabwean food and delectable feasts in Baltimore's Little Italy. In between, he caught himself singing.

Sol caught him, too. "What's that song?"

"Acuff Rose. From a band called Uncle Tupelo."

"I don't know them but I like when you sing their song."

So he sang it again – the verses that he knew – and the canoe, Sol, the lavish wilderness, and the music in his head blended into an incomparable feeling. It was Zen.

CHAPTER 31

H ap found the lone open stool at the Dushore Diner and reached for a menu. There was a tap on his shoulder. He spun around to see a pretty pregnant lady grinning back at him. It was the gal with the broken truck.

"How are you, Mr. Clay?"

"Please, it's Harold." He let out a deep, achy breath. "I've had better days."

"Why don't you come over and sit with me and my husband, Joe? He appreciates what you did for me."

"You don't need me interrupting your dinner."

"We're actually finishing up. You should join us."

It wasn't every day a girl, even a married one, asked him to dinner. "Alright, I suppose I can."

They went to the last booth, the same one where he'd met Lowell Orwell. Mary's husband stood to meet him. Joe Kambic was a giant-sized, moppy-haired teddy bear with a wrestler's handshake. He had on a new pair of blue jeans and a T-shirt about bass fishing. Hap would have tagged him as one of those fishermen who abandon their wives every weekend but he could tell Joe was crazy about Mary.

"Are you going to eat with us?" Joe asked.

"Yep, I'd be happy to." They weren't the right words. He wasn't feeling the least bit happy. He positioned himself next to Mary, careful not to sit too close.

"Mr. Clay said he was having a bad day so I thought he could use company." Mary spoke to her husband in the animated way a kindergarten teacher might speak to her students.

"We all have bad days. Today ranked up there for me. I broke a drill bit 250 feet down. What a pain in the you-know-what." Joe shook his head in frustration.

"What kind of drilling do you do?" Hap asked.

"Wells, mostly just for drinking water, but we've also done a few geothermal ones for heating and cooling." Joe exuded pride. "Those are supposed to be real efficient, environmentally good and all."

The last phrase made Hap's spine prickle, but he didn't dwell – he had a willing audience to share his woes. "My wife went to the hospital this morning."

Mary clasped his hand. "What happened?"

He relayed the events of the day with surprising acuity. The moments seemed so blurry just hours before. When he described Mim's current status and the bleak prognosis, he began to cry in slow drips. He paused to blow his nose.

Mary pressed his hand harder. "We'll pray for your wife, Harold. What is her name?"

"It's M-Martha." His voice faltered.

"I believe God answers prayer. Do you?"

"I... guess." Besides weddings and funerals, he hadn't gone to church since high school. The war had imploded his faith.

"Well, I assure you, He does. You can bet on it. Joe and I will do our part." Joe nodded in agreement.

"That's very kind." Hap appreciated their concern. No one else was pulling for him.

A limping waitress delivered dessert to the Kambics, and Mary asked about her leg. The waitress seemed embarrassed. "Would you believe I was gardening and stepped in a groundhog hole? Luckily, I only sprained it."

Hap thought of his gardening days and his beagle who loved nothing better than sniffing out a groundhog. Skipper was long gone... and his wife might soon be, too. His lonely stomach contracted from the sugary aroma of the slices of blueberry pie in front of Mary and Joe. He ordered Salisbury steak, a side of apple sauce, and coffee.

Before the couple left him alone at the diner, they asked for his phone number and address so they could check on him. He obliged although he didn't know why.

As he drove home, the sky was rosy purple in a sunset bouquet better than the one he bought Mim at the hospital gift shop. A barn and silo were fake silhouettes like someone doctored a picture. Ducks seeking refuge flew quick and determined across the scene. He pulled over to take a longer look and watched until the colors faded. Night closed in like a foreboding tide.

CHAPTER 32

It was a shitty start to Woodring's day. Sid Purillo called about the license plate. It belonged to a guy named Wisnoski, a reporter for a coastal newspaper in New Jersey who was known for his stories about crime and corruption. Sid's contact, the Chief of Police in Ocean City, referred to Wisnoski as a "pernicious prick." He knew him first hand. Woodring clicked his pen and stewed on the implications. Was it coincidence the reporter had parked on his land?

A second call came from the kinder, gentler Purillo brother, but Mikey and his piece of bad news was even more troubling. A subcontractor was having difficulty finding an ample yield of groundwater at Whispering Heights. There were a few perched water tables in the horizontal strata but not enough to support the needs of three thousand people. The state would require a reliable source and their meddling would stop progress faster than a tornado. Lawsuits from disgruntled home buyers or, God forbid, a class action suit, would be a colossal hurricane.

Hooking up to public water wasn't an option in rural Gifford County. The river was right there but it would be expensive to suck water all the way to the top of the mountain and there would be a cobweb of regulations standing in the way. The best plan remained a series of community wells to supply the townhomes and chalets. "Tell them to keep poking holes until they find a fucking geyser."

Woodring hung up and grabbed a cigarette, a bad habit learned from his father, the late lord of job sites for the Premier Land Development Corporation of Kissimmee, Florida. His pop wore a hard hat like a Roman gladiator enforcing Herod's rule, but that didn't prevent laborers from littering the construction grounds with unfinished smokes for the select harvest of a crafty kid. Woodring had watched his father facilitate the expansion of Orlando, and the deletion of ranches and orange groves, with agnostic precision and he could still hear his graduation advice: *"Clear your own path and leave others in the dust."* The father had remained true to his word in his relationship with his wife and his son.

Nicotine was still soothing. At least something was.

"I never even heard of Hunlock Creek," Reily said over his shoulder.

"You have now," Wil said from the stern seat of the tandem kayak.

"Yeah, but it was such a brief visit."

"That's your fault for rolling in so late. I figured you two had been knocked off by the Luzerne County mafia or abducted by ghosts from the Knox Mine disaster."

"What did we miss?" Reily hated to neglect the Odyssey programs but nothing could have taken him away from his day at the park with Sol.

"It was another short day. Good thing because I was more tired than a chronic insomniac. A catholic church did a fish fry for us. I think they used carp or maybe white suckers. It was pretty bad. There was a kickass slideshow about the 1972 flood. Alex closed things out with an impromptu concert around the campfire. Overall, it was a pleasant evening."

"Sorry to miss it. Well... not really."

"I want details, Watters." Wil nudged him in the back. "Where the hell were you yesterday?"

He was eager to share his good fortune but wanted to play it out slowly, to taste each moment again. He took a big, satisfying swallow from his water bottle and illustrated excerpts of the last twenty-four hours.

"You are primed. I can tell. You are back to your former Reilyness."

"I didn't know it was a documented condition."

"A state of mind and a state of being. So what happened after you left the lake?"

"We drove into Wilkes-Barre and found a sports bar with greasy burgers and fries. We gorged on them. Man, was I hungry. Then we talked for a couple of hours, each of us sipping pints of beer. It was picture-perfect." He bumped paddles with Wil to toast success.

"Everyone was worried about the two of you. Safety man was fuming. I thought he might give birth to a life jacket."

Reily laughed. It was good to be back on the water with Wil. Time and place had no meaning on the river but relationships did, especially one as eternal as the surrounding ridges. "By the way, I owe you a Wild Turkey."

"Huh?"

"Sol confirmed your accusation about Rick."

"I see. Well, I look forward to the libations and you'll be happy to know I've tried to be more courteous. I even extended a beer to him at the fire."

"My hope in you grows every day."

Sol wanted to be a log and drift along unnoticed. She watched Gabriele in the bow working the canoe they had borrowed from an older couple who decided the Odyssey was too difficult. Sol and her friends could use it as needed for the coming weeks. The couple would pick it up when the voyage ended.

Alex raced around them in Reily's solo boat like a duck on cocaine, but the mountains were ample company. Alex understood – he took off chasing an osprey. Sol loved how their friend sucked joy from everything no matter how trivial or circumstantial. She wanted to be more like him.

Gabriele blew her nose into a bandana. "So what were you telling me?"

"About my exhaustion."

"You slept with him again, yes?" Gabriele was always inquisitive.

"All we did was sleep, but he's fun to sleep next to." Even in his absence she could feel Reily's presence.

"Sol, I think he is the one for you."

The statement made her flush. "Maybe. Did I ever tell you about my boyfriend at Northern Arizona?"

"No, you must."

"We met late in my sophomore year and became inseparable. He was rugged and really smart – we'd do these mini-expeditions into the national forest and the San Francisco Peaks, but eventually his libido got the best of him. In the fall, he spent a semester abroad in Spain, atop a *senorita* he met during a wild weekend in Valencia. That was the end of it." The memories stung.

"Men can be so shallow." Gabriele scowled and tightened her ponytail.

"The experience haunted me. I left Flagstaff with plummeting grades, returned east, and enrolled at American University. My father was about an hour away at Mount Saint Mary's College. He'd already divorced my mother."

"Did you like living in D.C.?"

Sol switched sides with her paddle to keep the canoe on course. "For the most part, but a Saturday or Sunday poking around in nature with Dad was divine. No matter how weighty his own thoughts, he always listened and lent encouragement.

"Your father is an interesting man. I think Reily is interesting, too, and he is Wil's best friend."

"Maybe it's just my time of the month approaching, but I'm baffled why I'm so enraptured over him. He's much older than me."

"From everything I know and see, he is a good man. He is kind, yes?"

"Exceptional, sagacious..." Sol sighed. "I can think of many positives."

They entered the middle of a pair of extended lines of rocks – one on each side. The rock piles came closer together as they moved downstream. It was an eel weir used to trap the snakelike fish. From a program that very morning, they'd learned that the male eels make a harrowing trip from the ocean and up the rivers until they find small streams to call home. Eventually they depart, mysteriously drawn back to the sea to breed and die.

Gabriele turned her head to Sol. "The eels think love is worth risking their lives."

Sol pondered the remark. "You are right. They have an innate trust and patience, two traits I must practice." Gabriele possessed an uber ability to find the lesson in each moment.

"Then you should relax and enjoy the good fruit." Gabriele held up grapes she pulled from a knapsack and erotically dangled the cluster inches from her own mouth.

Sol was flabbergasted. "You are so weird." She shook her head and took another stroke. The landing at Mocanaqua was still miles away.

CHAPTER 33

From Mocanaqua to Wapwallopen to Berwick, Reily feasted on nature – a buffet of pattern, color, and light more pronounced than at any other time in the voyage. The river coaxed playfulness and he was in it nearly as much as on it. Trees watched, birds caroled, crayfish fled, and everyone knew the agent of his folly.

During the languid morning, he reengaged Alex. Behind the tough, angular face was a genial, social creature.

"Should politicians smoke pot?" Alex asked as he tied his kayak to Wil's.

"Probably, but an intoxicated judiciary might be a bad idea," Reily answered.

"Yes, but it would foster a friendlier, more collaborative legislative branch." Alex rummaged in his forward storage well and extracted a snack. "I'm considering petitioning the USDA for a recommended minimum of one ounce of pot per person per month. We all need a little happiness."

Wil dipped his visor in the river. "So long as George Bush is in office, I advise against alerting government agencies to your plan."

They stopped at a nuclear generating station in the afternoon. The power company assumed wrongly that Odyssians were just another tour group, civil and restrained like a gaggle of Rotarians, but there were ruffians in the bunch. Michael Blackman was the self-appointed general and Reily played along. The movie maker's case was that nuclear power could never be safe because humans were imperfect. Safety records were immaterial. Disaster or an unsavory contamination crisis was an eventuality.

The lower half of the Susquehanna was an energy-producing machine: nuclear plants at Berwick, Middletown, and the Maryland line; four hydro dams; a pumped storage project; plus a pair of coal burners. The river spun turbines and cooled reactors as electrons flowed outward into air conditioners, televisions, and dishwashers of thousands of oblivious homeowners. Befouled with nitrates and sucked viciously for its water, the river could have been a poster child for aquatic exploitation.

That evening, Alex shared another talent, photos taken the summer before on a road trip to federally-designated wilderness areas. "Best of the West" contained transcendent imagery of the Black Canyon of the Gunnison and the Cache la Poudre in Colorado, Hells Canyon in Idaho, the Havasu in Arizona, and the Gila in New Mexico. These were lesser known wild places but stunning nonetheless and all of them had a river running through them, nourishing life. Reily dreamed about those places. He had explored other parts of the West, mainly national parks, and even with the irritation of summer crowds, exultation was the emotion he remembered most.

After the picture show, Sol turned in but Reily reconnected with Blackman over a bottle of Captain Morgan. Blackman was one of the most intelligent people Reily had ever met, yet he could be as pedestrian as a trash man. One moment he might quote Socrates and in the next sentence complain about the Yankee's bullpen. Even with a degree of Hollywood fame and money, he was proletariat except for the backcountry Beemer.

Passing the bottle and pausing to burp, Blackman stood and steadied himself. He squinted at the steeple of a church down the road from the campsite. It was illuminated like a rocket on a launch pad.

"You know, there are two kinds of people in this world..." Blackman gestured like a preacher, "the living and the living dead. Most are the latter and don't even know it. I yearn to be the former but that's a hell of a lot harder. I'm talking risks and rewards. It may even kill you, but being dead is ten fucking times better than living dead. You understand what I'm saying, Watters?"

Surprisingly, Reily did, but maybe it was just the rum.

CHAPTER 34

Hap watched the sun rise without meaning through eyes raw and sticky from tears. Mim would have been seventy-two if she had made it to August. From a plastic Adirondack chair on his twelve by twelve slab patio, he heard one car then another zoom by on the familiar road, yet they could have been on another planet. There were so many things to do: funeral arrangements, contacting the few and far flung family members, sorting out insurance. The hospital would forward the death certificate; the government even had paperwork for dying. The idea of rooting through boxes and mementos caused another surge of tears. Mim was his universe. Was this tragedy punishment for his dishonesty? He needed coffee.

The calendar on the refrigerator reminded him it was almost the Fourth of July, the most patriotic of dates. If you wanted to rub salt in the wound of a decorated war veteran, steal his lifelong companion near Independence Day. Hap's trembling hand bumped the side of the coffee maker, spilling a scoop full of grinds. They littered the linoleum like a Jungian sketch of misery.

CHAPTER 35

A vibration in the hull was followed by a whiff of sulfur. It was the third such incident on the leg to Bloomsburg.

"Dammit Wil, I'm changing your diet."

"It's my prostate relaxing because of Gabriele."

Reily had other theories about Wil's turgidity but chose to change the subject. "What do you think of Michael Blackman?"

"The guy is full of himself. I thought he was an ass at first."

The comment was curious coming from someone with infinite ego. "So what do you think now?"

"During your protracted absence with Sol, we talked about my new book. He even made a few spot-on suggestions and, as you know, I'm very skeptical about feedback."

"He makes movies. I would think he knows something about telling a convincing, entertaining story."

"Absolutely." Wil pinched a mayfly off his cheek and held it up. "Family *Baetidae*, I believe. Blackman told me to get him a final manuscript before it gets published... said it has screenplay potential."

"That's great."

"We'll see." Wil seemed distracted. "I should call the office. Let's stop under the bridge."

In minutes they were aground on the sloping support wall. Wil jettisoned his lifejacket. "Are you coming along?"

Reily reclined. "I'll stay here and sleep."

He watched Wil jog away. A small plane droned past low, following the river before banking around to land. Even in the partial shade of the bridge, the afternoon heat reached an apex. Reily closed his eyes and received scolding chatter from a kingfisher. A car bounced overhead, thumping over the expansion joint. The plane elicited thoughts of his father. What would he think about this trip? He wasn't a conventional outdoorsman or one to frit away time, but he'd appreciate the conservation mission, the destinations, and the interesting people. Every day was a new chapter in a Lonely Planet travel guide.

"Were you out again?" Wil was staring down at him.

"I don't know." Reily stretched his achy arms and returned to a seated posture. "How long were you gone?"

"Twenty minutes, tops. You're not going to believe who called me."

"Jill?" He knew it was a rare event for Wil to converse with his first wife. She had anointed him a dung beetle in human form.

"That isn't remotely funny. No, actually it was Katy."

"Katy who?"

"Exactly, who the hell is Katy? I don't know a Katy." Wil was worked up. "I don't care that I have no clue who she is, it's what she was digging for."

"What?"

"She asked one of our dippy receptionists if I was vacationing in Pennsylvania because she thought she passed me on the highway. The dimwit said yes, that I was on some river rafting trip."

"That is weird. Are you sure you didn't meet someone by that name?" Wil was known to frequent casinos in Atlantic City where women were as easy to pick up as poker chips.

Wil shook his head. "Don't go there. You know I don't forget names or faces. It's part of the journalistic training."

"So if you don't know this lady, what does she want... or rather, want to find out?"

"I'm not sure." Reily knew Wil had a theory or two; he just wasn't ready to share.

During the final stretch to yet another riverside park, thoughts of mystery-Katy were replaced by Wil's elucidations about Gabriele's globetrotting childhood. She had lived in six different countries, attended universities on three continents, and knew five languages well enough to get by. Wil spoke with adulation never before witnessed. When he finished, there was silence except for the synchronized brush of water from their paddle strokes and muted sounds from town.

"You haven't been messing with your beard," Wil said.

"How would you know?"

"I know what I see or, in this case, what I don't see."

It wasn't a debilitating ailment, but Reily knew who to thank for its attenuation.

Reily liked Bloomsburg's spirit. Wil said it had pulchritude. Sol thought it was an upland version of Oxford, Maryland. To Gabriele, it resembled Heidelberg, Germany, but with more subdued architecture. The town had a plucky Main Street of respectable shops without boarded windows, professional offices with a dash of the ornate, a suite of eateries covering the culinary spectrum, and a vanilla university topping the hill like a cherry on a sundae.

They were sitting in a crowded pizza shop with walls covered by provincial Italian maps. Ceiling fans pushed warm air tinctured with garlic and oregano. The ladies were sprightly this muggy Saturday evening and even Wil, haunted by Katy-unknown, was blithesome. The eggplant parmesan wasn't half bad either.

Gabriele finished a glass of Yuengling with a suppressed burp. "I think beer is like men."

"As in having a head too big for their body?" Wil grinned at his own lame wit.

"No, in that brands, like men, are all different. Just a little, yes?"

"So what kind does Wil resemble?" Reily was curious to hear her answer.

Gabriele hesitated. "Grolsch from Holland. It is good but somewhat bitter – a little too much personality." She grabbed Wil's arm to placate him.

"What beer is Reily?" Wil asked to Sol.

"That's a tough one... maybe Sam Adams. Complex but refreshingly well-balanced." Sol exaggerated her points like an actress in a thirty-second ad.

"I'll drink to that." Reily gulped several ounces. Cold beer tasted extraordinary after a long day on the river.

Wil said the restaurant reminded him of a pizza joint in Providence when he was in college. Reily had heard the story too many times – about drunkenness, pepperoni, vomit, and banishment. Wil tended to add colorful embellishments each time he told the tale.

Reily floated off in his own thoughts. There was a gray, wide man behind the counter speaking in butchered phrases, probably the bulk of every day. He was polite but hurried with a gut ready to erupt from a stretched and stained polo shirt. Younger, slimmer black-haired men – relatives he assumed – worked the oven and the grill with zest. Counter-man acted as if he knew most of his patrons but no one could do that day after day if they weren't sincere. Maybe Blackman was wrong about his living dead lecture. If you loved what you were doing, no matter how meaningless it might seem, and made others happy in the process, wasn't that a life well-lived?

Sol waved her hand in front of his face. "You better eat up, space man."

Sol held Reily's hand on the downhill from town to camp. Their steps smacked the pavement and, like second-grade playmates, they attempted to synchronize their incongruent strides. When they almost reached the park, Sol broke into a run without warning, taunting him to race her to his tent. He kept walking, gratified by watching her from afar. With a quick gate and bouncing dark hair, she was Black Beauty.

The tent was easy to find, parked in the shadow of a giant willow and glowing from a battery-powered lantern within. Reily laughed out loud as he entered. Sol had rearranged in the moments since they parted. Her sleeping bag was on the right with the pillow against the back wall. His bag was in opposite orientation, the pillow by the door.

She was still breathing hard from her sprint. "Let's have reading time. It will be fun."

He didn't need convincing. Proximity was awe; her delicate scent and honeyed voice distillates of joy. It was too warm to be in the bag so he lay atop it, his grimy toes by her head. Reily regarded her small, tanned feet and pronounced arches, imagining all the places they had been. Petite hands held the latest issue of the *Journal of International Development*. He pulled Thor Heyerdahl from his duffel and settled in. Except for the crinkle of turning pages, all was quiet within the tent.

"Read to me from your book," Sol interrupted.

"That's an interesting request."

"I've never read Thor Heyerdahl. Enlighten me."

Reily leafed around for a meaty passage and narrated a description of the explorer's home and wife in Fatu Hiva.

"Sounds primitive but beautiful. I could live on fresh coconut."

Reily agreed so long as there was ample rum. "But it wasn't all pineapples and pina coladas for the nice couple. There were tough times, too. Thor was inquisitive but grounded. He knew he needed to walk in the shoes of his subjects and experience their pains and pleasures. Today, we – the collective we – are so high on ourselves, we don't realize how much we're missing."

Sol furrowed her brow. "We are an impoverished lot, aren't we... in the figurative sense?"

"I'm afraid we are, but maybe every little act of good intention mitigates us from a famine of spirit."

"That was a hopeful comment, but from the condition of your feet, Mr. Watters, I might guess you were destitute."

"Scarred from the wayfaring life."

Sol nodded. "The marks of *joie de vivre*."

CHAPTER 36

Woodring could still taste Jack Daniel's on his breath as he stirred his cholesterol medication. It looked like a mud puddle at one of his construction sites. Sirloin, bacon, and beer had been weekday staples, while eggs and Jack were weekend friends. Sundays only increased his longing for those carefree days of gluttony.

He worked on a second cup of decaf and turned to the lifestyle section of the Scranton *Eagle* featuring a two-page spread about a group of canoe and kayak nuts making their way to the Chesapeake Bay. A map showed the route of the so-called Odyssey and its progress day by day. According to the paper, the tree-hugging expedition was designed to raise awareness about environmental threats to the Susquehanna River. He skimmed pictures of the participants in their boats and lounging by their tents. He saw a guy he recognized – one of the whiners from the township meeting. The beard and long hair were unmistakable. Why would the guy leave his cushy camporee and weigh in like a concerned local? Then Woodring remembered the car, the license plate, and supposed rafting trip. Was beard boy the New Jersey reporter?

Woodring took his coffee and walked out the sliding door onto his deck, coveting the sweeping view of sixty acres and two prize-winning mares. The purchase of the property and equines was inspired by a trip to South America and the pampered pleasures of haciendas visited. Woodring called his mini-ranch "Wildcat Hollow" for the bobcat he'd spotted, when first scouting the property, and later shot. Now its glass-eyed mount watched from the fireplace mantle.

Sitting down on a chaise, Woodring decided that the river trippers warranted closer scrutiny. A yellow jacket resting unseen disagreed and speared the underside of his forearm. The instantaneous scream – and subsequent cursing – persuaded one of the horses to lift its tail and soil the pasture in apathy.

CHAPTER 37

M im's lifeless shell was spruced up like she was going to a ballroom dance. She wore a pink dress and pink lipstick, neon against her pale, powdered skin. Her body looked too small for the big, pricey coffin but it underscored the permanence of her condition. Hap ached to see her again – to hear her voice and feel her quiet presence – but he had significant doubts that such opportunities would ever materialize.

Mary, his pregnant friend, had made the fancy new church and its efficient preacher available for the crappy occasion. She was waddling around somewhere getting the social hall ready for the luncheon to follow. The preacher didn't seem half bad. He was to the point and had a nice way of putting people at ease.

A whispering line snaked to the coffin. Gaudy dresses, ugly enough to mark highway construction zones, revealed Mim's quilting buddies and friends from the Daughters of the American Revolution. They clashed with the grove of white birches planted in the courtyard beyond the picture windows. Hap's heart dropped as the room-stretching figure of Lowell Orwell squeezed in the back door.

When Orwell reached him, Hap was exhausted from the endless repetition of condolences.

"Hap, I'm real sorry about this." Orwell exhaled an arduous breath.

"Me, too."

"Hope you'll get your feet back under you soon."

Hap questioned the deeper meaning of the beady-eyed statement. "Me, too," he replied.

Lowell shimmied away and entered the sanctuary, but the most surprising visitor was one of the last people in line: Gertrude Bunting, an unsightly pear of a woman who could challenge Orwell in a wide-load contest.

"I was sad to hear about Mim. She was a good woman." Gertrude hugged him like a long lost baby doll. "This may not be the place to tell you this, but I appreciate that you weren't too hasty with that rezoning vote."

Hap wasn't sure what to say. "You do?"

"Yep, I don't know what I want to do with my land but it would be best if it could stay a farm. That's what Don would have wanted." Her eyes were moist.

"He was a fine man."

Organ music blared from the sanctuary, a signal it was time for him to take the reserved spot in the front pew, but Gertrude grabbed his hands and sniffed tears. "You take care of yourself."

Hap knew that wouldn't be easy.

CHAPTER 38

A morning breeze out of the north pushed the canoe downriver. Reily pulled a rain jacket from his dry bag and tied the sleeves to two paddles. Sol watched from beneath a floppy blue hat intended to ward off sunburn. On any other adult it would have looked silly but on her, it was entrancing.

He handed her one paddle. "Hold this upright."

"May I ask what we are doing?"

"It's a makeshift sail to get us to Danville more quickly." He adjusted the position of the jacket and felt the canoe accelerate.

"I think we're sailing." Sol appeared amused. "I didn't know you could do that in a canoe."

"Have you ever sailed... I mean prior to today?"

"I helped for a day on a fishing boat that had a sail."

"Very cool, and where was that?"

"Zanzibar."

"You really have been all over." Reily wrestled the paddles against a stronger gust and anchored one between the cross supports for Sol's bow seat.

"Clever boy." It was a different voice.

He dropped the sail contraption and turned. A kayaker was searching for morning tea on the wrong continent. "Where have you been, Frances?"

She paddled closer. "Giving the two of you your space."

"That's very thoughtful, but unnecessary," Reily said.

"Both of you will have to come visit me in Eleuthera. We have a bit of everything – sailing, diving, superb beaches. The island is quite extraordinary."

"I'm sold." He was beguiled with the thought of going to an exotic locale with Sol.

Sol was listening. "I'd love to visit. I've been to the Bahamas once... to Nassau and Paradise Island for a long weekend. It was very nice but I'm sure Eleuthera is even better."

"Worlds better, my dear. One hundred miles long and in most places not more than a mile or two wide."

Reily tried to envision the island but was diverted by Sol's use of "I" instead of "we." The inevitable questions about the implications of their relationship had been avoided to this point.

"I'm actually leaving all of you tonight," Frances said. "I can't even remain for the meeting about that awful development but I'm not sure there's much I can do. I'll give you my information and you two come see me. But don't tell Alex... he'd smoke all the 'material' in my garden." She dropped a heavy wink on that final point and peeled away. She was one of a kind.

Reily directed the canoe and calculated the best way to speak to Sol about their mutual future. Every moment he spent with her, his long term interest compounded. Everything she said and did, every motion, emotion, and expression delighted him. He kept waiting for an irritating revelation or a palpable behavioral flaw but neither materialized. Her stroke was purely synchronous with his. She was magnificent by every measure.

"I don't think I ever told you about my travel plans." Sol's words sounded cautionary.

"You mean for the Odyssey?"

"Yes, I hope you're not upset but... I can't stay through to the end."

Reily's paddling ceased. "When do you need to leave?"

"Tomorrow, after we're off the water. Gabriele has to go, too."

"I thought you were heading to Havre de Grace." A half dozen mallards erupted into flight as if trying to escape the bad news.

"I'm sorry, but I have to be back at work. It makes me sick to think about it." Her words were forlorn. Maybe she really did want to stay.

Never had Reily succumbed to a woman so completely, so quickly. Wil's counsel was needed but Wil, too, would soon abandon him.

The Susquehanna turned slightly, a mountain wall on the south side and a flock of islands dead ahead. There had been other islands throughout the trip scattered here and there like pre-ordained rest stops on a river highway. There was something special about them. Maybe it was their unspoken independence or tenacious survival. Each was its own small world, a chance at paradise regained.

They slipped into the archipelago through a constricted passage. The arch of the trees made a surreal green tunnel animated with chirps, whistles, and the commentary of water. The island to the right rose higher than others and supported larger trees. He wanted to stop and explore although he wasn't sure why, considering his state of mind. He nudged the canoe into a ribbon of gravel along the toe of the bank.

"Bathroom break?" Sol asked.

He tied the bow painter line to a tree. "No, I just want to see the island."

They climbed the steep bank to discover a silty path winding between clumps of spicebush taller than Reily. Sol said it smelled like the McCormick plant in Baltimore. Patches of exotic day lilies were showy but out of place in the fluvial wilds. Someone had assembled a tree stand between two stout river birches using scavenged shipping palettes and plywood. Pieces of 2x4 were nailed into one of the trees, making a ladder to the platform. The structure, fifteen feet off the ground, merited closer inspection. He climbed while Sol watched from below. Atop the creaky deck, the view gave him a fuller appreciation of the size of the island. It was big enough to build a house on.

"Is it safe for me to come up?"

He felt like the bad boy in the neighborhood, secure in his fort, away from troublesome girls. But this one was still worth the trouble, he hoped.

"Sure, but be careful on the ladder."

When Sol reached the platform, Reily extended an arm and guided her to a spot beside him. They sat with their legs dangling off the side. A cicada's crisp exoskeleton, proof of its transformative liberation, adhered to the birch bark. He removed it and placed it on Sol's shirt.

She examined the specimen with her eyes. "It's... charming."

"I wanted to give you a gift... to bribe you to stay."

Sol ignored his comment. "Can you imagine living underground in darkness all those years and suddenly emerging into fresh air and sunshine? For them, it must be like going to heaven, although I doubt they have conscious thought."

"I can relate."

"I didn't know you were a burrowing insect?"

Reily stared straight ahead. "I wonder what it would be like to live on one of these islands."

"Lonely and challenging I would imagine, but I think your Thor Heyerdahl would approve."

Reily was pleased she remembered. "He would definitely approve. If you had a boat, you could visit civilization whenever you needed, although winter could get interesting."

"You'd have to build high like the Swiss Family Robinson."

"I loved that movie. I took Casey to Disney and we visited the treehouse three times. I'm not sure who liked it more, me or her." Reily pictured himself chasing his daughter around the structure.

"That movie was a little before my time but I've been to the Magic Kingdom. I enjoyed the treehouse although some of the furniture was far-fetched."

He put his arm around Sol. "Wasn't there a piano or an organ?"

"I think so. I'm not sure how you get one of those up a tree."

"It would make for a compelling alternative existence, far from some of the lame lifestyles we lead... speaking of the general population, of course."

"I could see myself doing that, if it was done well." Sol bit her lip in reflection.

"You'd make an excellent island woman."

She laughed in the fond way he loved. "You'd be the preeminent island man of your day."

There was nothing to lose. Reily had to trust in providence. "I think I am in l-love with you." His voice trembled. "No, actually, I know I am *madly* in love with you."

Sol peered at him with a mixed expression suggesting surprise and disquieted happiness. "I may be falling in love with you, too. It's somewhat overwhelming yet satisfying at the same time. I'm notoriously cautious about love but you are causing me to explore my own feelings like never before."

Reily digested each sentence and attempted to dissect the meaning. It was promising but guarded.

"Don't look so concerned. It's okay." She pulled him in for a kiss.

The juicy connection of their lips quenched his anxiety. They climbed down from the platform and returned to the boat, pausing to admire the island, the perfection of the secret passage, and the smooth and tumbled rocks beneath their feet. He inspected one and held it up for Sol to revere. The flat rock was the size of his hand and displayed a '2' etched by nature. The number was aberrant but obvious.

"I'm taking this with me. I think it has deep significance."

"I see." Sol stepped into the canoe while he held it steady. "I want you to know that even though I'll be leaving, I may come back. I have a little more vacation to use and I can't think of a better way to expend it."

Reily felt lighter. "I'll keep an eye out for you."

CHAPTER 39

D anville High School fulfilled every whim of a river traveler: flat athletic fields for camping, a spacious cafeteria for eating, a modern locker room for showering. Reily cherished the swank library where he lolled on a brushed denim loveseat. The room had a heady collection of books and quiet alcoves for getting lost in stories. A thick, pale Berber carpet subdued noise and movement. He didn't know if the students valued the facility but on this July Fourth evening it was a cozy slice of America's diminishing educational luxuries.

Odyssians dripped in, including Sol who flopped beside him wet-haired and smelling delicious. Alex entered the room wearing a Led Zeppelin t-shirt and cutoffs too short for a guy. A graying but nimble older couple from Richmond, Virginia, came in next and finally, Wil and Gabriele. She looked as precocious as ever... though Wil appeared somewhat reticent. The last arrival was Dr. Rob Murray, a few minutes late, checking his watch and closing the door behind him with care. He positioned himself in the center of the room, using a low-rise bookshelf as a lectern as he placed his papers before him and moved his glasses from the top of his head to his eyes.

"At risk of offending some of you, let me start by saying that there's nothing pretty about a suburb. You may live in one as I did. Their aesthetics are subjective but there's no denying that they can be a desert in terms of biodiversity. This meeting is to figure out how we can prevent the property known as Whispering Heights from becoming the Sahara of Gifford County."

The Virginia gentleman interrupted. "How can we help? Some of us come and go every day and there are just a few weeks left in this journey."

"I think all of you can help." Murray directed his eyes to every corner of the room. "It might be the ideas you offer at this meeting or perhaps some of you can get more deeply involved. There's no pressure. I simply appreciate your time and interest."

Alex stood. "Peace will not come out of clash of arms, but out of justice lived." He immediately sat down.

"Thanks for the Gandhi, Alex." Murray cracked a smile. "I'd like to open things up. The floor belongs to all of you. I'll moderate and record your ideas."

The lady from Virginia asked clarifying questions about the scale and timing of the project and the actions taken to oppose it. It was difficult to pin down such a leviathan – weather, subcontractors, site conditions, bureaucracy, approvals, and financing made development projects woefully complex.

"Houses, in some configuration, could be well underway by next spring with the first residents moving in by the end of summer. Roads and other infrastructure will likely go in this fall. The ultimate size of the project will depend on the final actions of the township. SURCOS has focused on public education so far. Our hope is to get locals informed and have them pressure their elected officials... but it's time to try new strategies." Doc Murray knew how to use his pulpit.

Little Carly's father, who looked like a preppy hippie, suggested organizing multiple protests – at the project site, at meetings, anywhere it might make a difference. "We'll drive the developer nuts."

Kim, who'd stepped in unseen, recommended forming a committee to review development plans and examine them for deficiencies. A staid couple from Lancaster – the husband could have been lifted from the pages of a Sears catalog – asked about involving the press.

Wil tuned in. "Absolutely involve the press. They'll not only drive the builder crazy but might dig up a thing or two you can use against him. Gather press lists, cultivate the interest of key writers, issue press releases when there are specific events or actions, possibly meet with editors or editorial boards, and always write lots of letters to the editor."

Doc Murray furiously scribed the ideas on a flip chart.

Alex rose again. "I can take pictures of events or the property... just tell me what you need. I can also take more pictures of the township trio and the developer. They'll love that." The group laughed.

The man from Lancaster cleared his throat. "I have my own plane – a Cessna with four seats – and my pilot's license. As time permits, I'd be happy to take Alex or someone else for a ride to see or photograph the site from the air." His wife rolled her eyes in disapproval.

Reily thought more about the nighttime exchange between township officials and the developer: it was bribery plain and simple. "Is the development contingent on the rezoning of the land?"

"There are two tracts of land. The larger one is owned by the developer, Mr. Woodring, but it is less developable. Regarding the second tract, Woodring has been in negotiations with the landowner, Mrs. Bunting, to purchase it." Doc Murray slowly paced the floor as he answered. "More than a third of the houses would be constructed on this property as well as the major access road into and out of the development. This is Woodring's ideal scenario. It is possible that he could obtain the Bunting property and build without a successful rezoning, but that would greatly diminish the number of homes he could construct. So, in summary, the short answer to Reily's astute question is no, the development is not contingent on a rezoning."

Reily wasn't satisfied. "Do you think developments like these involve impropriety by the developer, elected officials, or both?"

Doc and the group seemed surprised by the question. There was a pause before Doc Murray answered, "Sometimes I think that happens. In this case, I have no evidence or suspicion of anything illegal occurring, but a word of caution: fighting development is like stepping on an ant hill. There's action everywhere and the ants climb and bite from all sides. You have to be nimble and know when to evade and when to use the right tools in your arsenal. The bigger the developer, the more ants – attorneys, friends in high places, you name it – and the larger the project or hill, the harder they'll fight to defend it."

When the meeting ended, Reily and Wil corralled Doc Murray and enlightened him about their ordeal at Whispering Heights and the interaction witnessed.

Murray scrunched his face in disbelief. "You're sure about this?"

Wil put his hand on Doc's shoulder. "The downside is that our testimony would be gutted in a courtroom. No one would believe we could see or hear anything in the big, bad woods at night. Not to mention, they would question our sanity and our motives about being there in the first place."

Reily leaned in. "Tell Doc about your new friend, Katy."

Wil relayed the odd inquiry made to his office in Somers Point.

"You think someone saw you or your car that night?" Doc Murray asked.

Wil took a deep breath. "Perhaps."

Murray rested against the wall. "Why would they go to all the trouble to track you down... unless they royally fear what you know?"

Reily folded his arms across his chest. "So what do we do?"

"Maybe just wait and see. If we pursue some of the other things we've discussed tonight, they'll feel more pressure. But you should document everything you saw and heard and let me know if there are further inquiries from Katy or other aliases." Doc's expression was clearly worrisome.

"There's one thing I don't get," Reily said. "The old supervisor, the scrawny one, made the motion to table the zoning request. Why would he do that if he's getting paid off to support the project?"

Wil shrugged. "You watch... at the next meeting it will pass unanimously or at least two to one."

Walking out of the school with Wil, Reily bridged another disquieting topic: "So you're out of here tomorrow?"

"After we get to Sunbury. I wish I could stay. This has been a trip I'll never forget."

"I'm glad you came." Reily wanted to say more but the words captured his good feeling about the past days. "So what about Gabriele?"

"She's leaving, too." Wil was predictably evasive.

"I mean what about the two of you?"

"We're going to see each other as we're able."

Reily wanted to deck him. "You better see her again. You two are great together."

"I know."

CHAPTER 40

Thunder effervesced into a thousand self-extinguishing sparkles over the river. The succession of color and sound lifted Sol's melancholy but it snapped back into place with the shortest lull in the display. Reily's hand clung to hers as if afraid to let go, or maybe it was the other way around.

They were afloat on their blanket on a grassy sea surrounded by people, some as big as boats, contentedly anchored, their eyes gleaming when the sky exploded. Were their faces veiling a deeper disenchantment? She second-guessed her own emotions... she wasn't disenchanted, just confused. The man beside her was whole and gratifying but it was as if an invisible rope coiled around them both. It was a warm, dizzying knot but was it too tight?

Sol took a deep breath and Reily squeezed her hand. Despite his aura of tranquility, his forehead revealed apprehension. It was time to leave, although she feared the moments of inevitable angst. She'd rely on her belief in the intentionality of life – if she and Reily were meant to last, they would.

Reily paddled alone. The flat water caused by the dam at Sunbury and a headwind out of the southwest were a drag but he welcomed the exertion and distraction. He tried to think of nothing but each stroke. His aquatic meditation worked until something interrupted; a train rushed alongside the river, loud and indifferent. Reily's thoughts were like freight, tucked away in dusty corners, headed to destinations unknown.

Wil changed his mind and left after breakfast in a rush, leaving Gabriele to paddle with Sol. The cars were already shuttled. When they arrived at the state park on Packers Island, the ladies would be finished as well.

Sol was waiting for him to paddle into shore, her car idling on the park road, Gabriele beside her. Gabriele delivered a mighty hug and reminded him to stay in touch and keep an eye on Wil. Then he turned to Sol and they embraced for what seemed like minutes. He wanted to say something profound but couldn't.

Sol lifted her eyes to his. "I'll talk to you soon, okay?"

Reily nodded and they parted. Sol Messina, the woman of his dreams, got into her little car, her spunky blonde-haired friend at her side, and drove out of sight.

He felt as heavy as a tombstone.

CHAPTER 41

The mower belched a black puff of smoke and bucked to a stop.
"Goddammit." Hap dismounted knowing it was out of gas.
The uphill walk was more of a challenge every year, especially on a summer afternoon hotter than a bonfire. He slid open the backdoor and entered the relative cool of the house. All was still. A floorboard groaned underfoot, inducing the skin-crawling sensation of another person's presence.

Out of the refrigerator, he took a yellow plastic pitcher and poured himself a glass of instant lemonade. He added a handful of ice and went to the patio, positioning himself on a favorite chair. Jets headed to New York or Boston traced contrails in a cobalt sky. Planes made him think of the war. There were single-engine bird dogs used for observation, P-51s, and F-80 jets. With that kind of technology, how had the Korean War come to a stalemate?

Hap closed his eyes then heard the sound of a car entering the driveway – some lost and stupid city person turning around. A car door slammed. This prompted Hap to go inside and through the house to open the front door; there stood Mary Kambic, the pretty pregnant gal, holding a casserole dish.

"Joe and I wanted to see how you were making out." Mary sat beside him on the patio drinking a glass of his lemonade.

"I'm alright, I suppose." Hap was pleased to have her company. "Thanks again for bringing the macaroni and cheese. I bet it's good."

Mary smiled at the compliment. "I know Joe likes it. He'll scarf down a dish of it in one sitting. I'm lucky to get my own serving."

"He's lucky to have a chef for a wife."

"I don't know about that." Mary put the glass to her lips and surveyed the grounds with perky blue eyes. "You certainly have a nice place here."

"We..." Hap caught himself. "I've been here a long time. I like the peace and quiet."

"Me, too. That's the best part of living up here. I hope it stays that way. Everywhere else is changing, but around here things are the way they're supposed to be, more or less. I love the woods. Joe and I hear coyotes all the time. I always wonder what they're saying."

"I don't think it's going to change much." He tried not to sound defensive.

"Me neither, unless the big development goes in." Mary looked down, embarrassed for bringing it up. "Our place is only two miles from where they'll build."

Hap finished the rest of his drink, not sure how to respond. "It may not happen." He knew it was a lie.

She made eye contact again. "I was happy you voted against it at the township meeting."

"Well, I just voted to table the rezoning. There'll be another vote."

"Still, I'm glad you're representing us. It's been awkward because Joe's company's doing the well drilling at the site. He's got to be careful... that developer's a real something. I shouldn't repeat what Joe called him. Let's just say he's not a nice man."

"Joe's right about that."

"Now, please don't repeat this, but Joe told me they can't find much water there. They keep drilling deeper but there's not enough for all the houses they're going to build."

This was news to Hap. He wondered if Orwell knew. For some reason the disclosure wasn't upsetting; it was having the opposite effect. "Keep me posted about this, as much as you're comfortable sharing."

That night Hap slept fitfully, wiggling around like a noodle in a pot of boiling water. After midnight, a storm brought strobe lightning and dreams of interrogation. His mind jumped back and forth from Mim to the proposed development.

At 5:45, he ended the torture and stumbled to the kitchen. As the coffee pot babbled, he stared without focus, pawing through his options. While he drank his first cup, the gray of dawn gave way to an epiphany of muted colors. Hap reached a decision and would not waver.

The coffee tasted unusually bold that morning.

CHAPTER 42

The West Branch was a wilderness river. The first hour, two miles from Keating, a bull elk with a rack like a candelabra emerged from a grove of shoreline aspens. It stared at Reily as if he was the first human to make the descent. Two hours later, a bear loped along the other shore. The second leg of the three-segment Odyssey was off to a lively start.

Life was charitable on the land but not in the river. The water was meretriciously clear in the shallows and aqua in the deeper pools. It was attractive, inviting, and unequivocally dead... no fish, no frogs, nothing. Evidence was found at the river's edge on rocks brandishing a rusty, caustic precipitate – the legacy of the coal industry. Strip mining had sullied what may have been the most gorgeous river in the east, and its small towns were festering as badly as the water. Except for the terrestrial fauna, everything was scribbled in a gloom that couldn't be shaken.

In Renovo, Reily avoided his friends who remained on the trip – Alex, Rick, Kim, and Blackman, the feral filmmaker. The others were gone, even little Carly and her yellow slicker. He retreated to his tent and reentered the existential world of Thor Heyerdahl, living off Nutri-Grain bars and water that tasted like warm plastic. He tuned out drunks gunning their motors and juveniles attempting to disfigure themselves with fireworks. Soon the weather defended him with a slow, steady bombardment of rain.

The next morning was gray, sodden, and surreal. Nothing – not the contrasting boats or a rich cup of Ugandan coffee prepared by Rick – could lift him from his catatonia. Reily wondered if he could keep going. The comforts of home tempted but he paddled on.

In the afternoon, they left the boats under the Route 120 bridge and a school bus took them to an overlook where, beneath two spacious tents, a local hunting club laid out a spread of barbecue wings and ribs. Reily ate bullishly, the spicy calories stabilizing his mood.

An after lunch program about food plots for deer and turkey failed to hold his interest so he walked away to a stone wall atop the plateau.

The view was guarded by a stubborn mist but Reily knew the river was far below going through its motions, working without complaint. He stretched out on the wall, feeling the hard, gritty sandstone against his back. The rocks and the setting reminded him of that perfect night at the Heights. How was Sol readjusting to life in Baltimore after their adventures? Was she thinking about him? Rocks were fortunate to be free from the agony of uncertainty.

Late in the afternoon, Reily washed ashore at White Oak Camp. The retreat for city kids was closed for renovations but temporarily opened for the Odyssey... austere river runners didn't mind sawdust. The facilities were far less derelict than he was. His last haircut had been two months ago. Showers were MIA. He coined a new term: Hygiene Deficit Disorder.

Rob Murray was the contrarian. He dropped in at dinner, polished and genteel, wearing a navy blue golf shirt and off-white slacks. Later, the Doc was deep in discussion with the camp manager, but excused himself to say hello.

"How are you, Reily?"

"Hanging in there. This was a pretty stretch of river today, except for the mine runoff."

"Yeah, it's sort of an undiscovered wonderland. We're making progress on cleaning up acid mine drainage but it's going to be a long process. Restoration is tedious work. The West Branch may never fully recover."

"We have to avoid the impacts in the first place."

"Exactly, that's why we have to seriously curtail the Whispering Heights mess."

Reily hoisted his jeans. He had shed pounds in the past weeks. "I still want to help with that."

"You want to see it from an airplane?"

"When?"

"Day after tomorrow. Mr. Samuelson, the man from Lancaster, will be flying in to Lock Haven. Alex will be joining him." Doc gestured with his glasses. "You're welcome to come, too."

"My father was a pilot but I'm lukewarm to aircraft with propellers."

"Come on, we could use your keen perspective and another set of eyes."

"I succumb, but it's against my better judgment."

As darkness fell, Reily retreated to his hammock suspended between two pines behind the dining hall and beside his tent. The land was quiet but dense with earthy scents. He watched fragments of clouds scrape the mountains until the stars turned on. Soon they were thick as flowers on a summer prairie. Damp webbing stuck to the back of his shirt. He closed his eyes and labored to accept unconsciousness. A slight squeak paired with a perceptible beat of acrobatic wings. Then there were footsteps, a human shadow at his feet. It was Alex seeking kinship and a smoking partner.

A substantive social interaction in the outdoors required a noble log, heavy and humble, to listen and offer support without speaking. Scouring his memories of multi-day adventures, nearly every one included such a temporary bench. This one was particularly comfortable. He sat facing the river beside the slumped figure of Michael Blackman who was rolling a joint by the light of his headlamp.

"You two are a bad influence. I was quite content in the hammock."

"C'mon Reily, you've got to live a little… nothing like a little sweet Jane to amplify contentedness." Blackman licked the edge of the cigarette paper.

"And compromise my faculties."

"Faculties aren't required this fine evening." Blackman slipped the joint to Alex.

"The stars are on high-beam tonight." Alex paused and ignited. "It reminds me of Wyalusing."

Reily remembered the night well. "That already seems like years ago."

"See what love does to you." Alex pontificated from his prophetic high. "You get sucked into a time vortex – don't even know what day it is."

"Dangerous shit," Blackman added.

"Time or women?" Reily received the joint from Alex but passed it on.

"Both. Look at you. You've been a lifeless stump since your chickie departed."

"Maybe, but I was having the time of my life while she was here."

Blackman jumped up. "You think they're a Godiva but they're really a medusa. You don't know which head will show up when. They're an addiction and an affliction. I've bedded women from Toronto to Tijuana. It's a full contact sport but other than expression of pleasure, interjecting emotion is a flagrant penalty. You move on. The season never ends but each game is a little victory. If – and that's a big if – you reach the pinnacle, it's only temporary. Live week to week. That's the Blackman creed." With that, he tripped backwards over a rock and hit the ground with a thud. The joint, still in his hand, sparked like a miniature rocket. Alex and Reily laughed out loud.

Alex caught his breath. "You're an opinionated sucker. Don't extinguish Reily's flame. It may be flickering right now but it will flare up again. Now give me back my reefer."

Blackman returned to the log. "It will engulf him, burn him to cinders."

"I hope Alex is right." Reily's mind felt shackled by the effects of indirect inhalation. Above the mountain, amulets hung by invisible strings dripping their pleasing photons. Then a flare of silver light burned over them, leaving a gossamer scar that disintegrated westward.

Blackman shook his moppy head. "What the hell was that?"

"A meteor, I believe." Reily peered upward. "I don't think I ever saw one that bright."

Alex rose and faced them. "Maybe one of us has been chosen?"

"We better smoke some more before we vanish," Blackman said.

"I think they want Reily," Alex said.

With the diminished joint between his lips, Blackman flicked his lighter and nudged Reily. "Dude, your buddy Wil writes like James Patterson, only better. I dig his manuscript."

"Wil's a fantastic writer but he never gets the recognition he deserves." Reily stood and felt dizzy.

Alex noticed. "Be careful, tall man, I should have warned you – that was power weed."

"Power weed?"

"Also known as one-hit wonder."

"Well, this one-hit wonder is retiring to his tent." Reily saluted his comrades. "If you're missing in the morning, I'll know what happened."

Blackman took an audible toke. "We'll leave a note."

CHAPTER 43

Reily's dream was invaded by semi-automatic hammering. Somewhere near his tent, a woodpecker was dissecting a tree, feasting on the perpetrators of the tree's death. Nature had a way of getting even.

The sun had returned from its temporary vacation to the apparent delight of every bird in the keystone state. Their raucous song and the growing illumination coaxed Reily outside still wearing yesterday's clothes. He followed his stomach to breakfast, a continental spread insufficient by traditional camp standards.

Blackman and Alex were present but as grim as reapers. They hadn't been raptured but they had learned that "one-hit wonder" had a dark side.

The day turned into a firebomb tempered only by the kiss of West Branch water. Reily's solo canoe bumped over shallow riffles and pushed through pools quarried by the river that filled them. They made for quintessential swimming holes and sweat and heat demanded such diversion.

At lunch, he learned more about the logging that had laid this land to waste a century ago. Towering white pines and hemlocks, coveted for toothpick-straight logs and tannins for leather, were erased in giant clearcuts. With the trees went the soil, wildlife, and wilderness that were Penn's Woods. Recovery had been accelerated by the CCC, forestry pros, and a rare breed of policy makers with guts and soul. There would be future defilement and vacation homes, but Reily was happy about the preponderance of trees. This was Pennsylvania's Amazon. Forested shorelines were a fortress interrupted only where streams tumbled off the plateau, chewing their way to the river and dropping their burdens at the edge like humble offerings.

Near Lock Haven, giant timbers were strewn along the river bottom, vestiges of cribbing that restrained log rafts so extensive they made the liquid surface a moving jigsaw puzzle treacherous to cross. There were probably skeletons of the workers in the sediments below.

He peered into the depths to spot more timbers until his neck grew stiff.

Now there were cabins along the shore and the river was a lake thanks to Lock Haven's dam. Surroundings unpretentious and demure became as rowdy as a rodeo. Personal watercraft buzzed the flotilla, and pontoon boats puttered past, coughing blue smoke. In front of a white-sided cottage less effusive than the rest, a mowed yard reached the water's edge. A sandy-haired girl maybe ten years old sat on the porch watching the canoes and kayaks paddle by, her head swaying to the rhythms of a boom box. She coyly followed his progress.

Reily thought of Casey. An outing in the canoe was a carnival ride to her and when they were driving back from their adventures, she'd declare with lemur eyes, "Thanks Daddy, that was fun." They could have flipped, swamped, or gotten stuck in the mud... it wouldn't have mattered. But then she became a teen and her mother's influences altered her mind and his universe.

He regarded his own maritime craftsmanship. Each unique strip bonded to the next, coated in glossy polyurethane to accentuate the wood. It wasn't bad work for an amateur.

"Is there going to be a test?"

Reily startled and looked around. Alex was approaching on his kayak. "What are you talking about, Mueller?"

"You were staring at the bottom of your boat. I figured you were reading a book, maybe a canoeing manual."

"Nope, just spacing out." Reily resumed a slow, deliberate stroke.

"You were thinking about your girl."

"Actually, I was, but not the one you assume."

"Of what girl do you speak, oh great one?"

"My daughter."

"You mentioned her previously. It was early in the trip..." Alex paused, "...paddling near Owego."

"I thought marijuana erased short-term memory?"

"I'm a biological repudiation of such myths. Where is your baby these days? Is she tall like you?"

"College, in Virginia. She's probably 5'9" and much better looking than her father. She'd have to have a naval escort on this journey to repel the advances of men like you."

"Why didn't you bring her along?"

Reily's face tightened. "She hasn't been speaking to me much."

"Reach out. Make contact even if she's a wall. Eventually, she'll crumble. Love pries open the cracks that form during periods of deep freeze."

"I wish it was so simple, but I appreciate your encouragement." Alex always made him feel better. The man could have been a psychiatrist but the easy access to narcotics might become a problem.

Wisps of smoke annexed their conversation, teasing with the smell of Worcestershire and charred meat. Twenty yards away, a thin, sunburned man with egret legs waved with metal tongs from the foredeck of a pontoon boat. An overweight wife or girlfriend stared from a seat, feigning a smile.

Reily's stomach growled. "That smells good. I couldn't see what he was cooking but I'm guessing sirloins, maybe T-bones."

Alex had a mischievous glint in his eyes. "He's grilling a piece of his woman's ass."

"You're bad, Alex. You talk like that around your lady and I bet she'll crack you in the head with your guitar."

"It wouldn't happen. I self-monitor my speech around Erin."

"So that's her name. You've alluded to her existence many times, but never dropped a name."

"She's the best. Tolerates my smoking. Well... most of the time, and she's super laid-back." Alex opened a pack of jerky and tore off a piece in his teeth. "Erin tries to come to most of my gigs even though she has to get up early."

"What does she do?"

"School teacher... third grade. The kids love her."

"Are you going to marry her?"

"Doubtful. Erin says marriage is an institution of subjugation."

"What do you think?"

"I'm not sure we need to go through with such formality. We love each other and live together most of the time. It's great the way it is and she's fantastic about giving me a lot of independence. She was going to come on the Odyssey but had to go to Massachusetts for a continuing education workshop. Normally she'd eat this up. Erin loves kayaking."

Alex had made a winning selection. *The odds seemed to collude against such pairings.* For the first time in days, Reily caught himself tugging at his beard.

"Tall man, are you going to join us for tomorrow's flight?"

"Doc Murray hit me up last night. I said I would, but I have trepidation."

"You'll be fine. I think we have to be at the airport at 7:30. Do you mind driving?"

"Only if you promise to keep my irrational fears secret."

"I'd never betray someone who looks like Jesus."

Reily rolled his eyes and noted the takeout ahead on the left. Boats were being carried from the water and lined up in the grass like cars on a lot. A flood control levee spanned the other bank, the buildings of downtown Lock Haven cowering behind the fortress. His knees ached from miles of sitting and kneeling. "Alex, faithful follower, I may need your help leaving the water."

That night, after the politicians had visited and painted the town in hyperbole, Reily followed Alex, Rick, and Blackman across a bridge to the closest bar. A spotlight lit a hanging sign with the words "Cub's Pub" in forest green letters etched into wood. Inside, Cub's had a shiny bar, a dozen or more taps, and plenty of empty, high-backed stools.

Reily bought the first round and ogled as dark and sticky Guinness overflowed the pint glasses. Two guys in work boots slouched at the near end of the bar, one of them shaking his head in drunken disbelief as the other bitched about his girlfriend. At a round table in the far corner, four young women of college stock avoided eye contact with his band of paddling degenerates. They were all pretty. Three wore combinations of sweatshirts and tight-fitting workout clothes, but one – a slender, vivacious, artificially-colored brunette – wore black dress slacks, heels, and a pink top that matched her lipstick. From her sanguinity, she had to be the cheerleading captain or president of a sorority.

Blackman, the epicurean of the opposite sex, was enraptured. He ordered a shot of Sambuca to quell the potential for scurrilous deeds. Alex suggested she was an erotic specter sent by the motorboat industry to impede their paddling. Her salacious presence even seemed to stir Rick who called her "saucy."

While the co-ed was undeniably stunning, the length and luster of her hair switched Reily's mind to Baltimore and the laugh of one of the girls exhumed his daughter for the second time that day. He'd gone too long without talking to either of his gals.

Unable to suppress primal urges, Blackman promenaded his way to the young ladies, leaving Alex and Rick to venerate his audacity. Reily summoned the bartender, asked a question, and left the bar. As directed, he found a pay phone a block away. It appeared as worn and neglected as he felt. From between two credit cards in his wallet, he found Casey's phone number scribbled in pencil. He dialed her first, figuring if she was as irascible as he feared, he might need Sol's solace. After the fourth ring, an answering machine picked up with a recording of a familiar but diffident voice. He cleared his throat and waited.

"Hi Casey, it's Dad. I wanted to see how your summer is going. I'm still on the paddling trip on the Susquehanna. It's been a great experience. I think you'd enjoy it up here. The scenery is amazing. I was thinking about you." His throat knotted. "I miss you. I'll try you again as soon as I have a chance. Take care."

He hung up and took a steadying breath. Sifting through his wallet again, he pulled Sol's number. Drops of perspiration trickled down his side. Her phone rang to a different pitch. A convivial, saffron voice acknowledged the call and, after a brief salutation, dissolved to a frosty beep. He struggled to dispatch a worthy message but the words seemed banal and deficient. A motorcycle roared past as he said goodnight.

The plume of exhaust paired well with his misery.

CHAPTER 44

At 11:15 A.M., the mail was delivered to the office like any other day, but this time it included an envelope from Harold Clay. Woodring had never corresponded with Hap through the U.S. Postal Service. In fact, he had specifically told the man to avoid contacting him.

His nosey office manager, Terri, had received the mail and opened each piece before placing it on his desk. Atop the pile was a menacing hoard of familiar cash and Clay's letter. She must have read every scribbly, hand-written word:

Mr. Woodring,
On second thought, it seemed best for you to have your money back. I'll do what I think is in the best interest of Conroy Township. I have to live with myself and my decisions. I hope you understand.

Harold Clay

Woodring's hand shook with rage as he read the supervisor's note again. The simpleton had no concept of the pressures, the mind-blowing details a businessman had to endure. Big projects meant big rewards for everybody involved – from the builders and loggers to pavers and even incompetent local governments – but the entrepreneur, the visionary, had to assume all the risk, every dime. It wasn't right. In the last thirty years, America's business acumen had crash landed and never gotten back off the ground. Every Pennsylvania jurisdiction was a different country. You never knew what they were going to accept or reject. He'd pegged Hap Clay as a featherweight, a power-happy pragmatist with the discernment of a skunk. But the skunk had grown moral stripes.

He frisked the contents of his top drawer, desperate for a cigarette.

How could he keep Terri from spreading insinuations about the cash and correspondence all over northeastern PA? She wasn't a rumor mill, she was a rumor turbine and if her body wasn't *Penthouse* perfect, he would have found a more taciturn replacement long ago. But first, he needed to let fat Orwell in on what happened.

The chairman of the Conroy Township Board of Supervisors picked up on the second ring as if he had nothing to do except sit by the phone.

"Lowell, this is Carl."

"Carl who?"

"Carl Woodring, the guy hoping to propel your despondent fiefdom to prosperity."

"What's up?" Orwell sounded uncomfortable.

Woodring recanted his sullied morning. "Now what are we going to do?"

"I suppose we could talk with Hap some more."

"That hasn't done anything, nor has cold hard cash."

"Maybe we could get it done without him. I could work on Larry Wilson."

"Jesus, that's a reassuring strategy. He's already voted once to table it." Woodring made rough calculations in his head. Without Gert's land and without the rezoning, Whispering Heights would lose its profitability and panache. His Shangri La vision was wasting away.

"Maybe I can persuade him. Larry's a heck of a nice guy."

"I don't need nice, I need a green light."

"But you don't even have Gert's land yet."

Woodring began to wonder if Orwell might cave. Did he lack balls, too? He was round enough to be a eunuch. "That's my problem, one more in a growing list. You just keep thinking about options."

Orwell stammered. "I'll give it a shot."

"Please do or I might ask for change." Woodring snuffed out the cigarette. It was already down to the filter.

Chapter 45

B ob Samuelson was serious and focused in the pilot's seat. He scanned the horizon, interpreting the geography below. "That's Williamsport to the right at about three o'clock," he shouted over the growl of the engine.

Reily stole a glance and then another. The patterns of civilization impressed him: mosaics of green, geometric streets, sinuous highways, a stalwart ribbon of river to the south. Away from the city, the density and quantity of buildings diminished progressively. Except for an occasional town or crossroads, it was *Sticksville*. Forest stretched in every direction undulating like a bad carpet installation until tarnished by a house or unpaved road. Some of the homes had acres of lawn to tend. If the suburban reenactors had their way, the rural frontier would vanish beneath the tires of Cub Cadets. He had designed plenty of big, boring yards edged with exotic species. Now he was evaluating the mistakes of others, but they could have been his own.

The Cessna rumbled and climbed. The last time he'd occupied a co-pilot seat he was ten years old. Dad was Buzz Aldrin and he was Neil Armstrong and they were going places never gone before. That fantasy flight had ended with motion sickness and a brown paper bag, but vomit needn't despoil a good adventure.

Samuelson announced they were nearing the site.

Alex affixed a long lens to his camera. "How low can you get?"

"Close enough... but not too low. I don't want the FAA after me."

The plane performed a high arcing turn and aligned with the north branch of the river two thousand feet below. There was a matchbox community in the foreground with a barn and farmhouse surrounded by fields and woods. Reily spotted the dirt roads into the site and the beguiling outcroppings. An opening in the forest canopy contained trucks and a rig as tall as the trees around it. He looked for the place he had kissed Sol.

Samuelson swung the plane around to give Alex a chance to prep for the shoot. On approach, the wing dipped and Alex fired away at the discordant patch of drilling, the farm brushed with sunshine, the rutted roads gouging the interior.

Samuelson glanced over his shoulder. "Is that enough?"

"Another pass would help. I want to switch to a wide-angle."

The pilot circled, allowing Alex to capture broad images of the properties. Reily studied the bucolic scene. A rim of rock marked the end of level land and the precipitous drop to the river. There was movement below – a tan blur dashing under the cover of trees.

He pulled back from the window. "Did you see that?"

"What?" Samuelson said.

"I only saw it for a split second, but I think it was a bobcat, although it seemed bigger. It was running along the edge."

Alex smacked him on the back. "What have you been smoking?"

"I'm serious. There was a large cat down there." Whispering Heights retreated behind them. "Bob, would you mind going back one more time?"

"I suppose. What did we miss?"

'There may be a violation."

Samuelson swung the plane around and checked his gauges.

"Drop as low as you can go and aim for the middle of the woods. Alex, you might want your long lens."

In thirty seconds they were over the target. "See the small clearing... get a picture of that," Reily motioned to Alex. "It must be a staging area for construction vehicles. I think it's next to the wetlands Doc Murray talked about."

"I thought I saw a little water," Alex said.

Samuelson goosed the throttle and adjusted course. The bearing indicator displayed 260 degrees. Alex began to repack his camera gear.

"I didn't see any silt fencing. They're probably required to have it." Reily tightened his seat belt. Anything *required* was anathema to a developer. For a prick like Woodring, cutting corners on erosion control was business as usual and penalties were as scarce as enforcement. It was a subtle "screw you" to the dwindling population who still cared about the world around them.

CHAPTER 46

Hap watched steam rise from a microwaved Swedish meatball dinner. It was a piss poor substitute for his late wife's cooking. The TV was now angled so he could view it from the dining room table. Eating there, with the volume maxed, he felt less alone than in his overstuffed chair. It was a new routine, one of many he should develop in the weeks ahead according to the counseling pastor from Mary's church. Adaptation was an integral part of a healthy grieving process. When the cleric led a prayer in his living room the previous night, Hap had been uneasy, but the rest of their talk was more than tolerable. Any friend of Mary's couldn't be too bad.

A ringing phone barged into his thoughts. He scrambled to pick up the wall-mounted receiver.

"Hello?"

"Hap?" said a deep voice.

"Yeah?"

"It's Lowell."

"Yeah?" He had zero interest in talking with Orwell.

"Woodring tells me you returned the money."

"That's correct."

"Now why'd you do that?"

"That's my business."

"You aren't going to throw a wrench into all of this, are you?"

Hap didn't answer but he could feel panic in Lowell's words.

"Jesus, Hap. We've come too far on this. Please don't screw it up."

"I'll do what I have to do."

"You better not wreck this. We have a vote in less than two weeks."

"I'm well aware." Hap's cooling dinner called.

Orwell panted like a pervert. "Are you on anti-depressants or something? You aren't acting like yourself. Look, I have to know how you're going to vote."

"You'll find out at the meeting."

"I need to know *now*."

"See you soon." Hap felt almost giddy.

CHAPTER 47

Reily had nothing but bright green water in front of him. How many variations of color could one river contain? Upstream it was almost aqua; on the North Branch, olive; today, beryl. Did minerals dictate the hue or was it a revelation of the river's secret mood? If so, today it was pert and insouciant. He wasn't.

It was Saturday but he was stuck in Monday. The routine was monotonous – same boats, same mountains, same river. One thing could cure his blues and he was tempted to take the offensive. All he needed was a full tank of gas. She would understand why he had violated their unwritten, unspoken covenant.

At Williamsport, Kim sauntered up to him trying hard to mask any embarrassment. "Hey stranger, want to walk into town for some real lunch?"

"Good idea. Know of any places worthwhile?"

"Zack's. You have to try their chef salad, it's enormous." Her eyes were wide and glowing.

He unzipped his life jacket. "Perfect. I was ready to raid safety man's dry bag for something to eat."

"I wonder how many Power Bars he has in there."

"I think he owns the company."

They walked along the top of a levee then across the Maynard Street Bridge. It was the first time he'd had an extended conversation with her since their drunken beach moment.

Reily checked his wallet for cash. "You're sure this place exists?"

"It should be in the next block. I was in town back in March plugging our inn at a tourism show. Zack's has excellent drinks, by the way. So how was the plane ride yesterday?"

"Good, I guess. The landscape looks surreal from that perspective."

"And what about the development site? Did you fly over it?"

He appreciated her interest. "Several times. It isn't so egregious at this point but there are signs that they're up to no good. That reminds me, do you have a cell phone with you?"

"Yep, you need to use it?"

"Yes, I guess I should."

Everything was big at Zack's: the booths, the floor to ceiling windows, and the drinks. Kim was transferring a mini-bucket of Long Island Iced Tea into her gut via a straw. He slurped an iced latte with a mountain of real whipped cream. For him, it was too early for alcohol.

While they waited for their salads, he called information from her phone and asked for the number of the Gifford County Conservation District. He was connected to their office voicemail, and a menu got him to a familiar name.

Reily left a message for Kip, explaining what he'd seen above Whispering Heights. He confirmed the best way to reach him and hung up.

Reily thanked Kim and handed her the phone. "I hope you didn't mind me giving him your number?"

"No problem." Her drink was half empty.

There was uncomfortable silence as he scrambled for other topics of conversation.

"Are you on the Odyssey for the duration?"

"I think so," she replied. "I was going to leave when we reach the main stem but I talked to my husband yesterday and he's decided to join me for the last stretch." She stared out the window.

"Is that a good thing?"

"Yep, I guess." She cracked half a smile. "He's making an effort and he hasn't done that for ages."

"I look forward to meeting this guy and seeing if he's worthy."

"You're too sweet. I don't know if you'll like Chris."

Reily vacuumed the rest of his latte. "Maybe he should meet my ex."

The afternoon blurred in a slow drift along the north face of Bald Eagle Ridge and past an infusion of cold water at the mouth of Loyalsock Creek. Now, Reily found himself feasting again. It was a legendary meal. If the rosemary chicken breasts and baby potatoes embodied the community's level of pride, the town would be around for a thousand years. Even this far into the journey, the generosity of local people continued to amaze him. Why did his rag-tag band of river runners deserve such hospitality from a historical society?

Blackman and a pair of society ladies led an after-dinner square dance, galloping down and across the weathered floor of the organization's restored and renovated barn. One by one, other recruits joined in. Reily focused on residual fragments of blueberry pie. To dance, he preferred libations to dilute self-consciousness. But no excuse could survive the determination of a particular society gal – one old enough to be in a display case – that grabbed his arm and hoisted him to his feet. She wore more makeup than a circus clown and perfume that suggested overripe bananas were stuffed in her girdle. Despite her pungency and his fatigue, her nimble moves made him smile.

When the caller was packing and tables and chairs returned to their proper place, Reily had another urge to call Baltimore. Forty-eight hours had lapsed since his first attempt. He found Kim outside by a cluster of tents smoking a cigarette and talking with a young couple. She handed over her phone.

"Just don't run down my battery."

"If I do, I'll treat you to lunch in the next town."

"In that case, stay on as long as you want."

At the edge of the property facing a sleeping street, he leaned against a giant oak and punched Sol's number into the illuminated keypad. The night air was mild and ripe for sleepy conversation. The phone rang, he waited. There was the sound of someone picking up and grave disappointment when it was the answering machine.

"Hey Sol, it's Reily again. We're in Muncy now. We did more than twenty miles today but even in my exhaustion I was thinking of you. Hopefully we'll get to talk soon. I hope things are good with you. Bye." He was frustrated he didn't say more.

Where was Sol at the moment? Out with friends? On a date? Reily felt a million miles away in this lonely corner of country.

CHAPTER 48

Woodring reviewed the brochure for the Poconos Home and Garden Show. Tobacco smoke swirled in the diffuse morning light of his office as he scanned the fine print. Each year the fees jumped... another pilfering of his hard earned money.

The phone rang in the reception area. Through the intercom, Terri announced a call from the Gifford County Conservation District. Woodring's neck constricted. *What do those imbeciles want now?*

The technician bumbled about inadequate erosion and sedimentation controls at the Heights. There had been a complaint and the situation had been verified. "Since you have repeat violations, Mr. Woodring, a fine may be assessed. You'll receive a letter from us within a few days."

"That's just goddamn great. So exactly how does someone prove that I have violations?"

"That's easy, sir. I found your fences down just like the man reported."

Woodring took a long drag of his idle cigarette. "What man? That's what I want to know. That land is posted. The sonafabitch was trespassing."

"I assure you Mr. Watters did not trespass."

Was the technician a retard? "How the hell not? I didn't give anyone permission to tramp around my construction site."

"Oh, he didn't walk around, he flew over."

Woodring laughed bitterly. "What? Who is he... Batman?"

"Mr. Watters flew over in a plane. I believe that's completely legal."

"Well, no shit." *Who do these by-the-book dingleberries think they are?*

"Look, I'm sorry about the need to intervene, but hopefully the issues can be promptly corrected. Have a nice day, sir." The technician hung up.

The guy was probably accurate in his findings; on occasion Woodring had been less than impeccable with his soil conservation practices, but there had never been significant problems from his recollection. What about the flyover deal? Who was this Watters? And who the hell can afford flyovers? Maybe it was a backdoor maneuver to sabotage his most ambitious project to date. Woodring's mind sifted through the regional competition in the housing business. There had always been a few jealous nimrods in the ranks, developers ready to feed their children to the lions for half the notoriety he'd achieved, but it still didn't add up.

As Woodring stewed over his predicament, his gaze lingered on the painting beside the door to Terri's space. It depicted a waterfowl hunter in a duck boat awaiting his bounty, the background awash in autumn splendor. The newspaper story about the flotilla of environmentalists invaded his head. Again, Woodring found himself dialing Lowell Orwell. The dependency, however slight, was unsettling.

"What do you need, Carl?" Orwell didn't sound as charitable this call cycle.

"Do you know the names of the people who commented at the last township meeting?"

Orwell hesitated. "I only know Roger... I never saw the others but I can check the minutes."

"Does a guy named Watters ring a bell?"

"Not really but let me see. I have them right here in the house. Give me a minute... "

Woodring replayed the meeting scene at the municipal building – and the inglorious remarks of others.

"I found him." Orwell breathed heavy over the phone. "A person named Reily Watters spoke. Wasn't he the tall guy who told the story about his parents' farm?"

Woodring remembered him too well. "So that was Mr. Watters." He thanked Orwell and terminated the call.

Was Watters in cahoots with the car at the construction site? Either way, the pesky little fucker was shitting on his business. Woodring drummed his fingers against the desktop.

Mr. Watters needed to be toilet trained.

CHAPTER 49

The ache came in waves like the pods of other paddlers who passed when Reily drifted. Petulant rapids performed an organic symphony. Streamers of foam bounced like fingerlings trapped in a seine. Sound and scenery were B-roll to addictive thoughts of reunion.

After the short voyage to Milton, Reily found his lovesick self under the roof of another pavilion. There'd been many on the trip. Maybe pavilion design called as a new career? Alex was at a picnic table scrutinizing bird's eye 4 x 6 photos of Whispering Heights and humming an unfamiliar song.

Reily leaned over him. "How did you get these so fast?"

"One-hour photo, oh great one. We're in civilization again."

"There must be a hundred pictures here."

"One hundred and eight. You have to take shots to make shots."

"You should go digital."

"In due time. Old things are passed away and all things become new."

"Look at that." Reily tapped on a zoomed image of a drill rig in a small clearing.

"Well drillers. You can see the company name on the side of that truck."

Reily squinted. It was hard to read but legible: *Northern Tier Drilling.* "I think I ran into that truck on my midnight dash through the site."

Alex peered straight ahead. "When was that?"

"The night we camped in Wilkes-Barre. Remember, I told you all about that craziness."

"But when was that? How long ago?"

"I don't know." Reily counted on his fingers. "Maybe eleven days."

"Okay, so we know the drilling was going on for a minimum of eight days."

"Drilling into rock is tedious."

"When you were there on that dangerous eve, did the trucks appear to have been there a while?" Alex's voice was more serious than normal.

"How would I know? It was dark and my mind was in survival mode."

"Here's my hunch. I'm no hydra-geologist but—"

"That's *hydro*-geologist."

"Immaterial. My less than fully understood perception tells me that truck has been there too long."

Reily examined the photo again. For a bulldozed clearing, there was an inordinate amount of greenery emerging around the rigging. "And your point is?"

"Could they be having difficulty finding water?"

Alex never stopped surprising him. For a stoner, he had many talents and insights. "That's an interesting supposition. We should bring it up with the good Dr. Murray."

Reily skimmed the other photos, finding several that showed silt fencing falling down and vernal pools still holding traces of water. Another shot could have made the cover of *Audubon* or *National Geographic*. It was an angled view of the river bending into the distance with dapples of white and gold creasing the surface and a sharp, craggy line of rock at cliff's edge. It could have been uncharted territory, a new frontier, but it couldn't appear more enduring.

Reily obtained directions to a drug store and set out for minor groceries and supplies. The town was a mélange of old and new, a collision of mom and pop and the ubiquitous chains flooding every corner of the country. Reily himself was an indelible, if not harrowing, sight – skin wind-beaten and bronzed, beard tangled and gray, hair long and seditious. Wearing shorts splotched with mud and sandals with failing Velcro, he was an itinerant vagabond in the flesh. The last bath had been the rapids at the mouth of Pine Creek; the last shower from a sun-heated bag of water in Lock Haven. While he plotted a future cleansing, a car loaded with three malevolent teens taunted him before making their tires scream in a masculine demonstration of territoriality.

After weeks of austerity, the store's motherlode dazzled. Shampoos and conditioners filled half an aisle. Condoms were stocked in amusing variety. He picked up a three-pack of disposable razors in case the will to shave came on a whim. Near shelves of bagged candy, he found slim selections of needed granola and breakfast bars. The paperback stand exhibited a Tom Clancy thriller and an archetypal romance with the anointed stud disrobing a fiery vixen on the cover.

The next great spiritual self-helper bared a new-age image of Jesus with uplifted hands sprouting a rainbow.

Reily witnessed himself in the mirror of the rotating sunglasses display. There was a paranormal similitude to the son of God. He wasn't sure if he should be alarmed or gladdened.

Back in battering sunshine, Reily spotted a vestigial pay phone on a brick wall. He was dying to check in with Wil. Deep down, he missed the scoundrel.

"What gives?" Wil complained that Reily had just interrupted his tutelage of the paper's spectacular summer intern.

"Sorry about that. I wouldn't want to derail any opportunities for deviance and scandal."

"No problem. There's a never ending supply of that. So how are things going on the cruise?"

Reily rehashed the past days: the scenery of the West Branch, the antics of Alex and Blackman, and the plane ride.

"So you have photos of the entire site?"

"Pretty much, plus I called the conservation district about inferior silt fencing."

"The developer's really going to hate your guts."

"He won't even know who reported him."

Wil cleared his throat. "I'm afraid he probably will."

"How's that?"

"From the letter to the editor you wrote."

"I didn't write any... hey, what did you do?"

"It was my way of helping. I'm a writer. You're on the river and have natural limitations to your advocacy. I live in front of a computer."

Reily liked the idea of boosting Carl Woodring's blood pressure. "So what did I say?"

"The basic stuff – beautiful place, worth saving, mentioned the Odyssey. I also said something about the river's potential for ecotourism."

"Nice. So when's it going to run?"

"I'd guess tomorrow. They called to verify that I, I mean you, wrote it."

"What number did you give them?"

"My seldom-used cell. They had no idea they were talking to a guy in New Jersey."

"Pretty slick. So, have you seen Gabriele?" The question was a tactic to get to news about Sol.

"She came to see me Friday night. I took her to the rides on the pier in Wildwood and later we rode each other at the southern end of Stone Harbor."

"I take it she was glad to see you."

"You know it." Wil had Donald Trump bluster.

Reily switched the phone to his other ear. "How long did she stay?"

"Until late yesterday and yes, I was glad to see her, too. Seriously, I never met a girl who was more fun to be with, and I don't just mean that in the sexual context."

"That's great. Did she say anything about Sol?"

"Not too much except..." Wil stopped mid-sentence.

"Stop screwing with me, Wisnoski."

"Sorry, actually Gabriele said Sol's been talking about you a lot. That has to be good."

"Depends what she's been saying."

"I think it was all good. I have a nugget of other info but I can't say anything."

"Come on, don't do this to me."

"I promised Gabriele."

"Please." He was begging like a punished toddler. It was no time to be proud.

"I can't, but don't worry so much."

"Come on, man."

"Hey, I hate to do this, but I have to be at beach volleyball at 4:00. Give me a shout in a couple of days. Talk to you soon. Bye."

"What the hell?" Reily spoke into a dead phone. *The bastard just left me hanging.*

CHAPTER 50

D espite miles filled with thoughts of Mim, and living with her interminable absence, Hap was relieved to be back at work. He tuned the radio to the jabber of a preacher as bland and repetitive as rows of corn. He enjoyed the news and folksy commercials of the religious station and no other signal was as strong. His tolerance of God talk was on the rise – probably because of the life changing crap he'd just been through. In an achy whine, the radio preacher quoted the fourth chapter of Ephesians: *"We must no longer be children, tossed to and fro and blown by every wind of doctrine, by people's trickery, by their craftiness in deceitful scheming."*

Why did they always have to use big words and complicated sentences? He caught the gist of the holy statement, though: Be careful who you trust because there are pastures full of spiteful bulls. Hap could name a few.

At a stop in West Pittston, the nurse couldn't find the paperwork and Hap lingered with unusual ease in the waiting room where a mounted television had on a morning talk show, the volume muted. The day's edition of the *Wilkes-Barre Courier* sat folded on an end table. He stood and skimmed the pages. A title for one of the letters to the editor piqued his attention: "Riverside Development Too Destructive." The first sentence eliminated any question as to which development the author, Reily Watters, was referring.

The name Watters swam in the back of Hap's brain; how did he know it? Regardless, the man's opinions were the kind of environmental silliness that Rush Limbaugh poked fun at on a daily basis, but deep down there was a smidgen of truth. How many projects can be absorbed that risk doubling the size of your municipality? Pretty soon they'd have to build a superhighway to move all the traffic. The possible ramifications made Hap's tummy roil. Would the Family Care Center mind if he used their bathroom?

After the evacuation of his bowels, Hap did something new: a walk along the river. The job entitled him to lunch, and too often it was skipped altogether. Some days he'd nibble a few stale saltines and wash them down with warm, flat ginger ale while he dutifully made his rounds. Today he would make Hap time.

Every stride was liberating but tiring – a tidy workout for his aging ticker. If Mim could see him now, her eyes would be bigger than supper plates. For the past twenty-five years, she'd nagged him about exercising, advice he haughtily ignored. He stopped at a boat ramp and watched with envy as a man close to his own age launched a fishing boat by himself. The motor started in a single pull, the stern wake frothed.

It felt good to be by the water.

The currents moved more or less on schedule but the ride was monotonous. To kill the hours, Reily hummed a raft of songs, an introspective soundtrack from the late '60s and early '70s. A slick, Kevlar craft knifed into a parallel position.

"You were channeling Neil Young, weren't you?" Blackman had a wicked grin.

"*Long may you run.*"

"Good tune from a good man."

"Do you know him?" Blackman seemed to know everybody.

"Nope, but I've been to a couple of his yowzy shows."

Reily remembered a concert from '79. "His lyrics come from the soul."

Blackman lifted his paddle from the water and hesitated like he was about to say something important... or at least something he thought was important. "My man, there are two kinds of people in this world – those that like Neil Young and those that can't stand him. I don't want anything to do with the latter." He made a shooting gesture with his right hand and laughed in a manner that might raise questions about his lucidity. "Take that to the bank."

Reily laughed, too, for the first time that short day, and pointed his bow toward the bridge marking another arrival. This time it was Lewisburg, known for Bucknell University and a federal prison. While he preferred open space over cinder block and iron bars, he felt increasingly chained by his own lamentations.

Perforating country melodies and cool, conditioned air, Woodring's cell phone rang. It displayed the office number. Why did

Terri insist on disrupting his driving? It was the only time he could escape the endless problems and inane surprises that came with his profession.

He answered over the sultry vocals of Shania Twain. "What's up?"

"Did you see today's paper?"

"It's the first thing I do every day." That was a distortion of the truth. Coffee and breakfast came first. About twenty minutes later, he'd stroll down his mini Blue Ridge Parkway, find the paper wrapped in plastic and take it straight to the john where he'd skim the headlines, speed read one or two stories, and check a few scores before discarding.

Terri vocally exhaled. "Guess you didn't see the letter?"

"What letter?" Her attitude had deteriorated in recent months but firing her was out of the question. She knew every tawdry detail of his business.

"The letter to the editor that makes you sound like a schmuck." With ingratiating enthusiasm, she read it aloud.

Every word made Woodring recoil, but the suggestion that Whispering Heights be "mothballed permanently for the betterment of the region" deserved censorship. It was treasonous Greenpeace speak and the author, Reily Goddamn Watters, had crossed the line. Woodring knew his projects often stirred nostalgic pleas for maintaining the character of this or that or avoiding some impact. Occasionally, he'd acquiesce and modify his plans in minor, infinitesimal ways but this motherfucker was persistent and ideologically warped. What was coming next? Tree spiking? Brainwashed college students chaining themselves to bulldozers?

Woodring ended his call with Terri and dialed Sid Purillo.

He needed another favor.

CHAPTER 51

The day began gray and muggy, the air as heavy as Reily's mood. The destination was the confluence of the river's branches where he had bid adieu to Sol days ago. It seemed like years. Alex was departing and so was Blackman. Kim would be reunited and preoccupied with her man. He would travel the remaining 120 miles to Havre de Grace without his posse; Watters on solitary water.

Reily re-read the torn and wrinkled itinerary. The remaining eleven days were easy distances but stuffed full of torturous fluff. Mail had to be piling up at home, the yard a hayfield, the house condemned. Life summoned.

Blackman called it "getting back to the track" but where would it lead? The Odyssey was supposed to have nudged him in the right direction, but had it? A grand arrival at the bay was compelling but what would it prove? No sane person would drag out this endless journey, especially as their friends departed. Sol's memory gnawed at him. She'd looked so believable when she said she might return.

Rick and his ponytail approached from starboard. "We're on the downhill run."

"Not far to go today." Even Reily's words were cheerless.

"I know but I'm talking about the run to the Chesapeake – the big ending. It will be a moment to savor." Rick was so upbeat, it was galling.

"I'm having second thoughts."

"What? No, you have to stay."

"I think I'm just worn out."

"You need more of my coffee." Rick positioned his kayak directly abroad Reily's canoe and asked him to hold on to the hatch cover while he filled a spare metal cup with black serum.

"Thanks." Reily was gratified at the timing of the intervention. He smelled the smokiness and sipped slowly. It was liquid Nirvana. "What kind is this?"

"An organic Italian roast from Zimbabwe. It's hard to find but worth the effort."

Reily attempted a smile. "I'll have to get some for myself."

The rig was eating oil and the bit was bordering on replacement; it had been another tough morning at Whispering Heights. After a much needed coffee break, Joe Kambic hopped back onto the machine and was about to start up when Earl Lukens, his supervisor, waved him to stop.

"What's wrong?" Joe eased his mammoth frame out of the undersized cab.

"We got a call from Woodring."

"Again?" Carl Woodring monitored their progress like a teacher on testing day. Joe pegged him as a control freak, worry-wart. It was bad enough they had Purillo keeping an eye on them like they didn't know what they were doing.

Lukens nodded. "He said drill to China."

"But we're finding hardly anything."

Lukens lit a cigarette in his greasy hands. "I know that. I reminded him that these wells aren't going to give him enough water."

"What did he say?"

"Wasn't my problem to worry about."

Joe shook his head in disbelief. "Maybe, but someone shells out big money for a place up here, they're going to be storming mad when the tap runs dry."

Lukens rubbed his forehead like he was trying to erase chiggers. "This isn't a good situation."

Photos of families, farms, meadows, and woods covered an exhibit at the Winfield boat access. Captions declared the amount of land each deal had protected. Volunteers from the local land conservancy stood at the ready to field questions and promote their organization for the edification of Odyssey goers.

Reily chewed a section of six-foot sub zesty with oregano. "So these were all properties you purchased?"

"Actually all of them were preserved through conservation easements," responded a small, fit man wearing a conservancy t-shirt.

"Oh." Reily knew the term, but wasn't exactly sure what it entailed.

The man sensed his uncertainty. "Easements are basically a covenant on the land that precludes it, in perpetuity, from being developed. The landowner still owns the land and can typically use it as before – as farmland or working forest – and we hold or manage the easement."

"What do the landowners get for the donation? It seems like they would be foregoing a potential windfall, at least in some cases."

"That's true. Sometimes we secure grants or otherwise raise the funds needed to pay a landowner for the easement. Usually it's an outright donation by the landowner, but there are tax benefits for them in either case."

"So once they've signed the papers, they can't clear the land or build any houses?"

"Generally, that's right, but there can be provisions for forestry activities, active farming, maybe even other home sites, but in that case the easement would likely be conformed around them, not include them."

Whispering Heights circled his mind but if there had been an opportunity to apply these techniques, Doc Murray or someone else would have tried. Reily continued to probe the volunteer about the conservancy's work and the man elaborated on their methods until a whistle from the water's edge broke the spell. Safety man was ushering the paddlers to push them onward like Viking slaves.

A headwind swirled deep in the backwaters of the Sunbury dam. It retarded Reily's headway but was no deterrent to personal watercraft. He hadn't seen their loathsome ilk since Lock Haven. One passed within fifty feet, generating a canoe-rocking wake. The expressionless teen at the controls probably had sociopathic interest in capsizing the boats; the fleet must have seemed a cannibalistic, tree-humping tribe. The dam enabled the kid's inferior form of boating and made a Berlin Wall to anadromous shad lucky enough to make it this far upstream. Multiple shotgun blasts to the dam's inflatable bladders would benefit the fishes' journey and his. It was a pleasing but terroristic premise.

Reily detected an observer watching from the state park overlook high above and resurrected a nagging thought: did anyone really care about his progress? He was becoming as cynical as his father.

CHAPTER 52

The workday neared a welcomed conclusion. Abigail Gordon was back from a showing and disgusted at the sight of her vapid cubicle in the cramped room she shared with an agent barely known. For a freewheeling developer, Carl sure skimped on the accoutrements.

Normally she could avoid her austere quarters but every Wednesday at 3:00 was the weekly meeting with Woodring – the "check-in" as he called it. It was a poor time of day for strategic thinking. Not that Carl was all that bad. Despite Abby's gross deficiency in real estate sales experience, he'd given her a chance and, so long as she was reasonably producing, granted her a long leash in how she executed her work. Occasionally their relationship would drift into the realm of friendship but she could only tolerate limited doses.

She picked up her appointment calendar, crossed the dim hall, and rapped on the side door to his office. "Carl, you ready?"

"Yep." There was an obdurate scent of a burning cigarette.

She entered the hazy office. "Can you put that out?" She always got her way.

Woodring rubbed out the butt and peered over his reading glasses, letting his eyes linger too long on her torso. "Have you lost weight?"

Abby sat on the high-backed chair opposite his desk and slid closer so he couldn't see her legs. "That's an odd question, but yes, I've been watching what I eat."

"You look good. So how are things?"

"Good week. Friday, I'm closing on the five-bedroom place in Dureye."

Woodring nodded his approval. "What about the little farm west of Tunkhannock?"

"Two parties are interested. One of them would be a stretch. The other wants to come back next week for a second walk around. They're bringing an uncle."

"Don't you hate it when buyers piss around? Let me guess, these people are in their forties?"

"Late forties, this would be the second home they've ever purchased."

"I goddamn knew it."

"Carl." She admonished him with a heavy frown.

"Sorry, but that's so typical. People like them look for a place to last them until they head to the convalescent home. You grow old waiting for them to make up their mind."

"It hasn't been that bad."

"Keep pressuring them."

"I will. Even though it's a far cry from a farm, I also told them about Whispering Heights. I assumed that if they like the area, they might be interested."

Woodring looked pallid. "I've been trying not to think about Whispering Heights."

"What's wrong?"

"A little bit of everything. This is the latest headache, although in the big scheme of things, it's meaningless." He handed her a newspaper folded over to the letters to the editor.

She found the offending letter and drew a startled breath. "That pompous turd."

Woodring cocked his head, "Who?"

"The man that wrote the letter."

Woodring leaned toward her, a pen in his hand clicking away. Tufts of his slick red hair fell down over his face. "You know him?"

Abby swallowed to calm her rattled nerves. "If it's the same Reily Watters then I sure do. He's my ex-husband." Leave it to Mr. Conscience to be mired in her business years after the split. What was he doing in this part of the state?

"What?" Carl stared at her in disbelief.

"Afraid so."

Carl sat back and glowered, his mind seemingly in another place. "Tell me about him."

"Well, what do you want to know?"

CHAPTER 53

The group trickled left to Packers Island, its grounds trimmed and pruned underneath a cool umbrella of silver maples. A uniformed park representative helped Reily carry his canoe to a spot in the grass beside the other boats. People mulled about, awaiting instructions on camping and shuttles.

Reily spotted Kim embracing an offensive tackle, or someone who could play the part. The guy was a mountain with shoulders. He had a wide, swooning smile and a nonconforming short swag of blond hair; it could only be her morally-deficient husband.

The gear truck seemed oversized and out of place in a half-empty parking lot. Tents and other belongings were piled behind it. Reily retrieved his stuff and again considered going home, but the first task was to take the shuttle back to Lewisburg and get his Explorer. He dropped his gear near Rick's Kelty, already staked and up, then boarded one of two vans. He slid in a row behind Alex and Blackman and between two older guys he barely knew.

He leaned over Blackman's shoulder. "I'm going to miss you crazy fools."

"Likewise," Blackman said. "Some weekend I'll invite all of you up to the big city for the night of your lives... if you think you can handle it."

Alex had a numinous gaze. "I'll bring special treats for the occasion."

Reily stayed silent for the rest of the ride on US 15. He was distracted and disconnected, unresponsive even to a line of billboards – a defacement of nature normally worthy of mind-lashing. The Clash's "Should I Stay or Should I Go?" looped in his head.

When he returned to Packers Island, he found a parking space three down from the gear truck. He sat for minutes searching for a decision while hope drained for a reunion with Sol. He opened the door and walked toward his gear pile, the overstory trees painting the ground with restless leaf shadows. Rick would be disappointed about his choice but there was living to be determined beyond the Odyssey. As he began to gather his things, Alex walked up and gave him a hug.

"Be good, wise one."

"You too," Reily pulled away and waved a pointed finger. "Don't smoke too much."

They were startled by a rude blast from Blackman's car horn, the madman at the controls. He swung a fast, wide turn into the lot with his sharp-bowed boat clinging on top. It was a rewind to the moment Reily first met him in Pittston. Blackman yelled something indecipherable out the window and saluted, the music already churning from his stereo. Then he was gone. Alex ambled away to his own car.

Reily slung his drybag duffel over one shoulder and reached down for a second bag. He stopped abruptly; two petite familiar feet stood before him. His eyes climbed up the apparition. He blinked but the beautiful vision remained.

"Aren't you going to say something?"

"I'm dumbfounded," Reily replied.

"You look well for a river rat." Their feet inched closer.

"It is you." He caressed her cheek. Her eyes were sweeter than cocoa. "You can't begin to know how glad I am to see you."

Sol put her arms around him, placing her head to his chest. "I missed you, too."

Reily breathed her scent. She was respiratory therapy. He lowered his face to hers and delivered an indescribable kiss.

Her lips lingered before pulling away. "Breathing is overrated but I have to pause."

The break allowed cogent thoughts to return. "Did Gabriele come with you?"

"No, it's just me. She was severely jealous I was coming back but she had to work. I should be working too but I wouldn't miss this chance." Sol seemed embarrassed about letting her feelings slip.

"Do you have enough vacation?"

She winced. "Barely, but that's okay."

"So where's your stuff?"

"It's still in my car."

"Would you like to move in to my tent, once I put it up?" He laughed at his own boldness.

"You better invite me. I didn't bring a tent."

He couldn't help but smile. The journey, their journey, was back on track.

CHAPTER 54

Woodring slept all of two hours. He was tormented by Reily Watters and the diminishment of Whispering Heights. The do-good shithead wasn't responsible for the water problems or Gert Bunting's intractability, but he had salted the wounds and caused new injuries with his public meeting testimony, the blatant snooping, a sneaky complaint to the district, and, most recently, the letter. Woodring had expected potshots from dirt-eaters like SURCOS and the Sierra Club, but not from a solo, renegade ghoul.

He got up from the breakfast table and stomped into his kingly bedroom. *The Best of Jenna Jameson* DVD occupied the nightstand. He found hardcore pornography to be calming, beneficial deviation, especially Jenna's bleached-blonde mastery. The lustful thoughts reminded him to call Abby Gordon. Maybe she'd do him a favor other than the kind imagined in his routine fantasies. He picked up his cordless phone.

Abby's tone was guarded when she answered. He seldom called her and her mood depreciated with each question. "I already told you that I never talk to Reily."

"He might be happy to hear from you."

"Trust me, our disdain is mutual. What exactly do you want me to extract from him?"

Woodring's wish was insidious harassment. He wanted to give Watters a jarring dose of stress but what could Abby really do? "Find out why he's so riled about the project and what else he intends to do."

"You think he'll divulge his plans to me? Reily's an ass but he's not retarded."

A wordsmith Abby was not, but the point was noted. "Look, I just want you to try. Maybe we'll learn something useful."

"Questioning a ferret would be more productive."

"Please." He reverted to begging, a common approach in his dealings with her. "Just make a coincidental contact."

"I can't wait to hear your plans for that."

Reily was glad to see Rob Murray experiencing a rare day on the river that he worked so hard to protect. Despite an encyclopedic familiarity with everything Susquehanna, Doc exhibited a newcomer's wonderment.

"The clarity must be pushing ten feet. If I had a secchi disk, we could confirm." Murray sounded like a nerd but maneuvered his high-end kayak with cool precision.

The river was a bulwark of protruding bedrock and ledges splitting swift water. Reily winced as he and Sol scraped bottom through a chute. They were paddling another borrowed canoe.

Limpid conditions returned. Sol reached over the side and plucked half an empty mussel shell from the aquarium beneath her. She held it up for Reily to see.

"Looks like a seashell, like the big surf clams you see on the east coast."

Murray also saw her prize. "*Eliptio's* solely a freshwater species. We're seriously concerned about their population. Their numbers are plummeting, especially the younger age classes."

Reily frowned. "Wish we could say the same about the human population, or at least stabilizing... although I do love my fellow mankind. Well, most of the time."

Murray had a pensive gaze. "We're certainly pushing our own carrying capacity."

"Speaking of capacity and how many people can be crammed into one corner of Gifford County, did you ever look at getting a conservation easement at Whispering Heights?" Reily directed the question at Murray but watched Sol's stroke. He wanted to be in sync.

"Not really. I don't think the developer has any incentive to do so."

"But can't he get tax breaks?"

"Yeah, but nothing that will approach the money he'll make if the site is built out as he envisions."

"What about the other property?" Sol chimed in. She was wearing her cute sun hat again like it was her shield against the worries of the world.

Murray eased his boat forward. "Mrs. Bunting's land?"

"Yes, I guess. If she's trying to get some income from her farm, maybe she'd be willing to consider it. I can't imagine that a lady who has probably lived in the area her whole life really wants to see it ruined."

Murray's eyes brightened. "You know, we've been so preoccupied with stopping the project that we haven't spent much time thinking about such a prospect. It's a great idea."

"So do we pay her a visit?" Reily rested his paddle across his thighs.

"Yep," Murray said. "I think we do."

"Good and what about the water?"

Murray shot him a confused look. "What water?"

"Alex and I were going over the aerial photos and found what appeared to be a well-drilling rig. It seemed like it had been there a while. I ran into it the night I was exploring the site. We were conjecturing that they might be having trouble finding water."

"We've been busy focusing on zoning issues, wetland rules, and endangered and threatened species but the water supply angle has been neglected, I'm afraid." Murray took off his SURCOS ball cap and scratched his head.

Reily made a corrective paddle stroke to prevent the canoe from turning. "Don't be too hard on yourself. You're leading a good fight and you've rekindled my conservation passions. I'm born again thanks to you." He wanted to unload all his thoughts about the Heights. "One more thing, what about that secret meeting in the woods? If the supervisor was being bribed, which had to be the case, shouldn't we call him out on it?"

"I can't imagine he would confess," Murray said.

"I doubt it, too, but he looks like the nervous and defensive type. If we talk to him, we might really shake him up."

Sol turned slightly, her face eager and defiant. "He just might vote 'no' at the next township meeting."

Murray interrupted a slow, thoughtful sweep of his paddle. "I guess there's nothing to lose, except for possibly alerting all the parties that we know of their secret meeting."

"Bring it on." Reily felt like a prosecutor ready to bring down a kingpin. He couldn't remember feeling so intrepid.

Murray appeared as if his mental load had been lightened. "Sounds like we better plan a country road trip. We have a few people to visit."

Hap wasn't sure what he was doing or why, but it sure felt right. For the past hour, he hadn't thought about his dumb doings on township matters. Instead, he focused on the here and now, putting a toothbrush and tube of toothpaste into the box that came from the left before passing it to the right. The delivering hand was wrinkled and worn, the receiving hand, Ivory Snow.

"Hap, you better slow down; the kids in Ghana will get these soon enough." Mary lowered her voice. "Plus, down there at the end, she moves about as quickly as the continents, God love her."

He chuckled. "Thanks for inviting me out. It does me good."

"Thank you for helping us. We really appreciate it." Mary seemed genuinely pleased to have him there.

The church basement smelled as new as it looked. Pleasant blue carpet ran wall to wall and long plastic tables lacked the scratches of the fake wood tables at the municipal building. The comparison reinforced the sad reality: he'd lost too much of his life posturing about minutia and wielding meaningless power. The bar was another road to nowhere. Mim wouldn't want him drinking himself to sleep and feeling sorry for himself, but she'd be flat-out tickled to see him helping out poor kids in Africa. His pretty new friend had shown him better priorities.

In tribute to his improving lot, Hap took a side route home via Gibson Ridge Road. Mim liked going this way at dusk when deer by the dozens would creep out of hiding and feast in the corn fields. It had been five years since they rumbled along the high, winding road but it seemed like yesterday. On that drive, they'd seen a ten-point buck. Mim said it was the biggest deer she ever saw outside the Columbus Zoo. He remembered the zoo visit on the way to Indiana. It was the last time they'd been back to see family.

Something bolted in front of him. Hap locked up the brakes, spitting gravel as the car careened to a diagonal stop. An unidentified creature vanished but another appeared. Before the high beams was a coyote as big as a German shepherd. With eyes glowing, it glanced toward him, scanning the danger before following its kin into the woods.

It was only the second time he'd spotted a coyote in the county. Word was they were back with a vengeance.

CHAPTER 55

Sol ordered soft serve twists at a corner ice cream shop and glanced at a wall calendar; it was July fifteenth but it could have been August or September. Time was being sipped and savored by the hour.

Reily hadn't stopped talking since she returned. He would paddle while he spoke, drift and listen, paddle and speak more. The pattern would repeat. He'd interject his stories or reflect on what she'd said and the volley would continue. She, too, had opened windows on her soul – sharing the emotions invoked by her work, frustrations with her parents' disassociation, dreams of things for which she still yearned. Her most candid revelation was a wish to teach and do research in a college setting... the opportunity to synthesize experiences and blend them with theory. The place wasn't of particular concern, just so it happened.

Last night they were in Herndon, tonight Millersburg – one step up in size and sophistication. The town had an operating ferry, the last of its kind on the river. They boarded with their ice cream cones and held hands. Sol felt ten years old again. On the crossing, they passed a collection of islands speckled with cottages and lesser shacks. Most were simple, rustic structures but a few had homegrown charm and creative architecture. She liked one with a white picket fence and a patch of orange lilies. There was a swing set in a small clearing and the cottage rose behind it. A giant sycamore made everything diminutive. Sol raised her hand, clasped with Reily's, in the island's direction. "It reminds me of Winnie the Pooh's house."

After dinner, with the north side of Berry Mountain aglow from the sun's melt across the broad water, they sneaked away in Rick's tandem kayak on a pirate's mission to scout the little cottage. A crude dock on the island's west side provided a suitable landing and, seeing neither boats nor people, Reily stepped out and helped her ashore.

Sol welcomed his gallantry. "Think we'll get caught?"

"Compared to certain nighttime adventures we've had, this is easy."

"Let's go peek in the window."

They tiptoed to the steps and up to a door whose handle bore a stout new padlock. A window to the left of the door presented their proportional reflections side by side. They pushed their faces closer and scanned the dim interior: a round table, two simple chairs, built-in shelves, a bible, a red Coleman lantern. A framed opening likely led to a bedroom. Beyond the table was a counter with a five-gallon water jug and the cottage kitchen.

"Daniel Defoe would approve," Sol said.

"Who?"

"The author of *Robinson Crusoe*."

"I should have known. I liked that book. I had to read it in ninth grade and write a critique."

She found humor in his recollection. "I hope you got an 'A'."

They sat down side by side on the steps, watching the sun celebrate day's end with smudges of lavender as pure as the fields of Provence.

"This is nice." She took hold of Reily's arm.

"Better than nice."

"We should get a place like this but build it ourselves. It would have to be bigger... not much, but it would need another room or two."

"And it would need to be higher. I'm sure a flood hammers this place every few years."

"It would have to be made of all natural stuff, driftwood and things collected from the river."

"What about power?" Reily seemed pleased with the island scheme.

"I'm sure we could figure it out. Maybe solar? Hydro?"

"We'd have to have a garden, too."

"An organic farm." Sol gave him a lighthearted shake to emphasize the grandness, if not absurdity, of their burgeoning plan.

"Imagine all the stuff you could grow in this soil." Reily gestured at the ground. "We'd be like ancient Egyptians along the Nile."

"Retro farmers." The notion was elating.

Reily digressed about silty loams and heirloom seeds then pivoted topics. "I guess Wil knew you were coming back?"

"Gabriele told him. I wanted to surprise you."

"You certainly did. So what's your take on the two of them?"

"Sporadic but steamy relations." Sol batted her eyes. "But I can tell she's poleaxed."

Reily placed his arm around her. "Good word. I think Wil really digs her, too. My boy has found his bearing."

One by one, stars congregated and katydids serenaded. The dissonant notes were as unconventional as their courtship, she thought, but they echoed hope, an ancient hope that summer brings.

CHAPTER 56

A chickadee's deliberate, repetitious notes coaxed Reily from the tent. Inside, Sol snored delicately, her face buried in a downy pillow. Outside, Saturday morning was warm and painted with dew. Seismic rumbles indicated an overtaxed diesel coming his way; railroad tracks and cooperative weather were Odyssey norms.

The engine crawled past and blasted its horn, shattering the silence of the town. Maybe it was a ritual of celebration. Trains, too, were followers of the river.

Reily carried his Heyerdahl book through an archway under the tracks to a failing bulkhead at the river's edge. With views of colossal water gaps in the mountain ridges, it was a fit setting to absorb Thor's wisdom.

Twenty-five minutes later, he closed the book with a sigh of refreshment and sense of accomplishment that accompanies the completion of noteworthy chapters. The author's transcendent spirituality was stirring. Heyerdahl spoke of the "joy of mere existence." Reily's own spirit was now entwined with the web of life around him: bass dreaming on the bottom, egret fishing from the marshy edge, crayfish sacrificed for a meal. It was testimony to a universal harmony intended but not maintained.

Late in the day, they neared clusters of uninhabited islands, a lost world juxtaposed against a city skyline and angular bridges stretching shore to shore. A riverside park interpreted Harrisburg as a peaceful, pleasant destination. From prior visits, the capital had a lot to offer: a science museum, state government buildings with pomp and stature, and a collection of good restaurants where lawyers, lobbyists, and lawmakers changed money. There were also streets bearing abhorrent decay and despair like the rest of the rust belt. Since his days in Philadelphia, Reily realized urban life shortchanged his sense of freedom. He longed for nature like the cormorants standing on the rocks he was passing. With their black shapes and hoisted, air-drying wings, they could have been scarecrows placed to frighten boaters.

He and Sol invaded City Island with the rest of the crew, landing on a concrete beachhead to secure a designated camping area beside a buzzing recreational complex. Harrisburg's minor league baseball team opened a home stand that evening against a club from Wilkes-Barre. The thirty-fourth night of the expedition was honored with a pre-game ceremony in the outfield and complimentary tickets. After the second inning, he left Sol's side in their bleacher seats and went in search of a restroom in the ground level concourse.

Exiting the men's room, a short, familiar, dark-haired woman walked his direction. He felt the searing agony of recognition. She came uncomfortably close.

"Hello Reily, of all places to run into you."

"Hi, Abby." He avoided her bituminous eyes and their diabolical noose.

"Why are you at a ball game in Harrisburg?"

Was it an interrogation? "I'm on an extended river trip. Tonight we're in Harrisburg." It was time to turn the tide. "Why are you at a ball game down here?"

"I heard about the Susquehanna travel group. Isn't it for some environmental cause?" She accentuated her pronouncement of 'environmental' as if it were a foreign word.

"Yes, an important cause, but what brings you all the way to Harrisburg?"

"The baseball game, do I need another reason?" Abby's veiny eyelids fluttered. "My boss's son-in-law plays for Wilke-Barre."

"So where are you working these days?" The sooner he exhausted the basic Q and A, the faster he could escape.

"I'm selling real estate."

"Where?" Reily wanted to gauge her honesty.

"I sell throughout the northeastern part of the state. The owner of the company is one of the region's premier developers."

"You must love it." Her esteem for creeps hadn't waned.

"During the good months it can be very profitable... but you don't care about money, right?"

"Not at all." Reily shoved his hands into his pockets and rocked impatiently on his feet. How could he have ever been in love with such a dreary woman? "How's Casey?"

"She's spending the summer at the beach. I told her to get it out of her system now. She needs to save money for her future."

"Yeah, she told me about the beach. Good for her."

Abby cocked her head toward the river. "So where are you off to next, all you rowers with too much time on your hands?"

He leered at her. "That would be paddlers, but you don't know too much about that sort of thing. We're continuing on to the Chesapeake Bay. We finish there next Saturday."

"And then what does Reily do next? I mean... since you aren't working."

Now she was pissing him off. "That's no concern of yours. Maybe I'll hike the last patches of Pocono wilderness or start a group to obstruct every asinine development proposal." His heart was pounding. Abby's greatest skill was provocation.

She squinted in the glare of the lowering sun, a vampire repulsed by light. "I'm sorry I've upset you. Believe it or not, it's been nice to reconnect." To his surprise and horror, she stepped forward and raised her toes, kissing him on the cheek. The spot turned numb as she walked off without turning around. He stared after her in disgust, but her angry odor lingered, a toxic combination of perspiration and strong perfume – Chanel Psycho.

In the Budweiser line, Reily replayed the events that had just occurred. It couldn't have been coincidence. While the attendant filled a plastic cup from the tap, he glanced toward the chain link fence enclosing the ball park. There she was again, the devil woman, outside the gate talking to a burly man with black, matted hair. The man looked his way and, startled by the eye contact, grabbed Abby's arm and guided her out of sight. Reily's confusion mounted but he had been conditioned well on one point: understanding Abby or her behavior wasn't worth the exertion of a single neuron.

On his return to the bleachers, he dwelled on Abby's comments. She talked of a big developer and he recalled the real estate ad for Golden Ring Realty. Then it hit him like a foul ball: the 'Ring' had to be for 'Woodring.'

Sol looked worried as he sat down. "Did you get lost in the bathroom?"

He stared at the field. "No."

"Will you share your beer?"

It was almost empty.

CHAPTER 57

Reily occupied the passenger side of Rob Murray's pickup, stewing over the prior day's encounter with his ex-wife. The anxious rhythm of the wipers supplemented his agitation.

"It's supposed to rain for the next two days," the Doc said from behind the wheel. "An occluded cold front's training moisture up from the gulf."

Sol sat between them and turned to Reily. "We picked a good day to do this. I wouldn't want to be on the water." Even in sodden weather, Sol saw a bright side. "So what are we going to say to the old man?"

Reily shrugged. "I'm not sure but I think we should tell him what we know."

"He may refuse to speak to us," Murray said. "He may not even let us in the door."

"I think he'll get rattled by us showing up... Maybe we'll be surprised." Reily gazed out the window and replayed his interaction with Hap Clay at the bar in Meshoppen. What would entice an old timer to take money from a sleazeball like Woodring? Did he need it that bad? Maybe it was an incipient need for clout and importance. "I think I have it figured out." He whirled around.

"What?" Sol raised her luscious eyebrows.

"Our strategy. We'll appeal to his need for relevance."

Hap Clay returned from services at the Beacon of God Church, his legs light and springy. The place felt less like a church and more like an indoor picnic with a bunch of friendly strangers telling upbeat Jesus stories. Their after-worship spread was better than a VFW pig roast.

He'd just sat down to make a list of projects—a coping strategy that the pastor had recommended—when there was a knock on the door. Hap opened it to find two bearded men and a cute doe-eyed gal standing awkwardly before him in a drizzle. If the taller guy put on some weight, he could have been Grizzly Adams. He recognized them from somewhere, but couldn't place it.

"Mr. Clay?" the tall man said.

"That's right."

"You might not remember us but we attended the township meeting where the rezoning was addressed. I also met you, prior to that night, at a bar in Meshoppen."

The man talked smoothly like he was college educated, and his long hair flagged him as a liberal. Hap recollected a hazy image of the guy irritating him at his sacred watering hole. He couldn't remember anything about their discussion. "So what are you doing here? I doubt you're out for a Sunday drive."

"We'd like to talk to you about the zoning issue, about your involvement. My name is Reily Watters, by the way." The man extended a handshake.

Hap didn't accept and he didn't like the way the man said 'involvement.' "You have a lot of nerve coming out to see me on a Sunday. This is God's day of rest." The additional point had been a centerpiece of the morning's sermon.

The cute lady inched forward. "We drove a long way to meet with you, Mr. Clay. Can we come in?"

Hap shrugged his shoulders. "I'm not sure we have much to talk about... but alright." He held the door for them. "I don't have a lot of time though."

The three visitors lined up on his long, stiff sofa, still in mint condition for something decades old. He sat in a rocker opposite them.

"I assume this area means a lot to you, Mr. Clay?" It was Grizzly Adams.

"Hell yes. I've lived here thirty-nine years."

"Then why screw it up by allowing a project that would change the face – for the rest of your life – of a place that you love?"

Hap fidgeted. "I don't think it would be too bad."

"I'm Robert Murray with SURCOS and I respectfully disagree." The other man spoke for the first time. He looked like a scientist. "As an ecologist and conservationist, I care most about the profound impacts to the natural resources but I think about the other changes – from doubling the traffic to ushering in other land use changes. The good life that you and your neighbors enjoy could be forever compromised."

Hap stared like a dying tortoise, his resistance waning.

"We know you really don't want to see this ugly thing happen otherwise you wouldn't have voted to table it at the last meeting."

Grizzly was trying to sweet talk him. "But we also know there have been attempts to change your perspective on the whole thing."

Hap snapped to life. "What are you saying?"

"I saw him give you something, money I presume, after the meeting."

"What are you talking about? Who gave me money?" Hap knew his tone was too defensive.

Grizzly stared like a stubborn mule. "Mr. Woodring."

"And when did he do that?"

"It was a few hours after the township meeting," the gal said. "You were at the development site. We were there. Reily saw the exchange, Mr. Clay." She was assertive but polite.

Hap's lips puckered but no words came out.

Grizzly Reily stood. "We're not here to condemn you, but we would like your help."

Hap had the urge to dispute their claim but sensed it was useless. "What do you want from me? What can I do?"

"We have a few ideas." Reily glanced at his companions. "But first I want you to know that you should feel good about what you are doing, talking to us and all. You're getting a second chance to make things better."

Half an hour later, the visitors prepared to leave. Hap actually felt compelled to shake each of their hands. His remembrances of pleasant days on the Bunting farm had been cathartic.

Before they reached the door, the doorbell rang.

He was dumbfounded that there would be another person coming by. It was even more shocking to find a stoic Lowell Orwell – as big and ugly as ever – occupying his front landing.

CHAPTER 58

"**W**hat a cool farmhouse." Reily appreciated the old, clapboard structure and a gray tabby resting on the porch railing, watching their arrival with curiosity. The rain had acquiesced to a fine mist that obscured the visibility of distant things but enriched the colors of everything immediate.

Sol stepped out of the pickup. "I hope this conversation is as productive as the last."

"Me, too," Doc Murray said.

Reily knocked on the screen door. He detected a creak in the floorboards that could only be caused by an oversized person in a tired house. A dog barked but sounded sick and muffled.

A cumbersome, globular woman materialized. "Whaddya want?"

On the way to the farm it was agreed that Reily would do the initial talking. "Mrs. Bunting, we'd like to ask you about your property."

Gert Bunting pushed past him and the others, holding a disposable aluminum pan with soggy corn flakes and milk, then flung the contents on the ground. "They're scraps for the chickens."

Reily waited for her to return to the door. "May we speak with you?"

"I'm tired of talking about it. I don't know who you all are but why don't you get going and leave me be?"

"My name's Reily Watters and this is Sol Messina and Robert Murray. Rob has been following plans for the Whispering Heights development. Sol and I learned about it on a canoeing expedition that traveled near here a few weeks ago."

She held them in a glazed stare. "I catered that group."

"I remember you." Reily felt as if he'd been reacquainted with a lost aunt. "You cook really well."

Mrs. Bunting broke into a partial smile, fracturing her stern face. "I can't waste much time flapping... I've got cookies baking that have to come out. If you want to keep talking, you'll have to come inside."

The kitchen smelled like a Nestle's factory. Reily's salivary glands rioted. Sol rubbed her stomach in agreement.

Mrs. Bunting stooped over the oven and extracted a rectangular pan rowed with gooey, molten circles. "I always get hungry for cookies on a rainy day. I don't know why." She invited them to sit down. The table was undersized, its metal legs spotted with rust.

Reily squeezed beside Sol. "Chocolate chip cookies are good anytime." The setting – and the treats – took him back to his childhood.

The older woman lowered herself into one of the chairs. "You behave yourself, I might give you some."

Doc Murray adjusted his chair to better face Mrs. Bunting. "So do you plan on selling to Mr. Woodring?"

"I don't want to... but I think I have to." There was solemnity in her words.

"You may have other options," Murray said.

"Now you want to buy my land, too?" She shot him a disappointed look. "I wish I didn't need to talk to any of you."

Reily knew they could win the old lady's trust. "I don't blame you," he said. "Who would want to sell such a beautiful place? But he was talking about something called a conservation easement."

Mrs. Bunting repositioned her bulky mass on the narrow kitchen chair, "Never heard of such a thing."

Doc Murray explained his affiliation with SURCOS and slowly presented the easement concept without his characteristic use of sophisticated terminology.

Mrs. Bunting seemed to get it. "So I get paid something pretty good – not enough to make me rich, but enough so I can pay my bills and stay put?"

Murray nodded. "Exactly, and the best part... the land stays as it is. Just the way you like it."

"Sounds too good to be true. What's the catch? There's got to be some briars in there somewhere." Mrs. Bunting hoisted herself up and brought the tray of cookies from the stovetop. "Help yourself."

Murray nibbled a sample. "As I mentioned, the only catch is that you won't be able to develop the property nor will a future owner. The other issue is where the funds will come from to buy the easement – I mean, to pay you for it. Many times easements are donated by the landowner, but yours is a different circumstance."

"I can't donate nothing. I'll be lucky to pay the fuel oil bill come winter."

"I understand." Murray removed his glasses as if making a gesture of legitimacy. "We would need to have an appraisal completed and, based on that figure, determine what we – actually the land trust organization – might be able to offer. You can negotiate to make sure you get what you need."

The corners of Mrs. Bunting's mouth lifted, her body straightened. "I know this isn't a done deal but it sure makes me feel good to think I may have another way to go. Mr. Woodring is gonna grow horns when I tear up his papers."

She insisted on walking them to the truck and waved as they drove away. To Reily, she resembled an ancient tree, rooted in place.

The pickup accelerated. "We're two for two," Reily said. He tasted chocolate on his lower lip.

"Yep," Doc Murray agreed. "I'll call the land trust tomorrow and try to get a very rough appraisal. From that, they'll be able to generate a number to pitch – assuming their board is amenable."

Sol leaned on Reily's shoulder and yawned. "The goods will follow the good deed."

Reily draped his arm around her and gave a light squeeze. "Who are you quoting?"

"Sol Messina."

He regarded her from an oblique view, admiring her chronic optimism. It was subtle but unremitting, an odd immunity in a world infected with cynicism. Sol's silky hair rolled past her shoulders. She was a benevolent fox. He must be the shaggy wolf... docile, for the most part, but never more determined.

Carl Woodring was watching Phil Mickelson miss a birdie putt on the satellite-fed Golf Channel when the phone rang. He picked up his cordless from a coffee table where blueprints for the Heights laid unfurled. Their margins were filled with notes scribed during repetitive commercials for golf balls and Buicks.

The caller ID displayed the number for Lowell Orwell. "Now what?"

"Carl, it's bad."

"What the fuck does that mean?"

"The speakers... from the township meeting, the folks trying to put down the project? They were just in Hap's living room." Orwell described each of them. "Hap called me the 'A' word and slammed the door in my face."

Woodring seethed. He was certain one of Hap's visitors was the Watters guy. It was bad enough that hopeless Hap was caving on their understanding, but now the sad excuse of a supervisor was meeting with the very people trying to nix the development. "What the hell is he up to?"

"I don't know. This ain't like Hap and I've known him a long time."

"Lot of good that's doing."

"What should I do now?" Orwell sounded like an overstuffed crybaby.

"Don't do a goddamn thing." Woodring banged the phone down, the force cracking the rigid plastic over the speaker. The call had poisoned his precious Sunday routine and he vowed revenge. A new strategy was required.

CHAPTER 59

"This part of the Susquehanna is so different." The headwind carried Sol's words.

"It would be even better without the impoundments." Reily forced another stroke, wondering how much further was Safe Harbor.

The biggest dams were still ahead, each a giant step down to the Chesapeake Bay. The water grew slow and tired. Deep under their hull, beneath slopes tangled in pawpaw and hickory, was the bottom of the vestigial river, once young and playful.

Sol turned around. "I like the river when we have it all to ourselves. Have I told you about my time on the Nile? I spent a week traveling it from Luxor to Cairo."

"Of course you did." Reily had never met a woman so well-traveled.

"Well, it wasn't that I had the Nile all to myself. It's a hub for a lot of activity, especially trade and agriculture. There were boats everywhere. Along the upper river though, there were places at night that were dead quiet, almost surreal. When you got away from the developed lowlands and out into the desert, the stars were unfathomable." Sol faced forward again. "I was a grain of sand on the plateau."

Reily pictured her, wrapped in a burka, awestruck in the shadows of sphinxes and pyramids. "You're a walking atlas. Tell me more." She indulged, dazzling him with savory stories of Egyptian cuisine and idyllic imagery of sailing feluccas. He was ever impressed by the way she had led her life to date.

At the mouth of Cuff's Run, the group was strewn amongst woody debris and hushed from hours of laboring against wind and chop. Sol handed Reily a tuna sandwich and retrieved one for herself. They spotted Doc Murray descending the last switchback of a precipitous trail. He stopped to greet a few of the participants then walked their direction.

"How's the paddling?" Murray stood before them inordinately composed for a mountain goat.

Reily shrugged. "Is that what you call it? I thought we were driving a plow."

"The wind?"

"Yeah, but it could have been worse."

"Sorry, I wish I could control the conditions, but I do have good news to report." Murray spoke with the enthusiastic authority of an Eagle Scout. "Yesterday, I had a conversation with the land trust. They valued Mrs. Bunting's land and buildings somewhere between $425,000 and $475,000. Rumor has it that Woodring offered her $500,000."

"So where's the good news?" Reily asked.

"I've been doing more thinking. I don't know that we can give her what she'll need through a conservation easement but maybe we can buy it outright if she agrees to subdivide."

"How can we compete with Woodring's offer?" Sol leaned against driftwood, her brow furrowed.

Murray smoothed his hair to the side. "I think Mrs. Bunting made it pretty clear that she didn't really want to sell to him, but we will need to be reasonable with our number."

"What do you think is reasonable?" Sol said.

"That's difficult to say, maybe $350,000. That should be enough to help her get by. I figure she'll want the house, barn, the other few buildings, and a small chunk of land... but maybe we could get the rest."

Reily hoisted himself onto the log beside Sol. "How hard is it to raise $350k?"

"Challenging, especially in that part of the state, but not impossible." Murray plucked an inchworm from his shirt. "In Noxen, where I temporarily call home, the locals scraped together $85,000 for a family whose house burned to the ground and they did it in two weeks."

Reily wasn't as confident. "But this isn't a tragedy, at least not that kind."

"You're right," Murray said, "but it shows what's possible."

Sol slipped off her sandals. "No worries. We'll get the donations."

Reily fluffed her hair. "You can count on mine."

"Tomorrow morning, I'm going to call Gertrude and see if she'll bite." Murray seemed determined to make the new angle succeed. "Keep your fingers crossed."

Doc moved on to talk logistics with the safety officer. Reily and Sol finished their sandwiches then exchanged globs of sunscreen for an afternoon greasing. Reily smoothed it over his nose and noticed Kim and her man coming their way. Besides polite nods and smiles, he hadn't spoken with Kim since the start of her new connubial chapter. The previously estranged couple had been keeping to themselves. Undoubtedly, they had a lot to talk about.

"Reily and Sol, I want you to meet my husband, Chris." Kim was bubbly.

Reily obliged. "Nice to meet you, Chris."

"Likewise." Chris over-squeezed his extended hand. The blond behemoth had a guilty mien.

Reily wondered what assertion of dominance might be next. Was Chris's gorilla stare friendly or was it Sol he was ogling? Reily caught himself cross-examining Kim's sunburned breasts. They screamed for freedom, incarcerated behind crosswires of an illegal one piece. She cuddled against Chris and complimented her man for his kayaking stamina. Maybe she was a good actress, but she seemed genuinely happy about the reunification. She must like being married.

Reily looked at Sol and imagined if she would, too.

Woodring saw raw nature – other than the rugged, decorative flare of taxidermy mammals or the trout rarely hooked – as an earthly hell to be defeated by a mortal trinity: bulldozers, backhoes, and boldness. His conquests bore a safe and sanitized uniformity that many a possessed homebuyer would consider heavenly. There was no remorse, only self-adulation in a steadfast drive to create high-end houses for eager shoppers.

The forests of Whispering Heights cast generous shade but not in the fresh cut he was admiring. Logs a foot or more in diameter were piled at one edge of the clearing and to their side, a mound of branches and brush that might have been deposited by a biblical flood. He was pleased with the expungement.

Mikey Purillo squinted at him. "The timber company returned over the weekend."

"The crew did this in two days?"

"They work fast."

"Nice to see someone does."

Purillo ignored the comment. "We left about ten feet on this side of the ribbon. That should be enough right-of-way for the west road."

"Parkway," Woodring corrected. The bedeviling sun began to sear his limpid forearms. "I want the road wider. Cars need space."

"What about the wetlands?"

Woodring glared through his favorite pair of Maui Jim's. Purillo was chronically thickheaded. "We paid a consulting firm to show us the wetlands and they did, so take the road to the edge. There'll be less berm to maintain and when the puddles have water in them, it will make the drive more scenic. The residents will love it."

Purillo sighed. "Whatever."

"I want to walk the boundary of Gert's property. You have the drawings?"

"Yep, they're in here." Purillo gestured with a cardboard tube in his pudgy left hand. "So have you heard back from her?"

"No." Woodring removed his cowboy hat and scratched his head, gazing in the direction of the Bunting farm. "I'm calling her today. I want to know exactly where things stand before the meeting."

"That makes sense. You know, we should probably talk about the water."

Woodring snubbed the request and scouted for the stakes he had personally impaled into the living forest.

"I need to know what to tell Earl Lukens." Purillo raised his voice. "He said the yields are what they are. He can drill deeper but he thinks it's a waste of your money and his time. It won't do any good."

Woodring whirled around. "It's good enough. As far as we're all concerned, it will suffice. No more drilling. Tell him to install the pumps, case the wells, and keep his mouth glued shut."

"So noted." Purillo sounded inanimate.

Woodring strode ahead, pushing through the undergrowth, leaving Purillo simmering behind him. The water decision was a gamble, but that's what he did: took chances. Luck was normally on his side but something told him it might soon run out.

In the artificial comfort of his air-conditioned Wilkes-Barre office, Woodring transferred his cigarette to his other hand and reached under his pant leg. There was a slight tickle by the band of his sock, an itch that needed scratched. He discovered a flattened, sesame seed protuberance and responded with an expletive-laced invective. The culprit was the common wood tick, something he despised more than poisonous snakes and environmentalists.

He used his Platinum Visa to excise the parasite and summoned Abby Gordon into his office.

She took her customary seat. "What was that commotion?"

"A goddamn tick was on my leg."

"Carl!"

"Do you have a soft spot for disease carrying insects?"

"It's the language. When are you going to get an air purifier? It reeks in here."

Abby's dark features had a way of darkening his mood but Woodring liked the tightness of her shimmering blouse and the subtle lift it gave her bosom. "Yeah, anyway, how was your weekend?"

"It would have been better if I didn't have to drive all the way to Harrisburg."

"I told you I'd pay you for your time. So what did you find out?"

"Not much. Reily's still the same old ex-husband, although he's tanner than I remembered."

"What's he doing?"

Abby took a deep, impatient breath. "He's still on the canoe trip thing and it sounds like he'll be on it for a few more days."

"That's it?"

"I guess so. I'm not sure what you expected." She looked at him coolly.

Woodring didn't know what he expected either. "I guess that's good. At least we know he's a couple of hours away and preoccupied with his jungle cruise. He shouldn't be much of a bother anymore." He doubted his own words. Watters, the shit flake, had paid Hap Clay a personal visit.

"You don't know Reily. One of his gifts – and curses – is his determination. You have to break his arms before he'll drop something."

Consolation was not one of Abby's gifts. Why did he always feel worse after getting her opinion? "Did Sid get a look at him?"

"Yes, I think so. I kissed him so Sid would be sure to know who he was."

Woodring stared in disbelief.

"It was crowded. I wanted to be sure he knew." Abby cocked her head. "Sid's not going to hurt him, is he? He doesn't seem like a very nice man."

"Nobody's going to get hurt." Woodring's tone lacked assurance.

When Abby left the room, Terri slipped in and closed the door behind her with cautious drama. She leaned against it and beamed toward him. "Mrs. Bunting called."

"No way, what did she say?" From his saucy receptionist's grand entrance, he expected only good news.

"The papers are in the mail."

"The papers are in the mail?"

"Yep, that's what she said." Terri remained peppy.

"But what does that mean?" Had she accepted his offer? Was she declining?

"I thought it meant you two had a deal."

"Who knows? Find me her damn number."

Two minutes later he was calling the evasive landowner, his lynchpin to new pinnacles of wealth. The phone rang nonstop and the room turned gloomy. A storm was bearing down on Wilkes-Barre.

CHAPTER 60

Reily positioned himself to get a better look. Just as they had been told, an ancient symbol was carved into smooth rock and oriented northeast. It pointed like a laser to the place where, on the summer solstice, the sun awakened. Only a few other petroglyphs remained exposed, the rest hidden for more than eighty years in the vacillating depths of Lake Aldred where hydropower trumped history. Some of the drawings were of human form, others suggested animals... the remainder were subject to interpretation. They induced a primeval shiver. He imagined the lost artists at work on a different summer morning, a thousand years ago.

Without saying a word, Sol traced her fingers over their impeccable lines. "Can we spend the day here?"

"I think many others have. You know who would really like this?"

"Alex?"

"'I'm sure. Actually I was thinking about my daughter, Casey. She loved Indian artifacts. She had a dreamcatcher above her bed until Abby questioned if it was a pagan symbol. We even found an arrowhead on one of our canoe trips on the Lehigh. You would have thought it was treasure."

"That's very cool. My grandfather gave me a piece of indigenous pottery he found on a farm when he was a teenager. I thought it was the neatest thing. He was a great mentor. I bet Casey thinks you are a great one, too." Sol gave him an assuring look.

"I don't know about that."

Sol sat down next to him. They were atop the largest rock in a vast reach of the river. "Call her again. I bet she'll be pleased to hear from you even if she never admits it."

There was more Native American splendor on display at the Indian Steps Museum. Reily's lips were sandpaper, his eyes grainy and sore from a light but steady wind. The last thing he wanted to do was drive hours to a meeting and witness municipal absurdity. He preferred to stay put and learn more about a people who had cherished their land.

Sol handed him a cold Pepsi. "I'll enjoy the drive with you. It will be fun."

"Maybe, but we only have two more nights."

"You have to give it to them like you did the first time." Her eyes were big and compelling.

"I'm not sure where things stand, especially with the old lady and her farm, but I guess we know what Mr. Clay may do." Reily felt a twinge of excitement. The vote would be a small but important victory.

"Exactly, so we should be there." Sol spoke with a subtle authority he'd come to adore.

"Okay, but first I'm cleaning up. No need to scare the locals."

Terri charged into Woodring's office as if she were the owner. "It's here."

Despite his irritation, Woodring couldn't help but notice the undone button of her white shirt and the pink outlines of a lacy bra as she bent over to drop the wad of mail on his desk. He suspected she extracted a sort of cunning pleasure from giving him sneak peeks of her ample rack. "What's here?"

"The contract from Mrs. Bunting, it's right there." Terri scurried from the room to answer the phone.

His eyes returned to the desk and Terri was correct, the second envelope was from Gert. He opened it like a starving chimp peeling a banana. There was a note scrawled into the top margin of the form.

"I decided not to sell to you, Mr. Woodring. I'm sorry if I wasted your time."

– Gertrude Bunting

Woodring dropped the papers. This was the a-bomb scenario he had feared. His mind raced like Daytona. He fired up a cigarette and, after several suffocating drags, clarity returned accompanied by numbness.

He would proceed with the smaller version of the development. There was no other choice, and minus the water problem, a downsized Whispering Heights was still a sure bet. Had he been too ambitious with the project? He puffed on his Marlboro some more. Without such risks he wouldn't be what he was today. And what was that exactly? He didn't dare chew on that question too long.

Reily sat close to where he had weeks before but the room seemed more ascetic. Sol was beside him but their Odyssey mates were absent... no one else could be persuaded to drive seven hours round trip for a two-hour meeting. Around him, municipal groupies licked their lips for a bout of verbal jousting. Township theatrics were a main event in rural Pennsylvania. Change the wardrobes and it could have been the middle ages. The building should have had a moat.

Doc Murray came alone and had taken a seat near the front of the room opposite a restless Lowell Orwell and the other supervisors. Lawrence Wilson was wearing another, or perhaps the same, plaid shirt. Hap Clay was still as a statue.

Big Lowell banged his gavel to bring things to order but a door opened and heads turned to see Carl Woodring in western boots and hat enter the corral he had tamed. In his infinite brashness, he went to the front of the room and asked Doc Murray to move his briefcase so he could have the end chair. Orwell waited in deference for the developer to take a seat.

The first matter of business was the tabled item on the zoning change for the Bunting parcel. Carl Woodring stood, removed his hat, and spoke. Reily couldn't believe what he heard.

Lowell Orwell contorted his face in confusion. "I'm not sure I understand your request, Mr. Woodring?"

"I'm no longer seeking a zoning change. Mrs. Bunting has declined my offer."

Cheers erupted from the audience. Doc Murray beamed like the proud parent of a newborn. Sol elbowed Reily... he was still in shock.

Orwell scrambled to maintain order. Larry Wilson remained calm and expressionless. Hap Clay scratched his head.

"So what does this mean for your development, Mr. Woodring?" Orwell asked.

Woodring folded his arms across his chest. "I'll revise my plans and resubmit them for the township's consideration."

Hap Clay leaned into his microphone. "Before we move on, I want to say a few words. I have concerns about Mr. Woodring's project."

Orwell was visibly peeved. "You can bring those up when the new plan is submitted."

"I'd like to do it now, before we go any further down this trail." Hap straightened in his chair. "You see, Mr. Woodring's got water problems. I know that for a fact."

Woodring stood stone-faced then advanced in slow-motion rage. "I have no idea what you're talking about." He seemed overly defensive.

Hap shook a quivering finger at the developer. "I talked to the well driller and—"

"Enough." Orwell's gavel hit the head table with sufficient force to take down a steer. The audience hushed. "This matter can be discussed later."

"Excuse me, Mr. Chairman." It was Larry, the silent supervisor. Reily had presumed he lacked vocal cords but his voice was crisp, his tone direct. "Our colleague has a right to speak." There was immediate applause. Orwell was finally put in his place.

Even Hap acted surprised. "Thank you, Lawrence. I just want to caution the township that the drilling company has had trouble finding water and these new neighbors are going to need a steady supply." He paused to drink from a paper cup in front of him. "Perhaps the state should be asked to come in and make sure the flows are sufficient."

Orwell shook his head. Woodring's cheeks turned crimson. Doc Murray scrawled notes on a tablet. What else could happen?

Orwell cleared his cavernous throat. "This matter is hereby acknowledged. Agencies can be notified as part of the consideration process when Mr. Woodring turns in his revised plans."

The meeting proceeded to less cantankerous agenda items. Woodring slipped out of the building, slithering for cover. Orwell resembled a lost dog – a Bassett hound with sad, sagging, saline eyes.

CHAPTER 61

"I think that's Mt. Johnson Island." Reily pointed to his left. A blunt summit covered with small trees emerged from the depths of the lake. It was the tallest thing behind Conowingo Dam.

"Did you say Big Johnson Island?" Sol said. While she was generally demure, she had a devious sense of humor.

"You're too funny for your own good, Ms. Messina. If you're so witty, why do they call this a pond, when it's clearly a lake?"

"Good question. Maybe they were worried about inflaming the opposition. Building a pond sounds milder than building a lake."

"Good answer." Whether it was fatigue from the late drive back from the northern tier or the culmination of thirty-nine days of paddling, Reily felt catatonic. The next twenty-four hours could be a defining point in his life, yet he was preoccupied by the symmetry of the powerlines swooping across the horizon and the cadence of Sol's voice. He tried to reconcile that he was now in Maryland and had navigated three states on one river. He was an Odyssey survivor, one of only thirty or so participants who had lasted since Cooperstown.

Even in sunlight, the neon words "Conowingo Hydroelectric Station" glowed like a "Jesus Saves" sign. The raw, crushing force of water spun steel turbines pulsing electrons into the northeastern grid while the blades fileted migratory fish negotiating their greatest barrier.

Anglers jockeyed to cast beyond the boiling outfall, competing with cormorants targeting the same prey. Past the riot of spray and sound, a bald eagle waited for currents to deliver carrion to its guano-shrouded throne. Sol's presence added to the rhapsody but his mood sobered as Rob Murray approached with an anxious frown.

"The supervisor's dead."

Reily struggled to process the message. Conroy Township seemed a world away. "What? The heavy guy?"

"No, Mr. Clay is dead from a car accident. That's what Mrs. Bunting told me over the phone."

"Oh." Those were the only words he could muster. The news was disturbing. After last night and the prior visit to Hap's home, Reily had been developing a fondness for the old man.

"When did it happen?" Sol asked.

Murray brushed a stonefly from his chinos. "This morning... he may have been heading to work. They're not sure of the cause. Mr. Clay's was the only car involved. Somehow he hit a tree."

Reily imagined poor Hap stressed out of his mind from the bullshit with Woodring and the township. "I wonder if he had a heart attack."

"I doubt we'll ever know," Murray said. "We can talk more but now I have to track down my contact with the utility and sort out tonight's camping arrangements. See you soon." Murray walked off in the direction of the powerhouse.

Reily led Sol to a bench overlooking the fishing area and considered the portentous news. "Could there be foul play?"

"I thought of that, too, but I don't know." Sol pursed her lips and hesitated. "Do you think Carl Woodring is that evil?"

"He's not a very nice person, we know that much." A siren wailed from the dam, warning of another turbine coming online. Maybe it had deeper meaning. Reily admired the liberated river running for the bay, carrying worries away without a second thought. It was renewal, grace poured out, Susquehanna-style.

Orwell called an hour earlier with unfortunate news. Woodring wasn't sure if Lowell was just floored by Hap's sudden expiration or mystified about the circumstances of the terminative accident. "He was there last night all fine and dandy," Lowell repeated in gasping monologues.

"I can't believe it myself," Woodring said more than once. Now, he was late for a meeting and waiting for Sid Purillo to return his call. The speedometer nudged past eighty on the interstate as he obsessed about the sequence of events. He had called Sid from the parking lot of the township building after Hap pissed all over his future. Woodring had communicated his wish to teach the supervisor a lesson with earnest but unspecific instructions. *"Do something,"* was the request he remembered uttering to the elder Purillo.

Now those words were haunting him. What had Sid done to the poor bastard? The old guy was somebody's uncle or grandfather – living, breathing, blood, sweat, and bones – and Woodring was complicit in the man's *murder*. The word and its weight made him want to wretch, but gastric expulsion would have to wait. From his side mirror, he watched another sickening event unfold – a state police cruiser closing in. His black SUV was easy prey.

Reily pitched his tent for the final time. The campground was far from busy roads, active rail lines, bars, ballfields, schools, and other cultural accoutrements. Like most of the previous days, Doc Murray and the others who planned the Odyssey had made a good choice. Tomorrow's goodbyes would be tempered by his gamble with Sol. It could be the best day of his entire life... or a slide to oblivion.

His tent was in soothing earshot of Deer Creek but he scratched restlessly at his beard, beside a campfire too hot for the end of July.

Sol returned from the Explorer barefoot with a bottle in her hands. Her hair was wet and glossy and she wore a floral print sundress that looked familiar and perfect. He couldn't help but smile.

"You even smell like a flower." He gave her a quick smooch.

"I got us something." She handed over a bottle of Great Western Brut.

"Where did you get this?" Shopping hadn't been a big part of the itinerary.

"When we stopped for gas in Rising Sun and you used the bathroom, I ran into the liquor store next door."

Reily peeled the foil wrapping the cork. "Very sly, but brilliant."

"You better hope I share."

Kim and her man appeared in the firelight. "So Reily, think we can have a little of that, too? We chilled it for you."

"Pull up a blanket."

One by one other people from the group trickled over to relive the trip – their highs and lows, pleasures and pains. They made overtures, likely to be forgotten, about getting together again.

Reily reclined on his elbows and regarded two dozen or more illuminated faces. He hadn't gotten to know the half of them yet he felt a common bond of shared experience.

Sol was sitting Indian-style playing with her toes as she talked, laughing more than he'd seen her do the entire trip. Kim sat across from him and gave a wink, not flirtatious, just affirming. Three skinny, blond-headed teenage boys – the Clark brothers from York, Pennsylvania – were goaded into performing a rap they had written for the occasion. It was called the "Odyssey Blues." Clever rhymes and a catchy refrain grew into a booming chorus. There was drumming on the ground, on bottles and one another, and the stars synced as the volume increased. Honeysuckle infused an epic sweetness to an already wondrous night.

CHAPTER 62

For receiving less than five hours of sleep, Reily overflowed with vigor. Crows cackled like drill sergeants. Deer Creek provided nature's morning radio. He gathered essentials and walked to the bathroom through grass sopping with dew. The world was cast in a diffuse, gladdening light.

Twenty minutes later, Reily kneeled by his lady. "Sol, you better wake up, it's 7:30."

She sat up and rubbed her eyes. "Wow, I was out of it. Did you take a shower?"

"Yep."

"Hey, what did you do to your face?"

"I shaved."

She ran her hands over his new façade. "I'll say. You look very nice, but I might miss your big beard."

"Me, too. They have a killer breakfast ready for us. Pancakes, I believe."

"Yum, I love pancakes."

After breakfast, the day accelerated: over Smith Falls and past Port Deposit, hard paddling to keep away from an overloaded barge, a sheer-walled quarry on river right. Garrett Island laid dead ahead like a ship in the middle of a mile-wide channel, while bridges – straight as planks – reached across the gorge. Ceaseless splashing and water fights celebrated the culmination. Beyond the festivities extended an endless shimmer of water and sky – the one and only Chesapeake Bay.

Then it was over, the past three hours and the past weeks an intangible blur. Reily thought of one-armed John Wesley Powell on the Colorado, Lewis and Clark on the Missouri, John Smith on this very Susquehanna. Now he, too, was a *bona fide* river adventurer of the twenty-first century. He aimed their bow for the lighthouse of Havre de Grace.

News cameras were ready atop tripods, reporters waiting. State dignitaries watched their arrival with feigned enthusiasm. Reily rehearsed in his head.

He and Sol carried the boat to the end of a growing row of watercraft. "We did it," Sol said.

"We did." Reily's mind was elsewhere.

"Let's watch the others come in." Sol led him by the hand to a railing upstream of the lighthouse. The sun accentuated the colors of the fleet of boats on final approach. Waves thumped against the wharf's riprapped shore.

He beheld the scene like a celestial observer. "The river told me something."

"I see." Sol seemed distracted by all the people and commotion. "And what did it say?"

Reily turned his head toward her. "She said that you and I should hook up."

"Hook up?"

"Yes." Now he was forced to utter the precise words. "I'm supposed to ask you to marry me."

Sol smiled and her cheeks blossomed pink. "And what am I supposed to say?"

He was embarrassed by the profoundness, perhaps over-hyped, of his proposal. " 'Yes' would be the preferred response, otherwise I'll dive in and swim off to Baltimore."

Sol encased him in a taut hug and rested her head on his chest. "Do you promise to be continually fun, caring, loving, and worldly?"

"I do."

"Then I say... yes." She punctuated her decision with a persuasive kiss caught by a newspaper photographer.

Reily lifted her and breathed ether. It was a monumental high.

Rick walked over with a friend – a small-framed guy in a white polo shirt and pleated tan shorts. He sported a fastidious beard. Rick nudged him forward. "I want you to meet Wes."

Reily shook Wes's hand. "Nice to meet you." He had to be the guy Rick had been fretting over.

Rick glanced at Sol, then Reily. "What's up with you two? You look guilty."

Sol didn't hesitate. "We're getting married." To Reily, the words sounded strange but pleasing.

"No way." Rick's volume made heads in the growing crowd turn their direction. Within minutes, the word was abuzz.

The Odyssey throng aligned in three great rows, the tallest paddlers in back and Reily dead center. Rick stood beside him, his earring sparkling in the sunshine. Doc Murray stood at one end. The safety man – who had diligently guided them 556 miles – sat deservedly in front, in the middle. Sol was behind safety man with Reily's arms on her shoulders. Kim also occupied the second row, flanked by the Clark brothers... two on one side, one on the other. Exchanges of cameras paired with requests for smiles.

Tears and sighs followed handshakes and hugs. Gear was sorted and stowed. Boats were lifted upon cars. The longest, greatest trip of Reily's life had ended, but a new one was underway. He was still wearing his lifejacket, forever bleached and faded.

Reily took it off and tossed it into the Explorer. "So what do we do now?"

Sol beamed. "Let's eat hardshell crabs."

"Excellent suggestion, but first I need to make a call. Actually, two. I have good news to share."

CHAPTER 63

onarchs tested the goldenrod, first two then three, diving and dipping as they moved flower to flower. They continued alongside the house, past the viburnums and over the "for sale" sign, before floating across the street on an autumnal breeze. They were trending south to Mexico on their fabled migration. His own momentous journey was now a hazy dream but it never strayed far from his mind.

Reily squeezed the hose attachment and directed a turbulent stream at the grime adhering to anodized patio chairs and a matching table. They were a few of the lingering props from his last life. Sol was in Baltimore preparing for their new one.

After the outdoor items met minimal standards for cleanliness, it was time to tackle the spider-infested 8x10 prefabricated shed. Inside, it reeked of mold and gasoline. Mixed-length scraps of lumber begged for reuse – he had a project in mind. On a shelf next to a can of motor oil, there was a small lamp splotched with mildew. Faces of Sesame Street characters decorated the yellowed shade. It was Casey's... for the "fort-house" as she had deemed the space.

Reily took a closer look and felt a perfunctory sadness. His conversation with her from Havre de Grace was upbeat until he mentioned his next round of matrimony. Casey became indifferent but not critical. She'd probably expected such a development sooner or later. She always had an uncanny intuition. When he asked her to be part of the wedding, she wouldn't commit. The mute gaze of Oscar the Grouch seemed menacing. He put the lamp back and retrieved the lumber.

For lunch, Reily microwaved a quesadilla and pulled a Sam Adams from the fridge. He regarded empty walls from the remaining chair at the kitchen table. They hadn't been so scant since he and Abby moved in over ten years ago. He took a foamy gulp from the bottle. Abby's relevance was fading fast... there were happier things to worry about.

Exactly how was he going to build a treehouse for two on a river island?

CHAPTER 64

From US Route 11, Rob Murray noticed a swath of fresh housing with lots too big, streets too wide, and trees too few. Daily reminders of stupidity were a curse of his occupation. Whispering Heights was the nightmare.

He requested the state's Department of the Environment to investigate the accusations of an inadequate water supply for his least favorite development. After months of follow-up inquiries, they called back only to assure him that there wasn't any problem. The wells were fine according to a water resources specialist with the charisma of a robot.

Meanwhile, construction was moving forward. Foundations had been poured at the first townhouse village and half the homes were already framed. The model on the end of the curving drive was under roof. Woodring hacked off two townhouse villages in the revised development plan but wedged extra units into the remaining clusters. With diminished cliffside frontage and insurmountable access challenges, the number of sky chalets was halved. Murray had done his best impersonation of a greener Atticus Finch, pleading for even more restraint, but with Orwell at the helm, approval was preordained. The wounds to the land wouldn't be fatal, just debilitating. The place would never be right again.

Murray found a sliver of solace with Gert's farm – still wild and fallow – but she was growing impatient at the slow pace of fundraising to buy it. The money could be found but would she cave to Woodring or another weasel before they reached the funding goal?

Southwest of Bloomsburg, he found the overgrown driveway to an unimproved boat ramp along the river. Reily's Explorer and three other cars were parked in a mown clearing obscured by thickets of spicebush and Japanese knotweed as dense as bamboo. He squeezed his truck into a makeshift space, offloaded his kayak, and launched. The destination was the island smack ahead.

Two kayaks and a canoe were pulled halfway ashore the unnamed island. Murray landed beside them and climbed the bank. The skeleton of a treehouse appeared to grow out of giant sycamore.

"So this is Isla de Watters?" He startled the workers.

Alex emerged from the shadows beneath the construction. "Robert Murray, welcome to the Republic of Reily."

Reily, suited with a tool belt, flannel shirt, and blue jeans with ripped knees, descended a stairwell that looked to be a fire escape, reclaimed and repainted a glossy brown. He put down the level in his hand and extended a long arm of greeting. Murray converted the gesture into a brief, masculine embrace.

"This is too cool. I want it to be my satellite office." Murray pointed to the ponytail inching down Reily's back. "I see you didn't rush to conformity after your Odyssey days."

"It won't be cut until the day before the wedding."

Murray glanced up at the elevated platform and a perspiring younger man with familiar ear jewelry. "So who's up there?"

Reily flexed his knees. "You remember Rick?"

"Certainly, how are things going?" Murray amplified his voice so Rick could hear him.

Rick put down a cordless drill and brushed sawdust from his hands. "Not bad, but there's a heck of a lot to do... Alex and Reily can't keep up."

Reily waved off the comment. "Let's get lumber for that slacker."

Murray followed him to a palette of 2x4s. "How did you manage to get this property? Some would kill for a place like this."

"We were lucky. We didn't know where we wanted to be. Sol was ready to leave Baltimore and I had no need to stay in Nazareth. We agreed that we wanted to live simply, nothing fancy, and the where didn't matter so much as the how." Reily pulled a pencil from the top of his ear and paused to align and mark a board. He seemed at ease in his new habitat. "Then we talked about the islands. We had joked about living on them during the Odyssey, but suddenly it became a viable consideration and then an all-out obsession about finding the right one."

"That's pretty bold stuff."

"Crazy, I know, but that's the beauty of it. We looked at topo maps and circled any island that looked promising. We were mostly interested in those near Harrisburg but the best ones were owned by the state. Then we thought about the islands upstream of Wilkes-Barre, but that seemed too far away."

Murray kneeled beside him to hold a board steady. "What about north of Harrisburg on up to Sunbury? There are hundreds of islands in that stretch."

"We liked that idea, too, especially near Millersburg but we thought there might be too much action, too many people, because of the water trail on that section. So it came down to this prime waterfront. We probably scoped out every island between Berwick and Danville. From the tax maps, we knew that several were privately-owned. We matched up the three best bets and contacted the owners."

"What happened?"

"The first guy told us to fuck off and keep away from his island."

Murray rolled his eyes. "Nice."

"The second family said they might consider selling if the price was right. They called me back asking for $150,000."

"That seems a little steep for Pennsylvania bayou."

"Exactly. I couldn't find a phone number for the proprietor of island three but there was an address. Sol and I visited the old guy's house – maybe *shack* is more accurate – off a dirt road in a place called Liberty Valley over the mountain from Danville. He was deafer than a tree but he warmed up to us, especially Sol."

Murray nodded. "She's good at that."

"What?"

"Winning the hearts of old men."

"Very funny. In any case, the man went on *ad nauseam* about his days on the island. His family called it Water Camp." Reily stood to stretch. "It was meant to be. Sol and I stopped here during the Odyssey."

"When you were supposed to be paddling, no doubt... no wonder my safety guy was at wit's end. No one followed instructions."

"Yeah, but if I would have followed instructions, we never would have discovered this." Reily cast his hands outward like Moses in his land of milk and honey. "I'll tell you more, but first let's cut some wood."

Reily yanked on the cord of the generator and it started immediately with a soft putter. The circular saw it powered was jarring and acrimonious but he kept his eyes intent on the cutting line. He was a natural. Murray carried the trimmed boards two at a time and stacked them below the treehouse. Gnats taunted, baited by his sweat.

Reily hit the kill switch and quiet reverberated. Murray had more questions about this construction adventure and took advantage of the lull. "What about the floodplain rules? How did the township let you do this?"

"They seem pretty lax. Their maps have the hump of this island above the 100-year line. We can build, but I have to pay flood insurance."

"Of course." Even friends had to comply with sensible – if not inadequate – rules. "Man, you'd be surprised at all the complaining I hear about floodplain protection. Have you ever seen this river really angry?"

Reily pulled more boards for marking. "Disgruntled but not raving mad."

"You saw the pictures during the Odyssey. When it floods, bad things happen."

"Doc, you're putting a damper on my island dream."

"Sorry, just be on your guard."

"You want to see the plans? I need a break anyhow." Reily led him to a card table on the opposite side of the treehouse in progress. Drawings were weighted with a rock at each corner. "Most of the ideas were Rick's except for the in-stream turbines. They should power the lower level lighting."

Murray delighted in what he saw on paper: photovoltaic panels, cisterns, wind turbines, and a composting toilet anchored with a recycled heating oil tank. "This is impressive, but where are you staying? I don't see a tent."

"I have a one-bedroom apartment, more like a tornado bunker, in Danville on a month to month lease. It's ample for sleeping and occasional hygiene—"

An anguished cry pulled their attention upwards. Alex was doubled over, holding his right hand, teeth gritted. Rick watched, suppressing laughter.

Alex slowly straightened. "He hit me with a hammer."

"Serves him right," Rick said. "I really am sorry."

Reily pointed at them with the tube that stored the drawings and shook it. "Be careful, you two. Workmen's compensation rules are null and void on my island."

Murray directed his attention back at Reily. "What about your job?" He remembered Reily wasn't working. "What are you planning to do for money?"

"I'm thinking about starting my own currency, or maybe selling my body, Watters Waterside Gigolo Services, LLC."

"Sol ought to love that."

Reily leaned against a support post for the new structure. "We'll be alright, at least for a while. Sol saved during her time abroad and her mom sends her money on a whim. I put cash away and I'll have residual from selling my house. If need be, I can raid my deferred comp plan or get a job of some sort."

Murray required more financial security. "What will Sol do? You two might go stir crazy out here."

"She wants to go back to school and there are a bunch of universities within a reasonable drive. Who knows, I might go back to school, too."

Murray stood with his hands in his pockets admiring Reily's balance of purpose and serendipity. "Good for her and you. You'll be the only students commuting by water."

CHAPTER 65

Falling leaves meant falling sales to Woodring. Shortening days signaled less time for golf and fewer hours for building things. October usually induced a kind of doldrums but today life was sublime. The big push, as he had called his construction offensive at Whispering Heights, had accelerated progress at Jameson Pond Village – the first of the series of clustered communities. Drive-by gawkers licked their chops at the townhouses and Mikey Purillo escorted couples on personal tours. Abby Gordon had reported a handful of inquiries just in the last week.

Now Woodring could see the fruits of his vision through a promising lens. Vinyl-sided, rock-faced conformity and the crisp, demarcated edges of turf farm fescue lifted him above the chiseling worry of the unfortunate detours of the past months... even the dreadful loss of the Bunting property and the misinterpretation that terminally abbreviated Hap Clay.

Echoes of hammers leapt from the townhouses and navy blue pickups wearing the red P of the simplistic Purillo Brothers' logo occupied a third of the driveways as if there had been a mass outage of television sets and an army of repair technicians had descended on the ripening neighborhood.

Like a bull elk reviewing his harem, Woodring strutted along the unblemished asphalt of Wildcat Way, the first of five cul-de-sacs soon to be christened with the names of displaced wildlife. Through the trees, an area labeled Fawn Meadow on the village map contained a rounded network of experimental sand mounds intended to treat residential sewage. He made mental notes as he walked, using a toothpick to dislodge particles of breakfast sausage from his dentition.

Ariat boots tapped a sluggish rhythm. A holstered cell phone swayed on his hip. At the turnaround, Woodring examined a small cinder-block building poorly screened by arbor vitae. It was pump house one, home to two state-approved water wells thanks to well log adjustments executed by Earl Lukens. A verbal lifetime guarantee of inflated drilling contracts at future developments had convinced the ruddy-faced foreman of Northern Tier Drilling to make the helpful corrections. Woodring took a deep, proud breath. Water problems, if they materialized at Whispering Heights, would be the unfortunate conundrum of the homeowner's association.

Mary teetered from the round weight in her abdomen and struggled to her feet holding a trash bag filled with withered flowers and plastic pots. Harold Clay's gravesite stood out against the older ones. Blades of grass stuck through the stony dirt. Their friendship had been brief yet important. Maybe the evangelism had paid off and he left this world a better person. Hap had similarities to her own grandfather but the baby would get to know neither of those good men. She waddled to the truck hoping the child had worthy role models one way or another.

By Dushore, midday hunger had the best of her. She stopped at the mini-mart and went straight to the counter.

"Can I have a six-inch tuna salad sub?" The young associate stared at her belly. The girl should have been at school, not working for minimum wage.

Mary waited for the sandwich and noticed a thin, attractive guy her age or a bit older checking out the menu board. His hair was side-parted and he had on glasses that made him look smart. His t-shirt displayed the face of a coyote.

She smiled at him. "I like your shirt. What does SURCOS mean, if you don't mind me asking?"

"Not at all, it stands for Susquehanna River Conservation Society. We're based in Clarks Summit."

"They do environmental stuff?"

"Yep, we do. I'm the director."

"That's great." Mary loved nature and even though many people she knew ranted about so-called tree huggers and preservationists, most of the time the environmentalists were right. "My husband and I love the river. We're even talking about buying a canoe."

"You should. They're a lot of fun."

She could tell he didn't want to get bogged down in conversation with a stranger but she needed his opinion. "Would you have a couple of minutes to talk?"

"I'm afraid I need to grab some lunch and get on the road."

"Oh, I understand." She was embarrassed. "I have to talk to somebody," she lowered her voice, "about some wrongdoing, or, at least, I think it is."

The man's eyes grew serious and attentive. "The environmental kind?"

"Yes, I think so."

"Sure, I can stay for a while."

The while lasted an hour.

CHAPTER 66

The north wind churned an opaque sky like a specter warning him to complete the treehouse before winter's arrival. Reily didn't need a reminder.

Rick brought in two reinforcements and Doc Murray returned for another bout of island punishment. The biggest surprise was heading his way: a tandem sit-on-top pushed by a tailwind and driven solo by Wil Wisnoski, still wearing a golf visor in early November.

Wil stepped onto the muddy shore. "I come in peace."

Reily dragged the boat up the bank. "You probably aim to infect my land with smallpox."

"Syphilis, actually."

"Damn those promiscuous Europeans. So how's Wil?" Reily smacked his friend on the shoulder.

"Better than ever." Wil looked over the progress. "I like your outpost. It takes me back to our Mannequin Creek days. Remember the lean-to we pieced together?"

"With the remnants of a picnic table."

"And fishing line."

"Wait until you chill in my new lean-to." Reily led him up a path to the base of the treehouse. "Sol calls it Hobbitecture although she's only seen the drawings. All that wood is rot-resistant native hemlock. Supposedly it was salvaged from Ricketts Glen."

Wil stood below the edifice, his jowls bent in a peculiar smile. "This is unreal."

A gangly guy in coveralls sat on the wood-shingled roof at one end of a photovoltaic panel. He waved to them without saying a word and went to work with a cordless drill. Below him, on the first level, a small octagonal window opened and the head of Doc Murray came out.

"Reily, do you want me to start a second coat of polyurethane?"

"Please. Do you remember Wil?"

"Oh yeah." Murray squinted Wil into focus. "Good to see you."

"Likewise." Wil turned to Reily. "Do you have all your friends slaving on this boondoggle?"

"It appears so but before I subjugate you, how's your woman?"

"Gabriele?"

"Is there another?"

"She's beatific."

Reily chuckled. "That good, huh?"

"She's suppressed all other longings, but I have big news to share."

"What's that?" Reily prepared for word of an engagement.

Wil inflated. "My novel has been approved for publication. It is now in conversion to a screenplay and in the hands of Blackman. He's shopping it with studios and agents. We talk about every other day."

"That's excellent. You work fast."

Wil's narrow eyes widened. "I still can't believe it. If all goes right, I could see serious cash."

"We need to celebrate." Reily wanted Wil's *magnum opus* to be revered – his friend never stopped writing. "Follow me upstairs, I want to show you the insides of this architectural marvel and hear more about your impending fame."

Inside the treehouse, the chilly air was laced with sawdust and solvents. The smells sparked a memory of him and Wil in their early teens, buying sodas at a Bethlehem hardware store, a jack of all things bizarre where you could buy paint in back and Tastykakes up front. "It smells like Bergman's in here."

"I haven't thought of that place for a long time." Wil pulled cord from a retractable spool mounted on the wall. "Is this for bondage?"

"Clothesline... for indoor drying. With the skylights and the wood stove, it should work fine."

Wil inspected a fixture. "So the lights are all compact fluorescents?"

"I got a steal on them." Reily gave an appreciative nod to Rob Murray who was moving a chair to finish the floor. "Doc here has a friend who works at the Sylvania plant upstream." Reily continued the tour. "That's where the kitchen table will go. The corner area will serve as the living room. My hammock will stretch to that wall when a siesta beckons. A couple of chairs should fit, too."

Wil eyed the spiral staircase. "What's upstairs?"

"The master suite. Rick and company are up there wiring solar panels to backup batteries."

Wil touched the ceiling without full extension of his arm. "You better not grow an afro."

"Tall people enter at their own risk."

"So what do you want me to do today?"

"Help me build cabinets... for right here." Reily traced a large rectangle on the bare wall above the counter and the sink.

"You trust me?"

"I do, but first let's have a scotch toast."

"I brought Red Label Habanos," Wil said.

Murray paused mid-application. "Is that tequila?"

"Nope." Reily gave a dramatic sigh. "...His cigar obsession."

Wil held up the smokes. "I'm a tobacco connoisseur. Let's enjoy these outside. Please join us, Doctor."

Reily poured three short glasses of Highland Park and delivered them to ground level. Wil stood and distributed plump cigars and a lighter.

A white cloud billowed from Wil's mouth. "What's going on with the Heights?"

Murray sat on the stairwell and puffed his own stogie. "I gave Reily the lowdown when I arrived, but it seems that Mr. Woodring has been back to his illegal ways... this time falsifying data, or at least creatively packaging it for submission to state regulators."

"Falsifying what?" Wil asked.

Reily sipped his smoky scotch. "Well logs, so it appears that the Heights are a groundwater oasis instead of a desert."

Wil was visibly flummoxed. "Where did you hear all of this?"

Murray recanted a convenience store encounter with a pregnant woman named Mary and her transfiguration into informant of surreptitious behavior by Northern Tier Drilling and Carl Woodring.

"Did she implicate her husband, too?"

"No," Murray coughed. "She said he wants to quit his job. Mary wanted to help somehow and was thinking about going to the state, but then she ran into me."

"So what's next?" Wil asked.

Reily took a drag on his cigar. "I suggested an attack on two fronts. Rob presents the case to the regulatory folks and I take it to the police and tell them about the conversation in the woods and everything we suspect."

"It probably is time to stick it to the bastard." Wil blew smoke up in the air. "Things could get messy."

Reily thought about the statement for a moment. "But what's life without a good old mess once in a while?" He raised his glass. "Here's to fame for Wil and justice for Woodring."

The whisky seemed extra strong and satisfying.

CHAPTER 67

Sol took a final look at the void that was once her apartment. Wood floors were scarred and naked; the kitchen faucet dripped... struggling to find a tempo for the new rendition of her life. Gabriele's crap was gone but hers filled boxes stacked by the door. Minus the local, short-lived relationship, Baltimore had been the right recipe – a pinch of her tidewater past mixed with other cultural flavors. The city was accessible yet escapable.

She wondered about her new home. Exciting, yes, but for how long? Sol had to trust the math. The equation was different now – there was a devoted, energetic companion in the mix. Gabriele had been good company, too, but they were independent spirits running parallel most of the time. Now, she was entwined in an exhilarating helix. The abstract model was frightening but not its reality. When Reily was present, there was no anxiety. She stopped thinking and lifted a box.

At street level, buildings cropped the sky and seagulls questioned the hauling abilities of her dying car. Hanging clothes seldom worn were loaded last, a cushion between boxes and the ceiling. When the car agreed to start, she looped through several blocks of Fells Point, feeling the bump of every brick through the chassis. Instead of getting on the Jones Falls Expressway, she detoured through Canton. The neighborhood was finding itself again, coming into its own. A hopeful patina replaced grime and decay. She turned onto an alley aligned with the sun. The marble steps of row homes sparkled with assuring radiance. She traveled north, comforted.

The perpetual trip was meant to continue.

After two and a half hours of channel surfing for decent music, Sol saw the promised sign along Route 11, her name scrawled in big, embarrassing letters. She followed arrows pointing to the water.

The car's undercarriage scraped over a gullied path pretending to be a driveway. She rolled to a stop when she saw Reily in jeans and a rugged work shirt. He was riverside where he belonged and placing rocks around the perimeter of a rough-cut parking area.

Her outdoor concierge strolled over, eager to guide and assist. "Are you ready?"

Sol got out and kissed him. "Heck if I know. What is that?" She motioned with her eyes toward a flat-bottomed boat tied to shore.

"That's the HMS Messina—my, or should I say *our*, new mode of transport. She has a 20-horsepower jet drive and, you'll like this, it's a four-stroke so it has much lower emissions."

"Very nice." Sol was proud of his planning.

"While I prefer paddle craft, I knew we needed more cargo capacity and a tough hull in case there's ice."

She shuddered at the thought of negotiating Susquehanna icebergs. "Speaking of cargo, did you see my car?"

He looked over her shoulder. "It's amazing you made it this far."

Reily steered the Messina, top heavy with her belongings, at an upstream angle fighting the current. Sol shivered at the bow. Three black and white ducks skipped ahead of them and surrendered to flight.

"What were those?" Her hair whipped in the wind as she asked the question.

"Buffleheads," Reily yelled over the racing outboard.

In the lee of the island, he throttled down until the boat crept into the proper channel. Even with the leaves dispatched for the year, their new home was difficult to see.

"Get ready to jump out and tie us off."

Sol braced for the landing. "Aye-aye, captain."

Reily nudged the boat onto a gravel beach and cut the engine. "Look familiar?"

"Of course." She took the line and looped it around the closest tree.

Reily approached her, ignoring his unloading duties. "Now close your eyes, I have something to show you." He led her by the hand and they climbed briefly before the terrain leveled. She enjoyed his affirming tug as they walked. Then he stopped.

"Open them up."

A vertical wind turbine spun as if it had been turned on for demonstration. Solar panels reflected clouds speeding overhead. Tall windows welcomed light. Her eyes mushroomed as she consumed the scale and splendor of the handiwork.

"And?"

"Magnificent." Sol ambled halfway around the structure, her head locked upwards. "I love the sepia grains of the wood. I love all of it."

"It was a team effort."

"Fine craftsmanship. May I see inside?"

She removed her hiking shoes and let her fleece socks slide across the polished floor. Heat radiated from a small, black stove. The room was tinged with the faint smokiness of a Northwood's cabin.

"I like the chairs and the table. Where did you get them?"

"The table was mine. The chairs are from the Salvation Army. Twenty-five bucks for the lot."

"The cabinets are stunning." Sol noticed a door in the corner. "I assume that's the bathroom?" It was all new, exciting, and overwhelming.

"You are correct. You'll find it to have a sink, toilet, shower, and vanity. We even have built-in shelves."

"Can we go upstairs?"

Reily wore a contented expression. "It's your place. You may go wherever you wish."

The bedroom, like all the rooms, was incomplete. It cried for a woman's sense of style yet Reily's limited attempts at decorating weren't half bad. On one wall, a painting showed a man rowing alone on a river at sunrise or sundown. The blurred background spoke motion, action.

"That's the Schuylkill at Philly."

Sol examined the painting up close. "I like the loose brushstrokes."

"It's my mother's work. She did it *plein air* on parents' weekend of my freshmen year. Dad and I were at a football game."

A framed print hung over the headboard of a timber-framed queen bed. In letter-symbols it spelled *coexist*. "I like that, too," Sol said and sat on the bed.

The mattress creaked as Reily eased beside her. "Peace, love, and understanding – that's me."

"This is cushy... the comforter's very soft." She reclined and centered her head on a pillow. "Was this stuff yours?"

Reily positioned himself parallel to her. "The bed was, but I made a few purchases."

"Don't go too crazy. There's a boatload of my things outside and I want to make sure they fit. I need to contribute to our home."

"No worries." He rolled on his side and placed an arm around her. "There is still so much to do. For one, we have to landscape around the steps and carve out space for a garden."

Sol made a false grimace. "I suppose you'll expect me to can vegetables and make quilts in my spare time."

"I'll help with the canning. We can buy the quilts."

"Good, because I hate anything that resembles sewing."

He tapped her cheek. "Look at that ceiling. What do you see?"

"Is that a mural?"

"Very funny, that's the real thing, the finishing touch – our personal skylight observatory... aka the magic window."

"Magic window?"

Reily rolled on top and met her eye to eye. "I'll show you magical."

She kissed him. "Promise?"

He buried his face into her neck. "Always."

CHAPTER 68

O n this windy February day, the Environmental Services Building in Wilkes-Barre looked colder than an igloo. The neo-gothic visage portended Rob Murray's two-year possession by the Whispering Heights demon. He'd let one vile project usurp too much of his life. It was time to slay the monster.

Coming off the elevator, Murray recognized a useless clerk who'd once refused to make him copies and Mr. Malawaskey, the consummate bureaucrat, in his fishbowl office reading the newspaper. The office of the enforcement division always smelled like stale bread. The odor probably leaked from the skulls of those who had worked there too long.

"So you *think* there's a water problem?" Malawaskey seemed irritated that anyone would bring an issue to him in person.

"Yes, I do. There's ample evidence."

"The photos don't tell us much."

Murray inched his chair closer to Malawaskey's desk. "I have an informant – the spouse of a man who works for the well-drilling company working on Mr. Woodring's development. According to her husband, they drilled for weeks longer than planned and had problems with drill bits and other equipment breaking. Even with greater depths, the yields were half of what they wanted."

The veins tightened in Malawaskey's neck. A coffee stain on his wrinkled dress shirt suggested a propensity for laziness. "We would need to see the numbers. If the flows are inadequate then we can make them drill more wells or develop an alternate water plan. Chapter 109 regs are pretty clear about this."

"You saw the numbers. They're in your files, remember? I'm sure they look fine... but they were doctored."

"Then the lady... or better yet the husband... would need to give us a detailed account." The bureaucrat groaned like a heifer with hoof rot.

Murray felt himself becoming agitated. "I'm not asking her to put her husband's job at risk until you get off your ass and check this out."

"Okay, okay, point made." A dribble of foamy saliva stuck to Malawaskey's lower lip. "We'll do an inspection and see what we find."

"And if the yields aren't sufficient?"

"...We'll make them correct the situation somehow."

"How about shutting down the development?"

Malawaskey lifted his hind quarters and raised his chair a few inches. His prolific weight must have exhausted the hydraulics. "I don't think we can do that."

"Wouldn't lying on an official document be a criminal offense?"

"Perhaps, but things could get sticky fast... the burden of proof and all."

Murray took off his glasses to wipe them, a compulsive habit accentuated under stress. "Then that will be a risk you'll have to take, won't it?"

Malawaskey nodded numbly.

A Dickinson Law School diploma was centered on the wall behind an executive chair big enough for a king. A framed picture of a freckle-faced boy occupied a shelf beside reference books about criminal statutes. In the hall outside, Reily heard banter about case scheduling and questions about weekend plans. He tapped his dress shoes on the tiled floor. Was the appointment a bad idea?

The door opened. "So what can I do for you, Mr. Watters?" It was a pleasant but to the point female voice. As he stood, the District Attorney met him in front of her desk. "I'm Leslie Page, nice to meet you."

Reily returned to his seat. The chair behind the desk was oversized because the woman occupying it was barely five feet tall. He wasn't fooled – a bulletproof stare, classy dress, and tight-wire bun spelled ruthlessness. "I'm here to talk about some wrongdoing." The words sounded goofy the second he uttered them.

"All I deal with is wrongdoing, Mr. Watters. What makes your situation special?"

"It seems pretty serious."

"It may be, but people typically talk to the police first."

"I was going to do that, but where the crime occurred they don't have a police force."

"Then the State Police would have been the next choice." She checked her watch. "I have to be in the courtroom in about twenty minutes so you'll have to tell me quickly about your matter."

Reily spoke fast and tried not to meander. He gave a little background on the development and Carl Woodring then dovetailed to the township decisions, the night in the woods, and the conversations with the late Harold Clay.

The District Attorney reclined in her throne and bit cognitively on a Mont Blanc pen. "And how did you get involved in all of this?"

"From a canoe trip." He told her about the Odyssey and the tour of Whispering Heights Rob Murray led from Camp Sullivan.

Leslie Page managed a slight smile. "My son, Cory, is going to the camp for a week this summer and I went there when I was a kid."

Ms. Page was actually pretty when she wasn't scowling.

"It seemed like a great place but there's another problem I wanted to tell you about." Reily explained the suspected deception regarding the water supply at the development.

She sighed. "We have a possible case of bribing a public official and falsifying official documents."

"There's one more thing, although we're not sure." He dove into the odd timing of Hap Clay's death.

"That's a big accusation, Mr. Watters, and a potential stretch based on scant evidence and likely coincidence. Furthermore, what proof do you have of bribery besides observations made in the dark where you were technically trespassing?"

"Mr. Clay basically admitted to us what Woodring had done."

"Yes, but Mr. Clay is now deceased. You lack a witness."

"Can't you look into this?" Reily wasn't willing to give up.

Leslie Page shook her head in slow capitulation. "This may be a waste of time but I'll see what we can find out. No promises though."

"Any efforts are appreciated."

She stood and grabbed a file off her desk. Her eyes evaluated him like she was selecting a juror. "Gifford County may seem like a backwater but we have the same crimes you find in the big cities – drugs, murder, theft, fraud, you name it. I'm up to my eyeballs in cases, but if we find any dirt on Mr. Woodring, I'll let you know."

Reily thanked her and exited.

Outside, the air felt warmer and the sun awoke... the long winter was breaking. The past two months on the island were cold and harsh, even necessitating a week of respite at a Bloomsburg motel. But as he strolled down Main Street in Tunkhannock searching for coffee, he was already perked by the potential imposition of justice, sweet and resolute.

CHAPTER 69

B y April, the ingenious island homestead, with its technologically-advanced Swiss family treehouse, was at a stalemate with the river. While the structure blossomed inside, a soggy March and fall work never completed had the grounds begging for attention. Poison ivy sprouted around the steps and pilings and a labyrinth of knee-high Japanese knotweed threatened to oppress the prospective vegetable patch. Reily knew what needed done. He organized a garden party.

On the Sunday after Earth Day, a fleet of boats landed on the island with crews armed with shovels, picks, and potluck dishes. Alex Mueller brought his lady, Erin, and Wil accompanied Gabriele whom Sol hadn't seen for months. Within the hour, Rick and his partner arrived and, to everyone's surprise, Kim – without her hubby who, to no one's surprise, again had failed to keep his pants on around easy women.

One group, led by Sol, chopped, dug, and extricated unwelcomed plants. They worked inside a serpentine boundary that Reily had outlined with driftwood selected from the surrounding islands. The bed-to-be extended from the base of the treehouse steps halfway to the primary landing on the narrow south channel. There, a selection of native riparian shrubs and perennials were stockpiled.

Reily took charge of a posse of two – Wil and Alex. They labored 100 feet down-island to liberate a rectangular transect of roots, vines, and other outlaws, transforming the rich soil into the Watter's seasonal vegetable larder. After an hour and a half of toil, Wil called for beer and a break.

"My hands are getting torn up. I won't be able to write."

Reily directed him to the nearest cooler. "Man up."

Alex grabbed a handful of soil and sifted it through his fingers. "You know what would be good right here?"

"A garden?"

"Cultivation."

Reily feared where Alex was going. "Isn't that what I'm planning?"

"Raising thy noble herb."

Reily cleared his throat. "Last I heard, that's against the law."

"Frances grows it... or so you said." Alex sounded like a kindergartener. Premature creases on his forehead proved otherwise.

"On a spread somewhere in the Bahamas. It could be two containers, for all I know." The comparison was ridiculous. "What she does is her business but I'd hate to have a fisherman stumble on this island and report me to the DEA."

Wil returned with beer in hand and caught the gist of the conversation. "Reily has a point... it's pretty damn risky. I can tell you many tales about decent people facing legal nightmares from their horticultural escapades with *Cannabis sativa*. I wrote a few of the stories."

Alex persisted. "I'm simply requesting a few square feet maintained for my enjoyment and yours, if you like. No one will find the motherlode."

Reily placed his hand on Alex's shoulder. "Blind faith can betray us. And what would you do with all that stuff?"

"I happen to go through record amounts of reefer."

Wil laughed. "We didn't notice."

Reily visualized the pot plot. "If I permit prohibited agriculture, you'll be my indentured servant, Mueller."

Alex bowed. "Of course, great Raja."

When the work was finished, Sol unfolded a clean tarp on the ground and Kim and Gabriele passed her covered dishes to set upon it. Erin placed rocks at each corner. The guys came down the treehouse steps delivering throw pillows and blankets for all to sit on. Reily put the *Best of the Band* in a CD player and adjusted the volume.

Music and laughter peppered their version of a Bedouin feast. Reily chewed flatbread smeared with hummus. Beside him, Wil ate fresh mozzarella Kim had brought from a raw milk dairy in Ithaca, New York. Reily noticed he was watching Sol talking with Erin at the far corner of their spread.

"They're both taken."

Wil passed him a plate of deviled eggs. "We do have exquisite taste in women, except Rick of course."

"Good observation, smart ass."

"I'm also observing a slight extension of Sol's abdomen. She better cut the fat out of her diet."

Wil had figured it out. "Eighteen weeks, brother," Reily gloated.

"Congratulations." Wil slapped him on the back.

"Island magic... what else is there to do when you're stuck here in the winter?"

Wil stood and raised a bottle of beer. "A toast to our hosts and to the little Watters on the way."

Bottles clanked around the perimeter but Rick pouted. "We didn't know. You should have told us, Reily."

A campfire followed dinner and the party continued. Wil had one beer too many. Kim and Gabriele intrigued Rick's man, Wes, with conversation about breasts. Alex and his guitar sugared the night, beneath the glitter of a North Branch sky and the boundless generosity of a big river. Then a second string broke.

On Sunday morning, the guests trickled off the island like stoneflies leaving the water. Each had an invigorating cup of Rick's coffee in hand. One guest remained: Alex Mueller. He was planting hardy seeds salvaged from his current stash.

CHAPTER 70

Fresh foliage cheered the lengthening days. Their green, unfurling aspirations complemented Sol's own sense of accomplishment. The long Thursday drive to and from Wilkes University was wearing, but she was finished until the routine resumed next spring. With a new baby, that would be more complicated.

Reily wanted to enter the teacher certification program at Bloomsburg University... what if they had classes the same night? The river created another hurdle especially when it was icy and swollen. Reily had been running her across in the motorboat and waiting when she returned.

The MBA program had been tougher than expected but the challenge motivated. Her advisor was impressed by her interest in fair trade models. "Most MBA students focus on increasing their earning potential. Few see it as a vehicle to better the system for all," he had said. The comment resonated. Sol would do her best. Research angles were already ruminating.

It was almost dark when she reached the west end of Berwick and saw a house with a homemade, weather-worn "Free Puppies" sign staked into the yard. Every child needs a dog, she rationalized. Her German shepherd in Michigan was as protective as the Secret Service and, at a time when her parents were bickering and their nomadic lifestyle made winning friends a chore, Kunzler was her best pal. Sol could still see him on the road, bleeding and anxious, and feel the sorrowed horror of his jaws slashing her face. His death had left a capacious, agonizing void. She turned around. There was never an optimal time to adopt a pet or heal an old wound.

Reily was there for her in the parking clearing. She smelled the smoke from the campfire before seeing the glowing embers.

He opened her door. "Up for s'mores?"

"Don't use up your romantic creativity so fast. We're not even married yet."

"It was getting late. I was hungry for something sweet."

Sol gave him a hug. "Likely story."

A whimper startled both of them. "What was that?" Reily said.

She suppressed a guilty face and opened the rear hatch. "Let me introduce you to someone." A dog with a dangling tongue lay sprawled.

"You didn't?"

"I did." In the dimness, the canine rose and came forward to meet its new master. Sol lifted it to the ground. A wet nose sniffed Reily's leg. The dog's tail moved like a windshield wiper on low speed.

Reily squatted to see their knee-high friend up close. It had long hair and shy, dark eyes. "So what do we call him, or is it a her?" The dog's tail quickened as he spoke. "I assume we're the owners?"

Sol loved how Reily could roll with anything. "It's a boy. Don't you want to know where I got him?"

Reily petted the dog. "I'm sure you'll tell me all about it."

"First we need to come up with a name for him."

They sat down on a blanket Reily had laid out. Their new friend paced and scanned the unfamiliar territory then plopped down between them.

"How about Keith? That was my father's name."

Sol shook her head. "That's a weird name for a dog."

"What about Wil?"

"Too confusing."

There was a long silence. The un-christened dog panted. Reily placed a log on the fire. "Okay, how about Whiskey?"

"That's still weird. Why would you call him that?"

"His coat looks sort of straw-colored, like booze."

"I have one but you better not laugh. What do you think of Journey?"

Reily grinned. "As in *Don't Stop Believing*?"

"No, as in a big adventure... like the Odyssey."

"Sorry, but that one's the weirdest yet. What if we called him John, short for Big John? Check out his paws. He hasn't filled out."

"I don't know. It's kind of boring."

"Maybe, but dog names are overused. John is a person's name – it would be cool to impart it to a dog."

"Let's test it. John, what do you think?" Sol slathered her words with excitement. The dog's ears perked and motion returned to his tail.

"Looks like a winner."

She wasn't sold but she wouldn't object. It would grow on her. From a childhood rife with interruption, she had learned to let situations unfold as they may.

The night cooled and the chill incubated the starlight. Sol finished explaining how the six-month old dog had been acquired. Toasty smoke swirled from the campfire. Reily, with his rebellious ponytail falling down his back, slipped marshmallows on a stick. She liberated graham crackers from waxed packaging. John stirred, sensing the presence of food. He approached Reily and sat before him.

"John needs Listerine." He waved away the invisible odor. "I haven't had a dog since childhood. I would have been reluctant to make the move because of the additional responsibilities, but I'm glad you were so bold. Thanks for stretching my comfort zone."

Sol patted his hand and leaned back, drinking the sky. Only the hiss of coals was audible and the rhythm of John's exhalations. She couldn't ascertain his breed. The free-puppy family only told her that the mother's mother was a pedigreed border collie. Her best guess was a hybrid of retriever and collie in some formulation. Like her father had taught, Sol spotted the small constellation near Orion, *Canis Minor* – the lesser dog. From the center, the star Procyon glowed in approval. Perhaps it was speaking for John who was preoccupied with the smell of chocolate and the sight of marshmallows ablaze.

CHAPTER 71

The baby wailed like a dying animal, flagrant disclosure of a diaper at capacity. Mary didn't mind. Months of exhaustion from her infant's demands couldn't neutralize the fulfillment of motherhood. Yesterday's visit from a well-dressed man from the District Attorney's office was more troubling. He'd come to their home and asked Joe dozens of questions about work and the job at the big development site overlooking the river. Joe wasn't rattled but she knew it bothered him – he couldn't hide worry.

Mary parked in the long driveway at Hap's former house. The yard grew as many dandelions as blades of grass. She'd tell the realtor lady about it. The property had been given to the Beacon of God Church through a handwritten addendum to a formal will. By the date on the letter, Hap wrote it last summer... in the days after he began to attend the church. It was a blessing but she had second thoughts of volunteering for the musty chore of disposing of his lesser possessions. The furniture and bigger items of questionable value had been auctioned months ago.

Mary carried the crying child in his car seat and took him to the kitchen for changing. She tucked the soiled diaper into one of the plastic grocery bags she brought along for such emergencies then laid the baby on a blanket on the empty living room floor. From the garage, she retrieved a box of stacked papers and magazines and began sorting next to her son. A pacifier wiggled in his mouth. His inquisitive eyes grew heavy.

There was a John Deere calendar from 1984; a discolored photo of a small dog – possibly a beagle; an oil-stained manual for a string trimmer; and, another manual, still in its plastic sheath, for a riding mower. A softbound road atlas was creased to a faded Pennsylvania. Five *Playboys* from the 1970s offered more provocative content. Mary pinched the explicit monthlies between thumb and forefinger and dropped them one by one into a trash bag. The pretty girls should have kept their clothes on, but the thought of quiet, old Hap sneaking a peek made her smile. At the bottom of the box was a property map, an

255

official document with blue lines showing the Whispering Heights mess. A cassette tape without a label was tucked into the fold. Something told her it was worth a listen.

The sports bar scene was safe and predictable. Guy friends bought her drinks wishing for sex but – most of the time – tampering their expectations. Terri didn't mind the attention since it had become less frequent. Explosive red hair and four-inch heels were an imperfect defense against hormonal injustice. Stress aggravated creases under her eyes that makeup couldn't hide. The wicked lines had worsened since her appointments at the courthouse.

"You're looking tired, girl." The barmaid had a knack for making her feel worse.

Terri stared into a glass of remnant ice cubes. "My boss has himself in a real shit storm." The place was dead tonight but it suited her mood.

"Yeah, you said something about that last week."

"I did?" The conversation vaguely resurfaced.

The barmaid dried a glass. "You said the police were investigating Carl... what's his name?"

"Woodring." Terri straightened on her barstool. "I've been talking to the Assistant District Attorney." It was exciting to be a resource, a go-to person. Carl took her for granted.

"So what's the latest?"

"I told them about cash that was sent to Carl from some township politician." Terri lowered her voice and leaned forward. "There was a letter with the money. It was being returned – like it had been a bribe."

The barmaid froze mid-wipe, tidying the counter. "Get out."

"No, I'm serious. There was all this cash sitting right there in an envelope."

"You want another?" The barmaid pointed to Terri's glass. Terri nodded. "Like how much cash are we talking about?"

"Twenty-five hundred. I should have kept it for putting up with all his crap."

"So what are they going to do next?"

"Who?"

"The D.A. people."

"They didn't really say, just that they wanted more evidence to make a strong case."

"Sounds like Carl's in a world of hot water." The barmaid spoke over her shoulder on her way to a new customer.

Terri felt a hint of remorse. "I think they have him by the balls."

CHAPTER 72

Reily paid attention for an upcoming turn. "It would have been faster to take the interstate."

Beside him, Sol inventoried the world through the windshield. "But not nearly as pretty."

"Do most people wait until fourteen days before their wedding to scope out the venue?"

"No, but we're different," Sol said.

"We sure are." Reily glanced at her in the passenger seat. The sun created a backlit aura around her head. She was still his river angel. "Hey, did I tell you I talked to Casey yesterday?"

"No, and...?"

He failed to contain his smile. "She's coming to the big day."

"That's wonderful. Maybe this will help align the orbits between you two."

Secretly, Reily feared a cold reception. He turned left on another country road. New yellow lines divided an unsullied coating of asphalt. Hydrocarbon vapors flowed through the downed windows. The pollen from a hayfield tickled his nose, triggering a succession of sneezes. June had arrived.

Sol laughed at him then twisted her head. "Was that the supervisor's place?"

He slowed and evaluated a simple brick ranch home in the rearview mirror. "I think so."

"Did you see the For Sale sign?"

"Yeah." The house seemed lonely, like it needed a friend.

"I feel badly about Mr. Clay, but let's discuss our wedding logistics." Sol folded her arms – something Reily noticed she did when discussing serious matters. "We're running out of time."

"I still wish we could do it at Ricketts Glen."

"Me, too, but Kirby Park should work fine."

"Cooperstown would have been cool."

Sol raised a fist. "You better stop."

"Okay, no need for violence. What about Havre de Grace?"

Abby Gordon cursed as a Ford Explorer, the same color as the one driven by her ex-husband, edged into her lane from the opposite direction. The passenger appeared to be pummeling the driver, the same thing she should have done to her old boss long ago. She'd had enough of Carl Woodring and told him so three weeks ago. Last summer's odd request to spy on Reily demonstrated his paranoia. There were also rumors of impropriety being funneled to her by Terri – free-range slut by any measure, but dependable sage for anything sordid.

An episode at Carl's house capped her decision. He'd asked her to dinner under the guise of needing input on the business but when he trolled his hand across her ass, it was clear he only wanted to get into her business. It was time to move on. Eddie Miller, a low-key real estate competitor, viewed Woodring as a walking bowel movement. Eddie welcomed her to his team like a sibling.

Abby arrived at the listing, a place as drab as sand, and parked on the driveway facing downhill – the same direction her life seemed to be heading. The ten o'clock showing was for a single man planning to relocate to the area. He worked for an oil company based in Louisiana. She hoped that meant a hefty salary and quick sale because the scant commissions of late were causing anorexia in her checking account. A dapper and datable client would be a godsend, but God had taken an extended vacation to another part of heaven. She was seeing none of the rewards Jim Gordon used to foment. Abby questioned how much her second ex really understood about matters of the spirit. The only thing that seemed to 'arise' when he was present was the little thing between his legs... and that was on a good day. Whether it was his past perfunctory behavior or the crush of a convoy of other disappoint-ments, it was adding up to a crisis of faith and she hadn't a clue where to turn.

At half past ten, she started the car. The man looking for a house had failed to show.

CHAPTER 73

The baby napped in the afternoon. The heavy languor permitted Mary time to cook, do laundry, clean the house, and once in a while, leaf through a magazine or the weekly newspaper. Today, she wanted to clip coupons. A Radio Shack circular boasting a sale on compact discs reminded her of the mystery cassette found at Hap's place. She wasted no time in finding her purse.

With the cassette secured in their stacked and aging stereo system, she adjusted the volume downward and hit play. The tape hissed. She strained to glean recognizable words, sounds, or anything of meaning. After long seconds of nothingness, she placed her finger on the stop button assuming the tape to be empty or defective. A sinister but muted voice declared otherwise.

She pressed her ear to the speaker and dissected fragments of conversation. It was unworldly but unmistakable – a bad deeds parable from the good book. Three men were talking and even called one another by name. They discussed land, time, and money and it was clear despite the poor audio quality that they were committing sin. She hurried to the phone in the kitchen and brought back a note pad and pencil. She listened to the tape again and again until the conversation was transcribed as best she could. Her hands trembled rereading the dialogue. *This was evidence of a crime.*

Peter "Talking Wind" Williams was on the cell phone. Reily was wet from the waist down after removing debris lodged against the instream hydroelectric turbine. He had spoken to the Onondaga chief and holy man only once since Alex made the introduction. Since the chief was co-performing their wedding ceremony, Sol thought it essential that they talk more. Reily obliged, leaving a message for Peter earlier that day.

"No worries, Mr. Watters." The chief's tones were as low as a great horned owl. "I have the standard service we discussed and I know Kirby Park well."

"We really appreciate you doing this."

"Thank Alex. He made me very happy at our events in New York. He is a friend."

There was something trustworthy and likeable about Peter Williams. The television public service ad of the Indian with the teary eye for litter had made an impression during Reily's youth and *Dances with Wolves* further enshrined a naïve perspective of native wisdom.

"May I ask your advice on another matter?"

Williams had a belly laugh. "Certainly, but I cannot promise that my words will be useful."

Reily quickly sorted the implications of a morning call from Doc Murray. The Department of the Environment was strangely quiet on the Heights case and wasn't returning calls. The District Attorney had been missing in action, too. Meanwhile Woodring was selling townhomes beside the biggest vernal pool. Reily pictured retirees spreading 2,4D next to salamanders, poisoning their squishy domain with weed killer. He strived for brevity but spent ten minutes telling Peter Williams too many details about the development in Gifford County.

"I knew of this wrongful plan. Now I know more. I'm not sure how my people or I can help but we will try. The Great Spirit listens and works in strange ways – ways we cannot understand – and the man who does not listen is foolish, very foolish."

Reily liked the chief's succinct reassurance. "I appreciate your assistance. So we'll see you on June fourteenth?"

"Yes, and I look forward to it."

Reily did, too. The wedding and its cast of characters guaranteed quite a day.

CHAPTER 74

Woodring sang off-tune to the only Ted Nugent song he knew while soaping his erogenous zone to a vision of Abby Gordon as a dominatrix. Even a shower couldn't wash away his warped hunger for her coarse wit and curvature. Clanking pipes reminded him that cheap water heaters weren't made to last. The tapping grew louder. *It wasn't the plumbing... it was raps on the door.* Someone was using the metal knocker.

He turned off the spigots, grabbed a monogrammed towel, and dried with haste. There was another series of raps and voices. Woodring stepped from the shower and pushed aside the bathroom blinds. In the double-wide driveway, a Gifford County sheriff's car seemed as out of place – and as frightening – as an alien spaceship. With bourgeoning dismay, he pulled his bathrobe from the hook and sulked toward the front door. It came alive.

"Carl Woodring, open up." It could have been the great and powerful Oz.

Woodring felt weak and dizzy but obeyed. Before him stood two deputies, pressed and uniformed, but less intimidating than they sounded. An officer with a thin face and nose like a shrew told him he was under arrest and rattled off charges difficult to process under duress. A younger officer recited the Miranda rights while watching him with an uneasy glare. The moment felt out of body. He longed for a whisky and his remote control.

After he dressed, they cuffed him. It felt far worse than the way it was characterized on television.

Woodring avoided stares of courthouse onlookers by concentrating on his own boots, more scuffed than he ever realized. His new friends in law enforcement led him through a series of humiliations, from pat-downs to fingerprinting to confinement in a holding cell – a live trap without lettuce or peanut butter.

After an hour in the cage, a Deputy D.A. named Greenfield made him sign a stack of papers nearly as voluminous as a mortgage settlement. The sardonic crush of the stoic man's last name brought an unbecoming moistness to his own eyes. Maybe it was caused by Greenfield's disclosure of a familiar name, a Mr. Watters, who initiated the criminal complaint. When he challenged the prosecutor about the absurdity of the claims, the man scanned his file folder and itemized the resounding evidence: sworn depositions from a well driller; a secretary who witnessed cash transactions; an audio tape documenting unlawful deeds.

Greenfield gestured with the folder. "I believe we have a tight case, Mr. Woodring. I suggest you find a competent lawyer."

Four hours and ten thousand dollars later, he was a limp passenger in the car of Mike Purillo. His construction Godfather had rescued him from his fresh, testicle-squeezing reality: felony charges of bribery and falsification of public documents. More charges were being considered. Purillo exhausted small talk in the first minutes of the drive. He knew better than to dwell on sensitive subjects.

"I heard Gert signed a deal for her land." Purillo apparently found courage to speak again, but Woodring wished the air conditioner would have muffled the words. "The conservancy is buying it. I thought you should know."

Woodring closed his eyes hoping to alter the moment or erase the day. His mouth managed to compose a question. "I guess her tract won't become part of the Heights?" It sounded like a statement of surrender.

"I don't think so," Purillo said.

"So where in the hell does some rural collection of earth fuckers get enough money to buy a goddamn farm?" Woodring reddened despite knowing that bouts of rage pole-vaulted his blood pressure. Reily Watters and his buddies must have had something to do with the deal... the ubiquitous sonofabitch probably coughed up his life savings for the purchase. Woodring thought about his limited options. The idea of being sodomized in prison chilled him as much as the evisceration of his accumulated wealth – the side effect of using a reputable attorney with any chance of winning.

But there was the Argentina contingency. It was a malformed retirement dream – living like a thoroughbred gaucho, washing back steaks with Malbec in the Andean foothills while submissive senoritas waited on his every whim. In 1996, he'd visited Buenos Aires, the Mendoza wine country, and Patagonia. In 1999, on a millennium hedge against Y2K pandemonium, he'd purchased ten brushy hectares southeast of San Juan with views of the Desaguadero River and snowcapped peaks in the hazy distance.

Before today, Woodring had given little thought to exactly when and how he might occupy the holding but now he envisioned a sunny window overlooking tall grasses bowing to the wind and a walking path to the river where he'd cast for rainbow trout. He couldn't imagine Argentine authorities expending resources to locate, let alone extradite, him plus, from what he heard, corruption increased proportionately with distance from urban centers. If he had to, he'd pay for anonymity. Major life alterations made him uneasy; being forced to do them made him angry. If he was skipping town, a final, vindictive overture was necessary.

"I need to talk to Sid." Composure returned to Woodring's voice.

"Again?" Mikey's fat fingers shifted on the steering wheel.

"Don't give me shit. Do you have any idea what I've been through?" Woodring stared at Purillo who refused to make eye contact. "Forget it. I'll get in touch with him myself." He checked his front shirt pocket for cigarettes but the courthouse gestapo had failed to return them.

Purillo's rearview rosary chastised him. Cars disintegrated on the frame in Bortner's Junkyard. A hill bled loose shale from a forgotten strip mine. Even an ice cream shop was dead and boarded. He was as ruined as the wretchedness around him.

It was time to begin again.

CHAPTER 75

"Why the hell did you come all this way on a Thursday? It's not like we're next door neighbors." Reily sat across the table from Wil and Gabriele at a Danville restaurant, Sol at his side. He eyed his friends with suspicion. They couldn't hide their excitement. Wil's t-shirt was abnormally bright and spotless. Maybe another wedding was in the works.

"I'll tell you, but first we need champagne." Wil waved over the waitress. "We have to make a toast."

The woman retrieved what may have been the sole bottle of bubbly and gave Wil the honors of popping the top. He filled four glasses. "Raise them up. Here's to the preservation of the Bunting property and to a movie in the making."

Reily almost spilled his spirits. "What?"

"Drink up. My book is going to be the next Blackman movie."

"Unbelievable." Reily delivered a congratulatory high-five. Ladies from a geriatric card club stared at the commotion.

"Oh, there's more. I made a donation to the conservancy working on old Gertrude's estate. It put them over the top. It's a done deal. No houses on that little hamlet."

Reily was dumbfounded. "I just talked to Doc Murray a week ago and he didn't say anything about this."

"He didn't know. It all came together fast. Moonrise Pictures completely bit. Late last week we had a call to sort out the terms. It was much less painful than I would have thought."

Sol looked concerned. "I hope you had an attorney review everything."

Wil bobbed his head in agreement. "We had faxes flying around, it was crazy. Meanwhile, I was at work. My boss would have freaked if he knew I was doing this on the clock. In any case, I'm expecting an initial check in the next few days and after that, there will be more."

"Blackman really took care of you." Reily slurped his champagne.

"It seems so..." Wil said with a hint of humility.

Reily still couldn't believe the conversation. His buddy had made it big time. "Tell us more about the Bunting deal."

"There's a ceremony tomorrow on site. Doc Murray is sending out a press release today and getting one of those banner-sized checks made. The conservancy is inviting county commissioners and other mannequins. I told him I'd connect with you. Can you two come?"

"You must," Gabriele added. Her outburst and Picasso makeup caused further glares from the card ladies.

Sol glanced at Reily for concurrence. "We can be there."

"Yeah," Reily nodded. "What time?"

Wil bit into his dinner roll. "High noon."

Reily looked at his friends. "So you'll stay with us tonight?"

"We were counting on it," Wil said.

After the meal, Wil finished sharing production details about the movie. The ladies excused themselves to the bathroom. He laid a credit card on the check.

Reily stared at him. "Why do you always wear that visor?"

Wil tapped it. "Protection – it helps me see things, understand things. It's my wisdom magnifier."

"You're a goofball."

"I can't explain it. I see things better with it and not just literally. Without it, I'd be a wizard without his wand."

Reily busted out laughing. "It hides your receding hairline."

"Screw you, hippie man. You're looking pretty girly with that mane."

"Look, I have no problem with my sexual identity, visor boy. My hair keeps me grounded. It's who I am."

"You need a good haircut."

"In any case, I really am proud of you. That was a fine deed you did for Mama Nature."

"Not a huge deal. I don't require much in this life, except women."

"Well, now I believe in miracles for I have witnessed Wil Wisnoski opening his heart and his wallet. But seriously, why did you do it?"

Wil hesitated. "It was the days along the creek. The creek made us who we are. I've never considered myself an environmentalist but when I think about our childhood, we had places to go wild. Kids need that. Everyone needs that – spaces close to home, larger spaces further away. After Blackman called with the good news, I looked out the window at my lone tree and thought of trees, creek floats, the river trip, and the woods we ran around in nonstop. We took them for granted because we could." Wil manipulated the salt shaker as he spoke, lost in his exposition. It was rare to see him so principled but Reily was moved by the tenets. "I want other generations to be able to take it for granted, too, but for the right reason."

Reily smiled. "With Gert's deal, you'll be saving a sweet set of woods."

Wil's expression turned snarky. "Don't think I blew my entire wad on that gig. I saved some for this." From his wallet, he pulled a picture of a small, cedar barn backed by a golden salt marsh with a row of tall pines bordering on the left. "I know the owner. Things are already in negotiation. I love this place. I'm hoping Gabriele and I can land there."

"That's an awesome property."

"I'll have you down. Time on the mainland will do you good. A man may be an island but he can't spend all his time on one."

The ladies arranged an impromptu trip to a mall in Shamokin Dam. Gabriele needed a dress for the wedding. Wil offered to drive. Reily wanted to tend the island gardens... an appropriate excuse to avoid shopping. He hated malls.

Upon return to the island, the sparkling river summoned. Reily coaxed John into the shallows or maybe it was the other way around. Their dog already had an unquenchable affinity for water. He never tired of retrieving sticks or submarining Reily on a cross-channel chase. By the end of their jubilant ceremony, both were irreverently washed from head to toe.

Reily weeded the legitimate gardens while John dozed in the dirt, content and indifferent. Heirloom tomatoes were beginning to flower and salad greens were as thick as small hedgerows. Ignoring the gripes of his knees and other unappreciative joints, Reily thinned the arugula and placed it in a bag. He sat the bag on the steps to the treehouse and followed a short path between stands of knotweed to check Alex's illegitimate crop.

Reily knew little about best practices for cannabis cultivation but from outward appearances, a healthy yield was in the making. Twenty-five pugnacious rebels were a foot high and in need of watering. The sky promised rain but the plants couldn't wait. He went for the pump kept beneath his towering home. An unnatural roar interrupted... there was an outboard motor nearby.

Reily dropped the pump and jogged toward the sound. John followed without complaint. Anglers in boats were common but they dared maneuver too close to islands ringed with prop-busting shoals. The boat was downstream, off the southwest tip of the island. Reily crouched behind a stout birch and watched with John at his side.

An overdressed, heavy, dark-haired man gunned his motor again and again – stuck on a patch of water willow. The man seemed uneasy in the boat and unsure of what to do. Scrambling to the stern, he glanced around. Either the guy knew nothing about water or was feeling guilty about something because it was obvious he was desperate to get away.

There was a familiarity about the man, even from afar, that made Reily nervous. The boater wasn't one of the usual fishermen who would wave or ask him about island living. They ran flat-bottomed boats and this was a v-hull. He combed his mind but couldn't make the connection. Then the boat lurched and accelerated. The ill-trained captain found deeper water.

A sudden, alarming thought struck Reily– had the man been on the island? The prospect was disconcerting but unlikely. The craft shrank slowly into the distance then suddenly angled to the north shore, toward a neglected municipal ramp. Reily squinted and made out a lone black sedan and trailer in the lot. *What a weird configuration.*

Reily stood and summoned John the direction from which they had come. There was a garden to irrigate and dinner to make. He headed back, a furry companion at his heels.

CHAPTER 76

T he farm smiled for all its fans. The pond shimmered, insects buzzed, songbirds whistled, a rooster cheered. The barn, a regal red, would have marched if it could. Cats wandered between cars, curious about so many visitors. Reily stood next to a portable table topped with a paper cloth and a cooler of iced tea wet with condensation. Sol stayed at home, struck by a bout of morning sickness.

Looking at Gert's house and the heat radiating in the fields reminded Reily of the Odyssey – the blistering days, crazy nights, and spontaneous road trips for the environment. The experience had been punishing and exhilarating at the same time, a forty-day dose of heaven and hell. He was a benefactor of the ordeal. So was the farm.

A familiar face walked his way. "What goes?"

Reily motioned with his eyes to everything around them. "Nice work, Dr. Murray."

"I just did what you, Wil, and other radicals and donors made possible – plus the conservancy, not SURCOS, did most of the fundraising."

Reily shook his hand with a poignant grip. "But you're the one that inspired me," he said. "You showed us the sorry state of things and we rallied. You made us believe in something better."

"Whatever." Murray shook his head. "You're making me emotional and I have to give a speech in a few minutes. Have you seen your buddy, Wil?"

"Not yet. He's probably in the hay loft with Gabriele."

"I was looking forward to breaking the news to all of you at the same time, but here's the preview: Carl Woodring was arrested two days ago."

Reily drew an excited breath. "Sweet justice."

"Unfortunately, he's out on bail but that may only be temporary." Rob, in habitual form, removed his glasses to wipe them. "I can't believe it myself. I'm not sure what it all means but we've protected this property and I imagine some or all of the current development will be curtailed by the legal fallout. It isn't a complete victory but it could have been a lot worse."

"Enjoy the moment." Reily placed his hands on Rob's shorter shoulders. "Celebrate now – there's more ecological persecution on tap for tomorrow. The struggle and suffering continues but the restorer perseveres."

Rob gave him a good-natured shove. "You're full of yourself."

Gert Bunting waddled from her house dressed in a violet frock that likely came out of the box only for weddings and funerals. What was she thinking on this day? Would she soon say farewell to her roots, or remain here, content that most of her surroundings would last beyond her years? Old Gert was a living lecture that Reily's better days were numbered, too.

A tour of the property ended for a small group of attendees. Others arrived, mostly men in suits with armpit stains and belts on their last adjustment. They were there to speak and split, an exercise perfected by politicians. Reily remembered them from the sleeper ceremonies for larger Sutton projects. He preferred the new life he was leading.

The conservancy president began to arrange the talking heads, but a red Isuzu SUV made a distracting entry on the Bunting driveway. Once parked, Wil and Gabriele exited as if time moved by their rules. It was classic Wil, yet his dress was atypical: no visor, pleated trousers, and a white dress shirt.

Reily waved him over. "I didn't recognize you."

Wil checked the buttons on his cuffs. "New man for a new day."

"Well Mr. Newman, I think they're waiting on you."

"No worries, except this." Wil reached into his pants pocket and withdrew a four-inch nail. "I ran over this, at your parking area."

Reily frowned. "That's bad timing. I wondered why you weren't behind me."

Wil laid the nail on top of a fence post. "I doubt it was accidental. One of those needs help to find a tire."

Despite Wil's tardiness, the bodies aligned on the Bunting Farm at noon as planned. A county commissioner competed with township supervisor Larry Wilson for the least inspiring comments. Wilson replaced Lowell Orwell, the chairman of the board of supervisors, who "regretted not being able to attend" according to a read statement. Reportedly, he was on bed rest for heart arrhythmia. Rob Murray spoke, beaming as if he were at his high school commencement, with a blinding reflection from the rim of his glasses. The ever-serious conservancy president made closing remarks. All the while, Wil stood there, illuminated in pride as self-appointed envoy for the wishes of the universe. At a minimum, he was a pallbearer to the avaricious schemes of Carl Woodring. A hawk circled and screamed high over the woods where Don Bunting and Hap Clay hunted. Even Gertrude seemed happy although her lips never parted. With a grand panorama behind them, it was visual poetry. Reily felt a deep, inexpressible satisfaction. This was the best of moments.

Wil and Gabriele talked Reily into an afternoon hike through the newly protected lands of the Bunting Preserve but before they explored, he called to check on Sol. Nausea had abated but she was still resting. "Enjoy your time with them," Sol said. "Visit our rock for me."

They gorged on the remaining finger sandwiches before setting out on a rough-cut trail winding into the property. No one had boots, but did it matter? Last time they hiked here, they were all barefoot. The trail traversed a field overgrown with brambles and old apple trees. An opening through rusted strands of barbed-wire led to a shady, hushed grove of hemlock, yellow birch, and American beech – with trunks the color and texture of elephant skin. A large beech bore initials carved by lovers of decades past. Mountain laurel thickened and blueberry covered the ground. Gaps in the view meant the escarpment lie ahead. Then, there it was, the Susquehanna, humble and unhurried in the silence far below.

Reily sat on a fallen log and smiled at Wil and his lady. "Does this look familiar?"

Wil peeked over the edge. "It's even better in the daylight."

Reily led them on a search for the 'reclining rock' where he first kissed Sol. When he thought he had found it, he requested his friends to sit down for a test. They obliged and embraced, exaggerating the romantic inspiration embodied in the location.

"Very funny." Reily waited impatiently for the smooching to cease.

Gabriele ended her role and gave a thumbs-up. "Good choice, Reily, yes?"

"Yes," he said, giving the rock an approving glance.

They followed the clifftop further northwest toward the boundary of the downsized Whispering Heights development. Reily hoped he could locate the giant outcropping of sandstone where he and Sol had played their version of hide and seek. Black 'No Trespassing' signs with fluorescent letters marked the beginning of Woodring's property – a zone of intentional destruction.

Turning away from the river, Reily ducked through a patch of rhododendron and stumbled into a muddy clearing patterned with bulldozer tracks... a road in the making. They followed it for over a hundred yards until it bent slightly right. Revealed, dead ahead, were the coveted rocks.

Reily tipped his head in the direction of the sedimentary maze. "That *was* the formation I wanted you to see."

Gabriele frowned.

"The new playground for the neighborhood brats," Wil scowled.

Reily felt morose. "Woodring will probably use them for building material."

"The kids or the rocks?" Wil asked.

Reily shrugged. "Both."

After touring more of the carnage, they tramped their way back to Gert's place and their respective cars. It was impossible to tell there had been an onsite celebration. The farm seemed timeless and at ease. A breeze out of nowhere rustled Reily's hair, a prompt to relish the small but significant triumph.

"Let's grab an early dinner somewhere," Wil said.

Reily figured Sol wouldn't mind. "Alright, but let's wait until we get closer to my place." He could even surprise her with a takeout meal.

Wil opened his car door and yelled, "You willing to put us up for another night?"

Reily nodded affirmatively. "Another memorable island visit guaranteed." He slipped into his Explorer and drove out Gertrude's lane, Wil tailing in his dust.

CHAPTER 77

Sol laughed out loud from the hammock of the treehouse and set down her Carl Hiaasen novel. This one was more outlandish than the last, but the author never failed to entertain. The dappled sunshine and antics in the story lifted her mood. Happy hour called. Tonic and a lime sounded revitalizing, and therapeutic to the growing baby in her womb. Gin would have to wait another six months.

She mixed her mocktail on their wooden counter, hewn from a slab of hackberry. Every corner of the place had a natural tale to tell. Reily had done well. John snored from his mattress in the corner, wondering when his buddy Reily would return.

Sol sauntered outside, careful to latch the screen door. From a hook, she retrieved a metal pail with an eye on the peas in the garden below. The stairs were descended with a drink in one hand and the bucket in the other. A train rumbled along the river's southern shore. She set her drink on a lower step and began picking.

A Goo Goo Dolls' song played in her head and she whistled along, paying no mind to a motorboat working the flats. Greenhouse smells of virgin foliage lingered in the calm interior of the island. Soon her container was half full, more than enough for her and her man.

A siren wailed from upstream. Curious, she placed the cache of peas under the house and walked the path to that end of the island. There was nothing to be seen but an expansive current, more leafy islands, and a colony of gulls rafting away the hours.

On the way back, Sol heard a splash in the channel. *Probably a restless fish.* The shadow beneath the house seemed darker, the river birches extra still. Then there were footsteps. A man she never saw before passed the garden, sneaking her direction. His eyes – wide with shock – discovered hers. He stopped in his tracks. One hand carried a gasoline can; the other, a flare. The man's expression turned sinister and he placed a finger to his mouth – the universal gesture to keep quiet, or else...

CHAPTER 78

Reily raced on I-80 East, aiming for the Danville exit. The meal in Hughesville could have been a year ago. Two calls to Sol had gone unanswered and during her pregnancy, she always kept the phone at her side. He swallowed hard to suppress escalating worry.

US Route 11 streamed with the last of the day's commuters and weekend travelers slowing his progress. Living on an island didn't alleviate all the hassles of civilization. Wil remained right behind him, likely surprised by the haste. Almost to the turnoff, Reily spied a car at the municipal boat ramp... it was a black sedan with an empty trailer. *The same one from yesterday?* His anxiety surged.

Reily skidded into his regular parking spot and dashed to his stashed kayak – a yard sale addition to the fleet, good for the back and forth to the island. He carried the boat past Wil, exiting the Trooper. With his free hand, Reily pointed at the kayak. "I should have used the motorboat today."

"What's wrong? You were driving like a psychopath."

"Sol isn't answering the phone."

"I'm sure she's fine. Maybe she dropped it in the river?"

"Then why was she on the river?" Nothing would makes sense until she was comforting him, firsthand. Reily pulled two sections of paddle from the hull and snapped them together. "I'm headed over. Why don't you two wait here and once I know all is well, I'll shuttle you in the big boat."

"Let me go with you," Wil said.

"No, just stay here. I'll be back soon." Reily sprinted in the kayak on a direct course for the treehouse – a fragment of roof and wind turbine visible. Had there been an electrical issue and Sol couldn't charge the phone? Had she fallen? What about the strange boat from yesterday?

He scanned up and down the river. There wasn't a boat to be seen. At first, he heard the call of a goose, but as the island loomed closer, John's hoarse barks were unmistakable. Reily churned faster.

Near shore, he slowed his strokes. The bow skidded into the muddy bank with a whisper. He scrambled onto level ground and listened. John's barking stopped. Reily inched forward. Ahead of him, the treehouse came into complete view. Caution overruled the urge to call out for Sol. He moved to the steps... a lime floated in a cup half full. The drink was still cool. Condensation puddled on the tread.

At the top of the stairs, he could see John, eager in dim light, behind the screen. Reily unhooked the door and comforted his dog. A slight breeze eased the warmth of the confines, scented by roses he'd given to Sol. Alone in a vase on the table, they seemed to share his unease.

"Sol, are you in here?" There was no response. The room appeared normal, unmolested. His heart accelerated.

Before descending the steps, Reily peered southwest down the long reach of the island. Nothing stirred. Then, beyond the garden, he noticed unnatural protrusions. *Are those hands?* He hurried to the spot, concern outweighing prudence.

Sol's wrists were handcuffed behind a tree. She stood, gagged and blindfolded.

"Sol, it's me. Are you okay?" There were no signs of harm. He reached for the fabric covering her eyes.

She nodded and tried to speak, the words muffled.

A twig snapped behind him. But before he could even turn, a crushing weight struck his skull with decisive force. Reality froze and the world retreated to a silent, endless void.

Wil and Gabriele wrestled his kayak from the roof rack of the Trooper. "I have a bad feeling," Wil said. "I'll give you my phone. If I'm not back in a half hour, call the cops."

"Please be careful, yes?"

"You know it." He didn't want to disappoint those imploring azure eyes.

Wil paddled warily. At this golden hour, Reily's island suggested a bucolic refuge but he couldn't shake the sense of doom. Usually he was the one snarled in a dicey predicament. His friend only had a ten-minute head start, barely enough time to reconcile even a minor issue. *Everything is probably swell.*

The safest approach was a wide, less obvious sweep upstream. The slower, longer route allowed a covert drift into the channel behind the treehouse. Ahead, the Watters' motorboat, *Messina*, lay tethered to the bank, slumbering at its private port. Wil observed a more concerning shape further down the passage – another boat, a V-hull anchored at the stern. Wil didn't remember any expected visitors. This boat's outboard was big enough for coastal action. *What the hell was it doing on this bony river?*

Wil secured his kayak to a root and snuck onto the island. The house loomed fifty feet down the path. No one could be seen or heard except for an oriole in the canopy, singing like there wasn't a care in the world, and Reily's new dog, sounding like he had a sore throat.

Wil advanced on the walkway, one cautious stride at a time. Thanks to Reily, his fluency with birdsong and the limitless ingredients of nature ever grew. He owed Reily so much, but assuring his old friend's wellbeing was priority one.

Wil rounded the treehouse and paused to listen. Without the slightest warning, two flashes – and simultaneous, earsplitting bangs – burst from the woods. His right bicep, then thigh, erupted in grotesque, brain-ripping pain. He floated out of body, writhing on an imagined bed of hot coals.

Despite having penned an anthology of articles about shootings and mob hits in Atlantic City, never did Wil anticipate the cruel sting now experienced. *Could anyone hear him screaming?*

Unidentified *booming* rebounded in Reily's head. His mind spluttered. He fought to part his eyelids but waited for the spinning to cease. He didn't remember drinking... the last time his body felt this awful, whisky was to blame. Dampness permeated his scalp. A cool, loamy redolence meant proximity to the ground. *Why was he lying on the ground?*

His eyes finally decided to obey. As they opened, and light and objects transmuted into forms, he verified his odd, prone state. A building came into focus – his elevated house. Angry mutterings entered his cognizance but they belonged to someone else. He didn't know the disgruntled voice.

"Don't try anything. You understand?" the voice spoke again. This time Reily heard a muted, illegible response... *Sol.*

Reily slid his head like a snail to see what was happening. A man with murky features had rough hold of Sol's arm and tugged her toward the channel behind the island. Even in his injured state, Reily recognized the guy as the mystery boater... his suspicions were corroborated. In the distance behind them, an object on the ground made a sudden movement and moaned. From the blotted white shirt, he knew it must be Wil.

Despite an excruciating cerebral ache, Reily yearned to act. His friend laid hurt, his fiancée in pressing danger. Incrementally, he lifted his upper torso and saw the weapon brought upon him – one of his own canoe paddles, now broken in two, the splintered shaft separated from the thick blade. The sixty-three inch Carlisle Beavertail, crafted of basswood, had been a Christmas gift from Sol. Its sorrowful state birthed an idea. There wasn't a second to lose.

Before this evening, Reily viewed Japanese knotweed as the enemy of his island. The invasive plant grew up to fifteen feet tall, forming dense thickets that shaded out native vegetation and created bare ground susceptible to erosion. Now it had an upside.

Conscious of the need for stealth, Reily crawled then slithered between crowded stalks, staying on the north side of the marijuana patch. The micro-forest held its own surprises: the stench of a rotting muskrat, ugly fragments of discarded plastic, a garter snake seeking a meal – or maybe an imperiled mate.

The island seemed so long. The earth turned unsteady... Reily waited for a spell of acidy reflux to pass. He heard cursing and the spit of a stubborn motor. With a surge of adrenaline, he pushed forward, tasting a salty trickle of sweat and residual blood, before veering left for the far end of the channel.

Toads scrambled out of the way, greenbrier piercing his side. Poison ivy mocked him. The moment Reily reached the spot where the bank became vertical and the soil sloughed away, the nearby motor came to life.

His pulse pounded. The foliage offered a hidden vantage point of the constricted exit and the boat was headed his way.

It happened in a blur. Sol occupied the front bench, the man sat in back with his left hand on the throttle control. Furrowed eyes probed getaway routes. As the man reached the critical point, Reily took to the air, bearing a jagged spear – before today, used only for peaceful canoe-propulsion duties.

The lunge elapsed in slow motion frames.

Preoccupied with navigation, the marauder saw Reily too late. The makeshift dagger, gripped by the flying Watters, plunged into soft tissue at the collar line. A geyser of blood attested to the surprising effectiveness of the daredevil maneuver.

Sandwiching the man against the outboard, Reily became drenched in rich juice as red as the embroidered P on the man's golf shirt. It was finished.

Fish were the only living things he had ever mortally wounded, and on those occurrences when catch and release went awry, he felt compelled to eat the unfortunate kill. Consuming the evidence wasn't an option this day – this would-be filet was enormous, fatty and unappealing – but the same pangs of sorrow and regret returned, with devastating intensity. Reily hadn't hooked a human being... he had speared one. Fatally.

He cut the motor and dropped anchor before removing the gag on Sol. Her skin was pale and cool, her body shaking.

"I'll take off your blindfold, but keep your eyes closed. The guy's dead," Reily said in a calm voice. "We have to help Wil."

Wading up the channel, he led Sol from the rescue scene, worried sorely about her and his friend. Energy drained with every stride.

They staggered to Wil's side, finding him unconscious but alive in a puddle of gore. His breathing was shallow. He needed a doctor, now.

Weak but alert, Sol pulled her cell phone from her pocket and called 911 for the three of them.

Wil awoke and Reily went to the house for water. He came back with John, who licked Wil's face out of apprehension or curiosity. Reily raised a cup to his buddy's lips.

Wil whispered something unintelligible.

Reily leaned closer. "What did you say?"

"You saved my ass again."

He gently squeezed Wil's good shoulder. "You're trouble, Wisnoski... Nothing but trouble."

With daylight in slow withdrawal, Sol tended to Wil. Reily mustered enough vigor for a crucial demolition. The dirty task took only a few minutes to undo six weeks of labor.

As he washed soil from his hands, a refreshing draft carried the rousing yelp of emergency vehicles, then the manic beat of rotors, reverberating upriver. Reily slumped his head in agony beneath a plaintive, cerise sky. Relief was imminent... and inbound.

CHAPTER 79

It was Woodring's last visit to Whispering Heights. Such finality was tough to take but Sid Purillo's corrective acts and airline reservations to Montevideo tenderized the sting even if he had to vacate his sprouting empire of real estate and life as he knew it. But why hadn't Sid called?

A morning appointment brought a teaspoon of satisfaction – an agent of Excelsior Energy wanted to lease the mineral rights beneath some of his holdings. A new technology called hydraulic fracturing enabled the recovery of natural gas trapped in shale 7,500 feet underground. They'd pay him now and he'd collect annual royalties. The latter could go to Mikey Purillo – the anointed receiver of his properties – but the lump sum chunk would sweeten Woodring's lifestyle in the southern hemisphere.

Woodring followed a tongue of compacted soil twisting through the forest. The unfinished road would someday enter another townhouse cluster once Mikey solved the water conundrum and legal issues in the wake of his departure.

On the future thoroughfare, he found an odd pile of feathers from an owl or a hawk. Not one or two, but a spray of ten were bundled with a vine. Where had they come from? The set reminded him of a brightly-colored Indian headdress he had when he was a kid. His father had taken it away as punishment for forgetting to take out the trash.

Unrepentant about his conquest of the land, Woodring left the road and entered the woods in the direction of the river. He wished to regale himself with the exceptional view one last time. It was the very reason he'd decided to buy the property five years earlier. People deserved to feel like a king if they could afford it. His company delivered, putting them in the thick of things – on top of mountains, next to lakes, or at the edge of the world. It was an addiction, to make each development more grandiose than the prefab crap his father once stapled together. Was it retribution that drove him, or an obsession to win his father's accolade from beyond? Woodring never reached a conclusion.

Dense mountain laurel impeded the path and he ducked under branches and slipped past outcroppings until he came to the edge. Even cigarettes didn't take his breath like this sight. Woodring peered at the water in the bottom of the void, moving like an endless conveyor. It was a dreamscape. He interrupted two dragonflies propagating their species, but who could blame them, it was the perfect spot to get laid. He remembered proposing to his ex-wife on Grandfather Mountain in North Carolina. The marriage lasted a year... he screwed up in every sense of the word, but their courtship was the best time of his life. Now, it was the worst. The depths of his situation changed everything. How had he fallen so far, so fast?

As Woodring turned to leave, the bushes rustled then stopped. He stiffened and listened but all he could discern were his own gasps. An oblivious doe must have picked up his scent.

Woodring thought of his rifle back at home and the security it provided, but he could hold ground without it. Something moved again. With arms held high and wide, he stared into the thicket and bellowed a mighty snarl. Echoes confirmed his lackluster skill at wildlife mimicry.

Nevertheless emboldened, Woodring resumed his contemplative, farewell walk, remaining on the rocky cusp. Now he found himself abreast a thicker patch of rhododendron, visually impenetrable. Faint indiscriminate sounds followed, parallel to his wandering... unless his imagination was getting the best of him. The trauma of recent days – and chaos of this decrepit year – may have taken a heavier toll than recognized.

Western hunting trips within the territories of grizzlies and mountain lions attuned him to risk avoidance, and peering into the distance, he noted the lack of escape options at his disposal. Fleeing to South America carried similar limitations. He scampered onward, picturing the dangerous fauna of that continent.

A turkey vulture with a bald pink head circled over the gorge, unafraid of heights. Stiff wings made it seem artificial – a sick, morbid kite. The woods crackled and crunched unequivocally. Woodring quickened his strides.

Ahead, the precipice assumed an unfriendly irregularity, with vertical gaps and notches near the top. The forest swallowed the edge. There was nowhere to go but through dense vegetation or atop precarious boulders big enough to squash a car. The next property line couldn't be far and the neighbors, with gardens and fastidious grounds, had tamed their land years ago. The preference for savannah and open landscapes by early humans made renewed sense... green grass and *occasional* trees represented safety.

To his left, branches swayed. *Keep moving.*

Woodring hopped across two boulders and stopped. *Was that a growl?* Without pause, the understory exploded from the motions of an immense animal with an acute prerogative. In desperation, Woodring leapt for the next rock... but misjudged, his cunning mind out of sync with a body degraded from years of smoking. The angled toe of his boot slid off the rounded surface. To his instant horror, there was nothing underfoot.

The apathetic cliff rushed by in abbreviated moments of razor sharp, all-consuming fear. Gravity afforded an express tour of the epochs of geologic time. The ending was severe, immediate, and permanent. Impact imploded skeletal structures. Organs disconnected and disgorged. Every atavistic thought faded to a cold blackness.

The developer's corpse lay sprawled beside the river, beneath sandstone whose silica grains cooled millions of years before the first spark of primordial life. Downwind, a pack of coyotes caught the scent of decaying tissue and followed shoreline rubble to his carcass. Chewing on bone and sinew, they took part in an un-promised feast – a sacred communion in nature's circle of humility.

CHAPTER 80

The wedding was a mini-reunion for the Odyssey. Rick and his partner arrived early to assemble a gazebo Rick had custom constructed for the occasion. A wind vane in the silhouette of a canoe with two paddlers topped its roof. Reily would swap vows with his bride under the shelter, but he already envisioned a permanent spot for it on the island.

Wil came dressed in a navy blue suit, self-modified to accommodate bulky casts on his arm and leg. His face and waistline were notably thinner but considering the ordeal recently endured, he acted remarkably well. Aiding his mobility, Gabriele, the maid of honor, glittered like royalty in a purple dress.

Sol and her mother were in the restroom making final preparations. All Reily could do was pace. Wil corralled him.

"You'll be great, Watters." Wil reached out and tightened his tie. "But you can't be a slob."

"I just hope Sol will be okay. She doesn't know what she's in for."

"Like marrying a killer?" Wil teased.

"That's not funny, I'm having nightmares. That Purillo guy was a thug, arsonist – probably a murderer – but he didn't deserve to die."

"It was self-defense. You're forgiven."

Reily shrugged. He hoped Wil was right.

Canoes and kayaks basked in the afternoon sun, arranged ornately along the river bank. Alex, festooned in a billowy dress shirt straight out of *Pirates of Penzance*, strolled and strummed his guitar singing nautical folk songs. "Wreck of the Edmund Fitzgerald" seemed a bit somber for the celebration but Reily didn't mind. Alex had almost cried when he learned Reily had yanked the pot plants and fed them to the currents before the police and EMTs arrived on the island, post-incident.

Alex switched to more contemporary songs as three o'clock approached and the audience moved to the boats. "Peaceful Easy Feeling" was being performed when a familiar Volkswagen sedan pulled into the lot, a silver canoe on top. Casey Watters, ever tall and beautiful, got out of the car and stretched. Reily went to her.

The minutes converged. Reily was back on the water in the pilgrimage known as life, surrounded by loving friends and his stubborn but acquiescing daughter. Sol was before him as radiant as the sun. Her dress was ivory with a gloss that glowed like her hair. Fuchsia flowers adorned her head. Even her skin sparkled. He wished his parents were alive to see her and share in the day.

Chief Peter Williams waited before the gazebo. A slender, female Presbyterian pastor with lengthy brown hair and kindly countenance stood poised to assist. Reily had met her in the hospital when during chaplain duties, she visited Wil. Either riveted from his close call with mortality or transfixed by the atypical splendor of the holy lady, Wil hadn't resisted. After chatting with the pastor and enjoying flashbacks to his earlier Presbyterian days, Reily asked if she would help with their wedding ceremony. He wasn't sure why.

Sol's father stood at the water's edge to take his daughter forward for the handoff. Chris Messina had a ragged head of hair and a forehead creased from too many years of pondering. Reily aimed the bow at his location. The other boats followed in two semi-parallel columns, a corrupted flying V. He and Sol landed them without incident and Chris assisted his daughter as planned. A hired flutist created a melody that carried them to the chief and pastor while the other boats clustered by the shore.

Wil and Gabriele took posts by the gazebo. Reily stepped from the craft and walked when prompted. He approached his dream girl. Words floated between them. Prayers were offered in their honor. The boats parted and Alex surged ahead. On the foredeck was a pillow secured with a bungee cord and carrying two artisan silver rings invisibly set with cobalt sea glass from Eleuthera. They were a spring gift from Frances in lieu of her presence. Alex, the reveler, emerged from his kayak and delivered the jewels. Chief Williams paused, head turned skyward.

A plane flew low in a laboring hum. It pulled a banner with large letters exclaiming CONGRATS TO THE NEW COUPLE.

Wil whispered, "That's Blackman's present."

More words were spoken by the chief, the pastor, then finally Reily was permitted to kiss Sol. When their approving lips parted, they were man and wife.

A never ending supply of wine purchased by Sol's flamboyant mother fueled the reception. It only seemed fit that they were all gathered under a picnic pavilion dancing on concrete in the open air.

At dusk, the party still roiled but Reily walked Sol to the water's edge for a respite. Swallows fed on mayflies. A blue heron hunted. He squeezed her hand and breathed in. It was a banquet for the living. Reily thought of the Heyerdahl book, freshly completed. It had been neglected since last summer's voyage, but in the nervous days before the wedding, he'd returned to the story, absorbing the explorer's honest, humble reflections on faith.

It was the author's last point that moved him most: that God, whatever His ultimate manifestation, must be intertwined with the salvation of the planet. It was a stewardship imperative, an expectation of the creator and a necessity of all mankind. The writings of other earth-defending heroes – Sig Olson, John Muir, Ed Abbey, Rachel Carson – were timeless and essential but Thor sent the message, subtly and sagely, that all needed to hear. Wear the proverbial green cloth or die trying.

A neon damselfly touched down on Sol's shoulder. Reily put out his finger and it climbed aboard.

Sol studied the creature and him. "It finds you as charming as I do, especially with that haircut."

He reached for the ponytail no longer present. "I feel lighter but now you can really see my scab."

"You're a survivor," Sol said, "but I don't know if I can survive a drive to Kim's tomorrow. I'll be exhausted."

"She said the cottage is ready for us no matter when we get there. We can take our time, but the next day she wants to take us to her favorite part of the lake." He interrupted himself and frowned. "She's trying to save it from becoming a two-hundred-room resort."

Sol sighed and looped her arm through his. "I'm looking forward to the trip – and to all our adventures together." She peered across the misty water. "You know, the Susquehanna has been pretty good to us."

Reily felt a quenching rush of gratitude. The same watercourse that etched landscapes, nurtured wildlife, grew economies, and inspired writers, artists, and theologians had reserved some of its magic – it brought him together with Sol... and changed his life.

He beamed at the water and reveled in its grandeur. "Yep, it's *some* river."

ACKNOWLEDGMENTS

Thanks to so many people who have inspired and encouraged me in this literary adventure.

It wouldn't have been possible without the support and patience of my wonderful wife, Deidre, and our amazing daughters, Sierra and Savanna.

Friends and family fortified the effort in innumerable ways with special thanks to Al, Allan, Allen, Amy, Andrea, Andy, Autumn, Ben, Betsy, Betty, Bill, Bob, Brian, Brooks, Bruce, Candy, Cheryl, Cindy, Claire, Dan, Dana, Dante, Dave, Dawn, Dick, Don, Doug, Drew, Ed, Elsa, Emily, Erica, Fran, Gretchen, Isabella, Janice, JD, Jill, Jordan, Jesse, John, Kari, Kay, Kelli, Lisa, Marci, Margaret, Margot, Mark, Mary, Michael, Mike, Natalie, Pat, Pete, Phil, Ralph, Ray, Rebecca, Rich, Ruenkauw, Sandy, Sara, Steve, Ted, Tom, Tony, Val, Willard, and all the Sojourners – past, present, and future.

And, of course, a generous helping of thanks goes to Demi Stevens, editor extraordinaire and wizard of the written word.

ABOUT THE AUTHOR

BROOK LENKER received his bachelor's and master's degrees in Geography from Towson University. He is a lifelong conservationist and currently directs the nonprofit FracTracker Alliance, addressing environmental and public health risks of oil and gas development across the United States.

Brook previously held positions with the Pennsylvania Department of Conservation and Natural Resources, Alliance for the Chesapeake Bay, and Dauphin County Parks and Recreation. Those roles – and volunteering for other environmental causes – provided memorable nature-based experiences which inspire his writing.

For many years, Brook was a regular contributor to *Susquehanna Life* magazine. This is his first novel.

When not exploring the great outdoors, he enjoys practicing 'the land ethic' at his home along the Yellow Breeches Creek in central Pennsylvania. Brook is proud to be involved with his local watershed association and the Susquehanna River Trail Association, which he helped found.

CPSIA information can be obtained
at www.ICGtesting.com
Printed in the USA
LVHW041653220719
624869LV00003B/409